# CASSIE EDWARDS
## Author Of More Than 5 Million Books In Print

### Winner of the *Romantic Times* Lifetime Achievement Award
"Cassie Edwards writes sexy reads! Romance fans will be more than satisfied."
—*Romantic Times*

## *SPARRING PARTNERS*

"Lynn, I've been appointed Program Director of the station," Eliot said.

"You *what?*" Lynn whispered harshly. "What did you say?"

He reached out a hand, but she slapped it away. "Lynn, I'm sorry. Really, I'm damn sorry. It wasn't my idea, believe me."

"You get out of my house!" she hissed. "How could you? Was this charming seduction all planned to soften me up? Did you decide to make love to me, then casually tell me that you've taken over my position at KSFC? How could you?" She covered her face with her hands.

"Lynn, damn it, I *am* sorry. You can't think I planned it this way. I've fallen in love with you."

"You get out of here this minute," she said in a low, threatening tone. "I want you out of my house—and my life."

# Island
# Rapture

# Cassie Edwards

**LOVE SPELL**  **NEW YORK CITY**

*With much love,*
*I dedicate this novel to my brother Fred Cline,*
*sister-in-law Sally,*
*and my two dear nephews,*
*Frankie and Freddie.*

LOVE SPELL®

April 1994

Published by

Dorchester Publishing Co., Inc.
276 Fifth Avenue
New York, NY 10001

The name "Love Spell" and its logo are trademarks of Dorchester Publishing Co., Inc.

Printed in the United States of America.

The fountains mingle with the river,
And the rivers with the ocean;
The winds of heaven mix forever,
With a sweet emotion;
Nothing in the world is single;
All things by a law divine
In one another's being mingle...
Why not I with thine?

See! The mountains kiss high heavens,
And the waves clasp one another;
No sister flower would be forgiven,
If it disdained its brother;
And the sunlight clasps the earth,
And the moonbeams kiss the sea...
What are all these kissings worth,
If thou kiss not me?

—Percy Bysshe Shelley

# Island Rapture

# One

LOOKING FROM her eighth floor office building window, Lynn Stafford could see only portions of the Golden Gate Bridge this early morning in September. The upper portion of San Francisco's grand tourist attraction was hidden beneath a shroud of fog so thick that it looked almost like snow capping a mountain. The wind whistled outside around the corner of the KSFC-TV television building, reminding Lynn of cool September mornings in her home state of Illnois. At this moment she was a bit homesick for the simpler ways of life of the rural community in which she had been born and raised. Caught up in the recent struggles for power at the TV station, Lynn had become disenchanted by it all, finding little or no glamour any longer in being one of the stars of "Morning Magazine."

"A penny for your thoughts . . ."

Hearing the familiar voice behind her made Lynn turn around. She smiled at her friend and longtime co-host Adam Lowenstein, who was leaning through her opened office door. "I didn't hear you come in," she said, laughing nervously.

Adam strolled further into the room. "You were

a million miles away," he said, settling himself onto the corner of Lynn's desk. "Anything you want to talk about?"

Hearing the resonant quality of his voice and seeing his handsome face made Lynn wonder again, as she had many times recently, why the management of KSFC-TV had refused to discuss pay increases with Adam when contract time had rolled around. Lynn silently studied Adam. There was no sagging jowl in evidence and only minute wrinkles at the corners of his eyes. It was hard for her to believe that the man standing before her would soon be fifty-eight years old. He was wearing a beautifully tailored brown tweed sport coat, a beige shirt with a slightly flared button-down collar and a dark red wool tie. He was deeply tanned and his skin was molded sculpturally to the fine, strong bones beneath. His short, curly hair had turned a distinguished silvery gray at the temples, and his blue eyes were clear and penetrating.

But his attractiveness wasn't his only asset. It had been his charm and his wit that had helped cover up for Lynn's many nervous bloopers when Lynn and Adam had first co-hosted "Morning Magazine" together.

Yes, he would be sorely missed. And she was bitter because management had decided to let him go.

Lynn settled down in the swivel chair behind her desk. She picked up a pencil and began tapping its eraser on her closed appointment book. "I'm still furious at Taylor for not agreeing to your terms on the new contract," she said. "It's not fair, Adam! No one is as good as you. And I most certainly don't look forward to meeting your replacement."

She slung the pencil away from her, across the desk. "I've been avoiding doing that, you know."

Adam leaned down closer to her, half smiling. "Who knows?" he teased. "Maybe Eliot Smith will turn out to be a white knight in shining armor. Maybe wedding bells will be ringing in the near future."

"Good Lord, Adam," Lynn sighed, rising quickly from her chair. The heels of her black pumps clicked noisily against the highly polished oak floor as she went to a filing cabinet. "I don't expect to even *like* the man, much less fantasize about marrying him," she quickly interjected. "It's the farthest thing from my mind, believe me!"

She jerked a drawer out, then a manila file folder. Absently thumbing through the papers inside the folder, she tried to avoid the amused glint in Adam's eyes.

"Maybe that's the way you feel now," he further teased. "But I do hear he's quite attractive and available."

His gaze raked over her. "You know that if I wasn't so devoted a husband and father, I wouldn't have wasted one minute trying to lure you into *my* corner," he added.

Lynn gave him a sideways glance, blushing, a trait that despite her sophistication, continued to embarrass her. Upon her arrival at college all those years ago, it had taken her a while to get used to the wolf whistles and stares of admiration that came her way. Even now, many years later, she knew that she was considered quite attractive, with her long and flowing golden hair and eyes the soft color of tender spring leaves. Lynn had never had a weight problem. She was tall, on the slender side, yet far from skinny, and wore her clothes with a certain flair. Ready for the TV camera this day, she was attired in a neat Albert Nipon black crepe de chine and cream polka-dotted "executive dress" set off by a white yoke and black bow tie.

"I'm going to miss you, Adam," she finally said with a sincere smile.

"I'm holding the position open for you at the radio station," he said, rising from where he had been sitting on the edge of her desk. "You're welcome there. Any time. Remember that."

Lynn placed the folder on her desk and eased back into her chair. "I might take you up on that offer," she sighed. "But first I have to meet the challenge of Eliot Smith. I refuse to let a total stranger chase *me* off the program, too."

Adam strolled to the window and gazed out for a moment, then spun around on a heel, facing Lynn. "You can't blame him for all that's happened," he said. "He's an innocent bystander, you know. The job was offered to him and he'd have been a fool if he'd turned it down."

"It's been in all the newspapers, Adam, about the contract dispute," Lynn argued, sitting back in her chair. "He must have read about it and had to have known that if everyone refused the job it would possibly have forced management's hand to give you that raise . . . to keep you."

Adam's face shadowed. "I wouldn't have wanted to be asked to stay under those conditions," he said firmly.

Lynn shook her hand. "Yes, I know," she said. "It

wouldn't have been like you. But, anyway, this Eliot person . . ."

Adam leaned down and sealed her lips with a forefinger. "This Eliot fellow did what anyone else would've done," he said. "He took advantage of one hell of a good job offer. None of us are in the business for charitable reasons."

Gently pushing his finger away from her lips, Lynn said, "He took advantage, all right! Of *you*, Adam. Of *you*."

Placing his hands in his rear pockets, Adam shrugged. "I need a change anyway," he said.

"But back to radio?"

"Yes. Back to what I did in the beginning."

"If you'd put out feelers, I'm sure you'd be grabbed by an affiliate TV station somewhere along the line," Lynn argued. "Why haven't you tried, Adam?"

"I like San Francisco. My family has strong ties here. It wouldn't be fair to them."

Papers rattled as Lynn once more began skimming through them. "Your children are grown now," she murmured, giving Adam a sideways glance. Her attention then moved back to the yellow, legal-sized pages on her desk. She rescued one page of script from among the others and began running her eyes over it, tapping a finger nervously on her desk. "Adam, your children have all left home and are married," she added quietly. Once more her eyes lifted to his. "Why would they be a factor in your career plans?"

"Do you forget that I'm about to become a grandpa for the third time?" Adam said, sliding back onto the corner of her desk. He crossed his arms and leaned down closer to her. "Hon, I wouldn't leave

11

my grandbabies behind, not for any job. They're only little once and I don't plan to miss any of their growing-up years."

Lynn smiled affectionately upward at Adam. "Grandchildren," she sighed. "I wonder if I'll ever even be a mother. If only Randy had . . ." She swallowed hard and lowered her eyes.

"Had lived?" Adam said, completing the words she still found hard to say.

"Yes," Lynn murmured, rising slowly from her chair. She went to the window and once more found herself looking toward the Golden Gate Bridge, glad to see that the fog had lifted. The bridge's red outline against the backdrop of blue sky shone brightly now beneath the sun's brilliant rays and advancing morning.

"It's been twelve years now, Lynn," Adam said, moving to her side. "Vietnam is a thing of the past. Why can't you place it behind you?"

"Randy died there," she whispered, feeling the familiar ache circling her heart when she let her thoughts dwell on Randy. They had been man and wife for only one year when he had been shipped over to 'Nam. When he returned, it had been in a sealed vault.

"Hon, you've got to make yourself forget," Adam insisted, rising and drawing her into his arms.

Feeling the comfort of his embrace, Lynn sighed and rested a cheek on his chest. "I'm going to miss you, Adam," she murmured. "You've been my pillar of strength for so many years now."

"Maybe that's been a mistake, hon," he said thickly.

Lynn eased her cheek from his chest and gazed

up into his eyes. "And why would you say that?" she asked.

Adam's brow furrowed. "You've depended on me *too* much," he said firmly. "I didn't give you enough space to look for another man. I just took over. I was always there, Lynn. I should've seen how wrong it was, how selfish I was being, and how unfair to you."

Pulling free from his embrace, Lynn smoothed the skirt of her dress. "You know that we've never been anything but friends," she said. "Everyone needs friends. And, Adam, I've dated. I just haven't found a man since Randy that I would want to settle down with."

"If you're hungry for children, you first have to let yourself get serious about a man," Adam said, going to her desk and picking up the script she had separated from the rest.

Laughing nervously, Lynn said, "How on earth did we get on the subject of children? I really must get moving. Especially if I'm going to show Eliot Smith a thing or two."

Adam's eyebrows raised. He placed the script back on her desk. "What sort of thing?" he queried with interest.

"That I can damn well carry my end of the show," she said stubbornly. "I have the funniest feeling that he's not the type to want to share a show with a woman, and I'm sure he'll try edging me right out of *my* job before too long. I've heard through the grapevine that he's a 'take charge' man. I'm afraid he's going to try to push his weight around here, forgetting I have seniority."

"Well, you forget this notion of yours that Eliot

13

Smith edged *me* out of *my* job," Adam said. "It's my age that's the culprit here. I'm sure Taylor wanted a younger, handsomer man in front of the camera." He cleared his throat. "These eyes of mine ain't quite as baby blue and this silver mane sure ain't as attractive as the dark hair I had when I wuz a kid," he drawled, trying to joke about what they both knew was no laughing matter. "Time the old goat was put out to pasture."

"But, Adam, age makes no difference," she argued. "You're even better at what you do because of the years of experience behind you."

"I tend to agree," he chuckled. He ran his thumb thoughtfully along the taut jaw line just below his right ear. "Experience is a very comforting thing."

"Too bad Taylor can't see it that way," Lynn sighed. "I hope Eliot Smith falls flat on his face. That would show Taylor that youth isn't the only thing that counts—even though he's managing director here at the station, he doesn't know everything."

"I wouldn't exactly call Eliot Smith a youngster." Adam further chuckled. "He *is* forty, hon. I even saw a stray gray hair or two the other day—he must have forgotten to use his Grecian Formula."

"Taylor must not have seen any flaws in Eliot Smith," Lynn said bitterly. "He hired him the very same day he interviewed him."

Adam went to Lynn and took her hands in his, pulling her up from her chair. "Hon, you're going to have to accept what's happened her," he said. "If you don't, your antagonism toward Eliot will show on the program, and you know our pal Taylor will never stand for that."

Nodding her head, Lynn sighed. "I know," she

said sarcastically. "While on camera hosting the show together we're to be all smiles and the best of friends. But I just may find that impossible, Adam. I don't like him and I've not even met him yet. I don't feel much like smiling, believe me."

"If you feel so strongly about this, why not think about making a change also?" Adam suggested. "Your contract runs out soon. Forsake the camera for good old radio. We could co-host the same type show together and have a hell of a lot of fun. Who needs TV? We'd draw the same morning audience on radio as we did on television—our fans wouldn't let us down."

Lynn walked away from Adam, slowly wringing her hands. She stood over her desk, seeing the strewn scripts atop it. "Adam, you know that wouldn't happen," she sighed. "Radio will never be able to compete with television. People are spoiled. They like the luxury of seeing things before their eyes. It takes too much imagination to listen, to try to visualize the announcer on radio."

"I say it's worth a try," Adam stated flatly. "And whenever you're ready to make the switch, just let me know. The big brass at KEZ-90 has given me free rein on programming. I'd have us back as a duo again so fast ol' Taylor's head would swim."

Going to Adam, Lynn took his hands in hers. "I do appreciate what you're willing to do for me," she said. "And I *will* remember."

"Will you also remember that if you need anyone to talk to, I'm your man?"

Lynn lifted a carefully plucked eyebrow teasingly. "I thought you were the one who said that I depended on you too much," she said, laughing softly.

He dropped a quick kiss on her pert nose, then said. "Forget I said that. My father complex was rearing its hoary head. The friend in me says call on me *any* time."

Dropping his hands, she hugged him instead. "All right, friend," she said. "I will."

"I must go and finish cleaning out my desk, hon," Adam said. He lifted her chin with a forefinger. "Just you keep that pretty smile on your face, you hear?"

"I'll try," she said softly. Then her eyes took on an angry brilliance. "I've been asked to meet with Taylor this morning. I guess now's as good a time as any."

"Don't get into a battle with him again, Lynn."

"Okay. If you say so," she said. She stretched her legs and kissed Adam affectionately on the cheek. "Now don't you dare leave this building without coming back here first to say good-bye."

"I won't, hon."

Adam winked at Lynn and walked from the room, leaving her with an empty, lonely feeling. Their relationship had been so special—some had even suspected that they were lovers. But Adam's love for his wife Patricia and their family had never permitted his feelings for Lynn to reach beyond the limits of friendship.

"I'll never again, ever, find such a good friend and co-host rolled up into one," she murmured. "Damn Taylor, anyway!"

But she knew that it was Taylor whom she had to please to keep her own job intact. Lynn knew that her job could be in jeopardy since she had on several occasions hotly defended Adam's position at the TV station. When contract time rolled around again, would she also get the ax?

"We'll just see about that. I may leave on my own," she further thought to herself. "But first, I've got to show Eliot Smith that a woman can hold her own in competition with any man."

Moving slowly from the room, she stepped out into a wide, bright hallway that stretched in many directions, leading to conference rooms, more offices, lounges, and the main TV studio, where different sets were partitioned off in smaller, soundproof, windowless rooms.

The plush beige carpet muffling her footsteps, Lynn moved on down the hallway, nodding a silent "hello" to others passing by and to the receptionists sitting at their desks outside various closed doors. When she finally reached the door that led into the executive offices of Jonathan Taylor, managing director and major stockholder of KSFC-TV, she stopped to compose herself before letting Taylor's secretary announce her arrival.

Lynn smiled toward Mary Thompson who sat smugly behind her grand oak desk. Mary's pink cashmere sweater looked expensive and she wore a strand of pearls draped ostentatiously around her neck. Her hair was a bright auburn, cut short, with tight curls framing her perky, somewhat square face. A soft color of blush had been applied to her high cheekbones and her lips gleamed from a layer of matching lipstick. Her fingernails were long and neatly filed and polished, proof that Mary's duties did not include typing.

Ignoring Mary's cold stare, Lynn lifted her fingers to her hair and smoothed it to fall silkily across her shoulders. Then she straightened the lines of her dress, cleared her throat and nodded toward Mary. "Will you please buzz Mr. Taylor for me now, Mary?" she asked briskly. "He's expecting me."

She listened to Mary's monotone announcing her on the intercom, then opened the door and stepped inside the spacious wood-paneled room. She closed the door and held her head high as she made her way across the vast room to where the seventy-year-old millionaire sat behind his huge desk, puffing away on a cigar. The room was bright with the morning sun spilling in through the wide expanse of windows at Taylor's broad, bent back. The smell of new carpet, waxed paneling and cigar smoke intermingled to create one rich aroma. A plush, upholstered chair placed in front of Taylor's desk was an open invitation for Lynn to settle into it.

Taylor nodded toward the chair. As Lynn sat down, Taylor eyed her through thick-lensed, black-rimmed glasses perched on a wide, bulbous nose. His face was too heavy to be wrinkled and his hair was suspiciously dark and thick for a man of his advanced years. His dark suit was impeccably pressed and a black tie lay perfectly in place on an immaculate white shirt.

Taylor leaned back in his chair, dissembling cool self-possession. "I see you've come," he said gruffly. He removed the cigar from between his teeth, flicking ashes into an ashtray. "Your timing is good. Eliot Smith is due here any minute."

The same bitterness Lynn had felt for Eliot from the beginning arose again, making her feel cold inside. She crossed her long elegant legs and met his piercing gaze. "So that's why you've asked to see me," she said icily. "To meet Adam's replacement."

Taylor leaned his full weight on his desk. His shoulders were thick and massive. "Lynn, your attitude distresses me," he said, furrowing his brow. "Don't you think I've noticed how you deliberately avoid meeting Eliot? God, girl, how do you expect to go on camera with him if you don't give him a chance?"

"He'll get his chance," she said, giving Taylor a grim look. "He'll have one hell of a chance. He signed the contract, didn't he?"

"If not him, someone else," Taylor growled, thrusting his cigar back into his mouth. He took two deep drags, then chomped his teeth angrily onto it and spoke out of the other corner of his mouth. "Adam Lowenstein had to go. You know that. His demands were becoming quite impossible."

Remembering that Adam's demands were not demands at all, but rather a reasonable request for an increase in his salary to match the increase in inflation, Lynn was once more ready to come to the defense of her dear, loyal friend. She rose from the chair and placed the palms of her hands flat on the top of Taylor's desk, leaning close to him. "You're aware of the public's reaction to Adam's leaving," she said. "He's been a part of the show for twelve years now. It's going to take a lot of hard work to get the public to accept a new face. Everyone loved Adam. Who knows? They may despise Eliot Smith."

Taylor jerked his cigar from his mouth and glared at Lynn through angry, squinted eyes. "You'd better not encourage it," he growled.

"I'm much more professional than that, Taylor," Lynn sighed. "As you very well know."

"Keep that in mind, Lynn," Taylor stated, then

glanced toward the door as Mary stuck her head in, announcing Eliot's arrival.

Lynn tensed, aware that the dreaded moment to meet Eliot Smith had come, a meeting that she could no longer avoid.

"Send him in," Taylor said to Mary, rising from his chair. He crushed his cigar out in an ashtray and coughed into a cupped fist to clear his throat. Then straightening his tie, he walked heavily to the door and welcomed Eliot into the room, a broad smile on his face.

Lynn rose from her chair and turned slowly to take her first look at this man whom she was prepared to dislike on sight.

"Glad you could make it," Taylor said, shaking Eliot's hand vigorously. "The airlines have been hell lately. You can't count on them anymore. It's the unions. They keep demanding but the service gets worse and worse, and costs more and more."

"We *did* circle a bit before finally landing," Eliot said, returning the handshake. "But I'm damn glad we finally *did* land," he added, raking his eyes over Lynn. "One minute longer would've been too much to have kept me from meeting *this* lovely lady." He removed his hand from Taylor's powerful grip and walked on toward Lynn, now offering it to her. "Lynn, I'm glad we're finally getting to meet. You don't know how much I've admired your work."

Lynn was stunned speechless by his unexpectedly boyish charm. She hadn't expected him to be so handsome nor so friendly. She had thought too often of him as cold, calculating, and brash. But instead he appeared just the opposite and was even causing her to blush by his obvious appreciation of her. Could he tell that she was quite pleasantly surprised by him? He had the tall, lean figure and broad shoulders of a man who didn't have to work at keeping fit. His short-cropped dark hair was very lightly touched with gray and his warm, brown, penetrating eyes were the kind that spoke without words. His perfectly shaped, sensuous lips appeared permanently curved in quiet amusement and his velvet-toned voice reflected gentleness, yet strength.

He wore a simple gray suit, white shirt and navy blue tie. He was obviously the kind of man who took great pains with his appearance, yet once the desired effect was achieved paid no further attention to his striking looks. He was casually elegant and perfectly at ease.

Eliot took Lynn's hand in his and gently shook it. "You *are* Lynn Stafford, aren't you?" he chuckled, amused at her deep blush and her silence. He too had dreaded this meeting, having become aware of how she had been avoiding meeting him. He had tried to understand her attitude, but what he had gathered by her devotion to Adam Lowenstein was that possibly there was a hidden relationship there that no one knew about. Seeing her now and feeling this sudden attraction to her made a tinge of jealousy begin to coil in his gut.

Lynn's eyebrows lifted. "Why, yes, I'm Lynn Stafford," she murmured. "But of course you know that. You said you even . . ."

"Admired your work?" Eliot said, looking down into her face.

"Yes . . ." she said. Damn it! Why did she have to blush at his each and every word? What would he think? She couldn't explain to him that she always

21

listened to a man's voice, judging his personality by the tone and manner in which he spoke. She knew that she had acquired this habit because of her chosen profession, where the voice ruled, sometimes even over one's physical appearance. And this time? With this man? She hadn't wanted it to happen, had never dreamed she'd react this way, but the velvet of Eliot's voice seemed to be slowly spinning a web of rapture around her heart.

"I thought maybe you had a twin and I was meeting her," he said, chuckling a bit beneath his breath.

"And why on earth would you think that?"

"Because you're even lovelier in person," he said, bowing gallantly, teasingly.

Lynn jerked her hand away from his, annoyed. She didn't *want* to like him! It angered her to realize that he was making it impossible for her to dislike him—which was probably exactly what he intended. For so long she had prepared herself for a meeting quite different than this. Now she actually had to force herself to concentrate on Adam and why she had taken such a dislike to Eliot from the beginning.

Taylor edged himself between Eliot and Lynn and placed an arm about each of their shoulders. "I'm glad you've hit it off so well," he said, beaming from one to the other. "That makes it so much easier for all concerned."

Lynn eased away from Taylor, stubbornly setting her jaw. "Don't assume too much too quickly, Taylor," she said, then made up a feeble excuse and left the room, wondering why on earth she had said such a thing as that.

Walking quickly into her office, she began slowly

pacing back and forth, trying to sort through her feelings about Eliot Smith. How had she fallen victim to his charm so completely?

"Hey. You're like a caged tigress, ready to pounce," Adam said suddenly from behind her, entering her office. "What happened, hon? Did you meet the new boy wonder?"

Lynn spun around and her heart grew heavy when she saw Adam standing there holding a box filled with his personal office memorabilia. The old bitterness toward Eliot Smith surfaced again, torturing her insides, as she was faced with the actual fact of Adam's leaving. Her gaze moved slowly up, seeing affection for her in the depths of his blue eyes.

"I must go shopping," she quickly murmured. She grabbed her purse and went to Adam. "I think I need a new hat. Let's put your stuff in your car—then you can help me pick one out, and we'll have lunch."

Adam laughed. "God, Lynn, something must really be bothering you," he said. "You always buy a new hat when you're upset about something."

Lynn's lashes felt heavy as she met Adam's questioning look. "Adam, I may have to buy *two* hats this time," she murmured.

# *Two*

WATER LAPPED at Lynn's bare feet as she jogged along the sand near her spacious beach house. In the far distance she could see lights from a passing ship twinkling like stars in the sky against the backdrop of night and she could hear a foghorn resounding hollowly across the water.

The moist night air felt chilly and damp against her bare legs and shoulders. She wished now that she had worn more than shorts and a halter. The evenings were getting cooler and the days shorter.

Flipping damp tendrils of hair back from her face, she lifted her chin and lengthened her stride. She had made one trip up and down the beach and was now only a few heaving breaths away from the steps that led up to her sundeck built on high stilts over the sand.

"Wait up, Lynn!"

Hearing the familiar voice of her friend Cathy coming from behind her, Lynn stopped and turned. Panting, she peered through the darkness, seeing Cathy's bulky silhouette only a little darker than the night. Cathy wasn't as tall as Lynn, but much

24

heavier and her figure was easy to identify even in the dark.

"Hi, Cathy," Lynn said as Cathy stopped before her, also panting. "You're out kind of late, aren't you? You usually jog before it gets dark."

Cathy laughed. "Yeah, I know. I usually do. It's safer that way," she said. "You know how I've worried about *you* running alone in the dark, Lynn. You should get a dog or something to protect you."

"I've thought about it," Lynn admitted, then added, "Cathy, why *are* you out so late?"

Cathy shrugged. "Pete's been called out of town again."

At this moment the moon came out from behind a cloud, revealing the hurt in her friend's eyes. Lynn understood why Cathy didn't want to talk about Pete or why he was gone again. Though they had been married for fifteen years, that fact didn't make for devotion on Pete's part.

"Come on in and have a glass of wine, Cathy," Lynn said, nodding toward her house. "Let's get some warmth in our blood. I didn't realize it was so cold."

Cathy wiped beads of perspiration from her brow with the sleeve of her sweatshirt. "I'm not a bit cold," she said. "In fact, I'm about to burn up."

Lynn's gaze moved over the heavy warm-up suit and sneakers. Cathy's auburn hair was in long braids, hanging down her back almost to her waist, and her mascara had run a bit from her thick, long lashes down onto her cheeks. "I guess you must be," she laughed. "You're dressed for winter, I'd say."

Cathy glanced down at her outfit. "Pete got these for me today," she said with a sigh. "He said maybe

I'd sweat off a few pounds if I wore this while jogging."

"So he *does* at least approve of you jogging," Lynn said, sarcasm apparent in her voice.

"He says it's the second best thing to dieting," Cathy said, shrugging.

"Christ . . . !" Lynn whispered under her breath. "Men!" She took Cathy by an elbow. "Come on inside. I have something to show you and *then* we'll have that glass of wine."

"Lynn, don't tell me you've bought yourself another hat," Cathy said, moving up the steps next to her.

"You've got it," Lynn laughed. "You know me pretty well, Cathy."

"What happened today to send you out on another shopping spree? More trouble at work?"

"Something like that," Lynn sighed. She stepped up on the sundeck and moved across it, and through the open glass sliding door into her living room. She shook sand from her feet and bent and wiped her fingers between her toes, then grabbed a towel from the back of a chair and dried her face which was damp from the mist.

Cathy stepped into the room, shoving the sleeves of her sweatshirt up above her elbows. "I love it," she suddenly said, plopping down onto a chair. She slipped her sneakers off and curled her feet beneath her. "Absolutely love it!" she repeated.

Fluffing her hair with the towel, Lynn looked toward Cathy with a lifted brow. "Love what?" she queried.

"The way you've chosen to remodel your house," Cathy said, leaning casually back against the chair.

"Thanks," Lynn murmured, gazing proudly around her. She had managed a "show-stopping contemporary look" without the assistance of an interior designer. Before the spacious copper-hooded fireplace she had placed a twelve-foot-long S-shaped sofa covered in camel duck with curved, mirrored glass tables at each end. Beige, industrial shoe vinyl gave the walls a slick, dramatic look and a beige area rug with bold navy blue trim covered most of the wood floor. A contemporary sleeper and lucite chairs provided additional seating.

"But don't you get lonesome way out here all alone?" Cathy asked.

Lynn draped her towel across the back of a chair. "Now how can I get lonely with a friend like you in your beach house within yelling range of mine?" she said. "No. I don't get lonesome." She felt a familiar empty feeling in the pit of her stomach, remembering the long, lonely nights, but she would never admit to it. She had only recently begun to worry that just possibly she *wouldn't* find another man to fill the void that Randy had left by his untimely death. Was she destined to be alone for the rest of her life?

Shaking her head briskly, she moved quickly toward where she had left a hat box on a table. "And now . . ." She laughed. "My new hat!" She lifted the lid from the box. "It's gorgeous, Cathy. Absolutely gorgeous."

Cathy rose to her feet. "Well, let me *see*," she said, moving toward Lynn. "Don't keep me waiting."

"It's sexy, Cathy," Lynn giggled, reaching inside for the hat. "I know you'll love it." As she pulled it from the box she heard Cathy's quick intake of breath.

"Put it on," Cathy said softly.

Lynn placed the hat on her head. "Well?" she said, making a slow turn in the middle of the room. "What do you think?"

"Heavenly." Cathy sighed.

"Do you really think so?"

"Smashing." Cathy giggled. "And with your green eyes, you look seductive as hell. Wish I could get away with something like that."

Smiling her thanks to Cathy, Lynn went to a mirror and looked admiringly back at her reflection. She turned her head first one way and then another. Yes, it was a perfect hat to match her current mood, a bold, sweeping 'padre' hat modified by Irene of New York, with wide, flat brim and a jeweled band. It was of this autumn's fashionable burgundy color and would exactly match Lynn's new classic wool suit of the same color.

Cathy leaned against the wall next to Lynn. "You still didn't say exactly *why* you bought the hat," she said. "I know you, Lynn. You always purchase a new hat when you're upset about something. But what? Tell me."

Lynn pulled the hat from her head and shook her hair back, over her shoulders. She placed the hat back inside its box. "I finally met him today," she murmured, avoiding Cathy's watchful stare.

"Who?"

"Eliot Smith. I met *him* today, Cathy."

"You did? What was he like?"

Lynn tossed her head with a dry laugh. "I was afraid you'd ask me that."

"Afraid . . . ?" Cathy murmured. "Why afraid? What do you mean?"

Still avoiding Cathy's questioning gaze, Lynn crossed to the bar at the far end of the room, next to Lynn's entertainment center where the latest VCR equipment, a stereo and speakers and TV were located. Soft splashes of moonlight filtered through the sheer, gathered curtains at the window to one side of Lynn. Another foghorn in the distance sent shivers up and down her spine.

"Lynn, you're daydreaming," Cathy said, laughing softly as she moved to Lynn's side. "Or are you purposely evading my question?"

Lynn handed Cathy a long-stemmed wine glass. "Cathy, I met Eliot Smith and . . . and . . ."

Helping herself to the wine, Cathy poured some in her glass. She took a sip, eyeing Lynn quizzically. Then she turned the glass around between her fingers. "And what?" she persisted. "Was he such a terrible person you can't even talk about him?"

Lynn shook her head softly. She poured herself a glass of wine and took a sip, then sank down onto a chair, drawing her legs beneath her. "No," she murmured. "He wasn't at all like I expected. He's even . . ."

The ringing of the doorbell drew Lynn quickly back up from the chair. She questioned Cathy with her eyes.

Cathy shrugged her shoulders. "I dunno, Lynn," she whispered. "Are you expecting anyone?"

Lynn tensed. "No," she whispered back. "Not a soul. I had planned to try and relax all evening for a change. I expect the next several days will be quite taxing."

29

"You mean dealing with Eliot Smith?" Cathy asked. Her hand flew to her throat as the doorbell rang shrilly again.

"I'd better see who it is," Lynn said, placing her glass on an end table.

"I'll stay till you do," Cathy said, taking her empty glass to the bar, and leaving it there. "But, first, let's take a quick peek. I don't like you being here alone so much. *Anyone* could see you on TV, like what he saw, and find out where you live."

"My phone number is unlisted and it's the policy of the station to never give the addresses or phone numbers to those who call and ask," Lynn reminded her.

"Someone could follow you, Lynn," Cathy whispered, tiptoeing to the front window.

"Oh, Cathy," Lynn sighed, reluctantly following her. "You read too many mysteries."

Cathy pulled the drape back a fraction and peered outward where a floodlight lit the whole front lawn and door as brightly as day, the one precaution Lynn had agreed to take. "God, Lynn," Cathy gasped. "Is he handsome! Who *is* that hunk of man?"

Lynn's eyebrows raised. She moved to Cathy's side, edging next to the window, looking out. "Who?" she whispered. "Let me see." Her heart palpitated and her face grew suddenly hot.

"Well?" Cathy whispered, once more quizzically eyeing Lynn. "Do you know him?"

"I can't believe it!" Lynn hissed, storming away from the window. She stopped and stared unbelievingly toward the closed door, crossing her arms angrily over her chest. "I just can't *believe* this! Who does he think he is? How on earth did he find out where I lived? If Taylor told him, I'll . . ."

Cathy grabbed Lynn by the arm. "Lynn, don't tell me that's . . ."

"Eliot Smith," Lynn grumbled between tight lips. "How *did* he . . . ?"

"I believe I smell a rat named Taylor."

"Taylor? Your boss?"

The doorbell rang again. Cathy jumped, then inched her way backward, toward the sliding glass door. "I guess I'd better go," she mumbled, stopping to rescue her sneakers. Then she stopped, eyes wide. "Or would you rather I'd stay?"

Lynn moved quickly to Cathy and ushered her on outside to the sundeck. "I can handle this, Cathy," she said dryly. "But thanks anyway." She dropped a light kiss to Cathy's cheek. "And you hurry on home. You shouldn't be out on the beach alone, either."

"Call me," Cathy whispered, edging toward the steps. "Tell me what transpires!"

Lynn laughed nervously. "Sure. Will do. Bye."

Cathy waved and rushed on down the steps and into the darkness. Lynn whirled around and hurried back into the living room.

"Oh!" she said, stomping a bare foot on the carpet as the doorbell rang again. "Why doesn't he just leave? I don't want to talk to him. Tomorrow morning is too soon as far as I'm concerned."

Her gaze caught her reflection in the mirror, seeing the way she looked. "Shorts, halter and sand still itching between my toes." She groaned. She ran her fingers through her hair. "And, God, my hair's a rat's nest!"

Another long, lingering ring and Lynn rushed

angrily to the door and swung it open in one fast jerk.

"Well, hi there," Eliot drawled, leaning cross-armed against the frame.

Seeing his boyish grin and the sparkle in his eyes set Lynn's heart to nervously racing. His face was as handsome as she remembered it, with a long, aquiline nose, square jaw and strong chin. His berry-colored sweater revealed classically molded shoulders and a stand of crisp, black chest hair protruding from its V-neck. His Levi's showed off the muscled strength of his legs and his narrow waist.

"What are you doing here?" she finally managed to ask, crossing her own arms defiantly across her chest.

Eliot's eyes passed slowly over her. "To see if we could call a truce," he said thickly. "And to try to find out why you've decided to dislike me before you even know me."

"If you must know, it's not that I dislike *you*," she said coolly. "It's what you've done and how you've managed to do it."

"Like what?"

"Like helping Taylor remove Adam Lowenstein from his place at the station."

"You surely can't . . ."

"Yes I can. Now will you just please leave?"

Eliot sighed and his eyes rolled back into his head. "So that's what this is all about," he said. His gaze moved back to Lynn. "I think I can explain everything. How about inviting me in and letting us talk this out?"

"I've things to do," Lynn said dryly.

"It's still early."

Lynn glanced over her shoulder, then back toward Eliot. "Oh, all right," she murmured. "But only for a few minutes. I haven't been home long and as I said, I have a lot of things to do." She stepped aside and stiffened as he walked past her, carrying with him a pleasant aroma of aftershave.

As earlier in the day, Lynn felt the same sensuous tremor edge its way through her. Now, as then, she tried to resist the feelings, not wanting to even like him.

Clearing her throat nervously, she closed the door and moved into the living room where he was making himself quite at home, strolling leisurely around the room, inspecting it.

"For a lady, you do quite well for yourself," he said, then hearing her gasp, knew that he had said the wrong thing. Flinching a bit, he swung around, seeing the flush of anger spreading across her face.

"For a *lady?*" she fumed. "So you *are* a male chauvinist!"

Eliot moved to her and drew her quickly into his arms, cutting off further words with a fiery kiss. He held her tightly against him in spite of her protests, while she beat at his chest with her hands.

What right did he have to grab her like that? If only Cathy were still there! He was too blatantly male! His kiss was causing dangerous feelings to erupt inside her, feelings she had thought dead even since Randy . . .

Enraged by these feelings, Lynn drew back one foot and viciously kicked at his shin. But the result wasn't as expected. She had forgotten that she wore no shoes. Her big toe snapped audibly as it made contact with his leg, sending messages of agony to her brain. She flinched and groaned and as he let her go, she grabbed at her throbbing toe and hobbled to a chair, easing down into it.

Eliot laughed a bit beneath his breath, and Lynn glared upward at him. "What's so funny?" she snapped. "I may have broken my toe!"

"I doubt that," he said. "Not if it's as hard as your head. I sense that you're quite bullheaded, a woman who's used to getting her way. Am I right?"

"Look who's talking," she hissed. "You've got Adam's job, haven't you?" When her toe throbbed even harder, she emitted a soft moan and held tightly to it, rocking herself back and forth.

"You're being unfair, you know," he said softly, ignoring her misery.

"Am I?" she said icily.

"Yes. You are," he said, kneeling down on one knee before her. "Now let me see your toe."

"No way!" she snapped.

"Let's see what damage you've inflicted."

"No!" she said, scooting farther back on the chair, drawing her foot up away from his hand.

"Why did you leave that TV station in Seattle?" she persisted, purposely ignoring his interest in her toe, and her own pain. She knew that his concern had to be forced. He wasn't concerned over anyone else, was he? Like Adam, for instance!

"The weather there gets pretty depressing," he said.

"It's no better here," she argued.

"I'm sure the sun has to shine here much more than it does in Seattle. And rain—God, almost every day."

When Eliot straightened up and moved away from

her, Lynn rose from the chair and tried to put her full weight on her foot, but the intense pain in her toe drew her quickly back down again. She squeezed her fingers about her toe and closed her eyes as another low groan rose deeply from inside her.

"Is it that bad?" Eliot asked, again dropping to a knee before her. He forced her hand away from her foot and gently examined the toe that was turning a pale purplish color and was noticeably swollen.

His dark eyes rose to meet her questioning stare. "It *is* that bad," he murmured. "Either you strike a powerful blow, or my leg is made of steel."

The touch of his hand against Lynn's flesh and his dark pools of eyes were making her acutely aware of the desire building inside her for this man. It had been so long! Why *now?* Why *him?* But she knew that sometimes nature took charge, even when least expected.

Lynn swallowed hard. "I guess maybe it's a combination of both," she laughed nervously.

Eliot rose to his feet, looking over his shoulder. "Where's your kitchen? I'll get some ice. We've got to get the swelling stopped or you won't be able to get into a pair of shoes for a week."

"Oh, no!" she groaned. Then her eyes snapped in many shades of green as she glared upward at him. "It's all your fault," she accused. "If you hadn't come . . ."

Then she paled a bit. "How did you know where I lived?" she asked suspiciously. "Surely Taylor didn't . . ."

A slow smile lifting the corner of Eliot's lips gave Lynn the answer she was seeking without his speaking. She doubled her hands into tight fists and hit the cushion of the chair on both sides of her. "How could he?" she fumed. "I value my privacy. He *knows* that!"

"He also knows that we need to iron out our differences before tomorrow," Eliot said. "We do have a show to do together, you know."

Lynn threw her head back with an exasperated sigh. "Tomorrow . . ." she murmured. Her jaw suddenly set stubbornly as she once more pushed herself up from the chair. "Yes, tomorrow. I do have to be all right. I've so much to do." Letting him appear on the show alone could be the beginning of the end for her. She couldn't let it happen! She would get to the studio even if she had to be carried! But, first, she'd prove to herself that she could move around under her own power!

She began hobbling back and forth, flinching as renewed pains shot from the wounded toe, on up her leg. Then, unable to bear it any longer, she sank back down onto the chair and looked defeatedly toward him. "Maybe I *do* need some ice on this toe," she murmured. She pointed toward the kitchen. "In there. And you'll find a washcloth at the end of the hall, in the linen closet."

"As good as done," he said over his shoulder as he moved away from her.

Lynn rested her hand against the back of the chair and closed her eyes. This was all unbelievable. Here she was, helpless and at the mercy of Eliot Smith, of all people!

"Eliot . . ." she whispered, testing his name on the tip of her tongue. Rather a nice name, all things considered. She'd been hypnotized by his charm, which he had no doubt been practicing for years, on women who probably fell all over themselves whenever he looked their way.

"I won't let him charm me!" she argued to herself. "I still don't trust him."

"One washcloth filled with ice coming up," Eliot said, coming back into the room and toward Lynn.

Once more she was aware of his torso sculptured to manly perfection and the proud way in which he held himself. She purposely avoided his eyes as he dropped to his knees before her.

"This should feel better in no time," he murmured, holding the ice pack against her toe while he let her foot rest in the palm of his other hand.

His gentleness, his nearness, was causing a wild, sensuous pleasure to soar through Lynn. She could feel the heat rising to her cheeks. But it was too dangerous to admit these sensations. "Here," she hurriedly said, brushing his hands aside. "I'll do it myself."

She forced a sharpness in her words and frowned at him. "I'm not completely helpless, you know."

"Maybe I can get you a drink," he said, rising quickly, eyeing the bar.

"No, I don't need a drink," she said. "In fact, I'd much rather you leave." Again she forced a cold sharpness into her words. "You weren't invited here, you know."

"But we haven't even discussed the programs that are scheduled," he softly argued. "You don't expect me to jump into this thing blind, do you?"

"I'm sure Taylor can fill you in on everything," she said dryly. She lifted the ice pack and wiggled her toe, wincing when a sharp pain once more engulfed it. "If this keeps up, I may have to appear on the damn set on *crutches!*"

Eliot placed a hand to his mouth and stifled a low laugh.

Lynn's eyes rose flashingly angry to his. "You still find this amusing, knowing that you may have made me an invalid?" she hotly accused.

"It's not broken," he said, sliding his hand partway into his rear Levi's pockets. "You'll survive."

"Sure," she hissed. "That's easy for *you* to say. You've got your shoes on. By tomorrow I'll be lucky to get my panty hose on!"

Eliot leaned down over her, placing his hands on the arms of the chair on either side of her. "Oh, poor baby," he crooned. He pressed a soft kiss to her lips. "Now why don't you let me get you a glass of wine? You'll feel better. I guarantee it."

She angrily shoved him away and wiped at her mouth, yet unavoidably tingling inside from the taste of him that lingered on her lips. "Will you just please *leave?*" she pleaded.

"After one very small drink," he said, moving casually toward the bar. "A bit of sherry for my lady."

Lynn groaned. "I'm not your lady!" she fumed. "I'm not your anything!"

He gave her a wry look from over his shoulder. "You're my co-host," he teased. "I'd say that's something, wouldn't you?"

"Not by choice. Or do you forget so easily?"

Ignoring her answer, Eliot poured two glasses of wine and moved back toward her with them. "Here. Drink this," he said, offering her one. "It's just what this doctor orders."

Lifting her chin stubbornly, she crossed her arms

across her chest. "I really don't care for any," she said through clenched teeth.

"Methinks you protest too much," he said, placing the glass close to her lips.

"Oh, all right," she said, circling her fingers about the thin, long stem of the glass. "I'll drink it if you promise to leave after you've finished with yours."

"I promise," he said. "Cross my heart and hope to die."

Lynn had to laugh. "Good Lord," she said. "I haven't heard that since I was a child."

Eliot settled down in a chair across from her. He took a sip of wine, then eyed her with a lifted eyebrow. "If I didn't know better, I'd think you were still that child," he said.

Lynn leaned forward. "Of all the . . ." She gasped.

"The way you're behaving over this whole thing," he said calmly. "Can't you accept change? Surely you've met other challenges and changes before in your career."

The doorbell's sudden ring was Lynn's reprieve for the moment. But then she had to wonder who else might be dropping in on her uninvited. This was becoming a night of surprises.

Groaning from the pain, she pushed herself up from the chair when the doorbell rang again, then began to hobble toward the door.

"I'll get it," Eliot quickly said, rising from his chair.

Lynn reached and grabbed him by the arm. "No, you won't," she said from between clenched teeth. "This is my house. You won't take charge here."

Eliot's expression was blank. "Huh?" he said. "Take charge?"

"I'll answer my *own* darn door!" Lynn said, hobbling across the floor. She cast Eliot a sharp glance from across her shoulder. "And since you've drunk your wine, please let yourself out as my other guest arrives. That's surely not too much to ask, is it?"

Putting his glass down on a table, Eliot walked past her and placed his hand on the doorknob as he turned to her. "I'll do you one better than that," he said. "I'll graciously invite your guest in, then most politely excuse myself. Kind of like a silent butler."

Lynn reached a hand toward him. "Eliot . . ." she began, but was too late. Eliot had swung the door open and Lynn was startled to see Eliot standing face-to-face with Adam in strained silence.

"You!" Adam growled, paling.

"You . . ." Eliot growled back. Color rose to his cheeks as he turned and gave Lynn an accusing stare. He had suspected something more than a business relationship between these two, and now his feelings were confirmed. It lowered his opinion of Lynn, knowing that Adam was married, and even had grandchildren. He was even old enough to be Lynn's father.

Lynn limped to the door and edged herself between Adam and Eliot, laughing nervously. Her gaze moved from one to the other. Though Adam had denied holding a grudge against Eliot, it was visibly there in his face. And she understood. "You've met before," she finally said weakly. "Now you meet again. How nice."

"Nice?" Eliot echoed, lifting an eyebrow.

Lynn could feel his dark eyes boring through her. She sensed much more antagonism on his part than the situation warranted. And most of it seemed directed at her, not at Adam.

"Hon, I notice you're having difficulty walking," Adam said, clasping his fingers onto her shoulders, swinging her around to face him. "What's happened?"

Eliot's fists doubled at his side. "Hon?" he whispered. Then he stomped out of the house, leaving Lynn and Adam standing staring blankly after him.

"He is a strange fella," Adam said, shrugging.

"You're telling me," Lynn grumbled. She watched Eliot's car speed away, not understanding him at all. But a chill wrapping itself about her bare legs and shoulders made her quickly forget him. She held onto the door as she limped back into the house.

"Come on, Adam," she said. "I need to get off my feet."

"I thought I'd check up on you, to see how things went with Taylor today," he said, closing the door behind him. "I never expected to find Eliot Smith here."

Lynn winced as a fresh pain shot through her toe. She crumped down into a chair and caressed it with her fingers. "To call a truce," she sarcastically laughed. "Can you imagine the nerve of him coming to my house? Darn that Taylor! I could wring his neck." She moaned as the toe throbbed.

"What happened to your toe?" Adam said, settling into a chair opposite her. "Christ, Lynn, it's all swollen and black and blue."

Lynn blushed. "I just—stubbed it," she murmured. "That's all. Clumsy me!" She would never confess to how she'd actually injured her toe. It sounded too utterly ridiculous, and if one more man laughed at her tonight, she'd probably scream!

# Three

THE SURF was loud, almost deafening as it crashed on the beach and then onto the rocky cliffs beyond. Lynn stood at a window in a heavy flannel robe, shivering, watching the angry ocean through the dismal gray mists of early morning. In all her years of living at the beach house, she had never seen the ocean so turbulent. It seemed to match her feelings. Her throbbing, aching toe was a constant reminder of Eliot Smith and the previous humiliating evening. In spite of herself, she could still feel his lips devouring hers and the strength of his body against her own.

A crazy glow rippled through her, as she remembered how much she had felt like a teenager being kissed for the first time. There was something magical in Eliot's touch, like no other man's since Randy's. Suddenly it was hard for Lynn to remember Randy's kisses and embraces. Eliot's face seemed to constantly be there, swimming before her eyes, taking Randy's place.

"No!" Lynn harshly whispered, tightly closing her eyes. "This can't be happening. I won't let it happen! I don't even like the man! Because of him, I missed the show for the first time ever!"

The doorbell ringing startled Lynn and her heart began to race. She limped around and eyed the door with trepidation. It surely wasn't . . .

"Lynn, hon?" Adam's voice broke through the silence. "Are you all right?"

A relieved smile eased across Lynn's face. Reaching from chair to chair, she managed to move toward the door. When she opened it she literally fell into Adam's arms. "Adam, I'm so glad you've come," she murmured, resting her cheek against his chest.

"Why? Has something else happened?" he asked, running his fingers through her hair. "You weren't on 'Morning Magazine.' A million things ran through my mind and everything led right back to Eliot Smith. He was smug as shit on the show this morning."

Lynn drew away from him. "I didn't watch," she snapped irritably.

"Lynn, why didn't you appear on screen this morning?"

Lynn lifted her bare foot up for his inspection. "My darn toe," she said. "There was no way I could get a shoe on this morning. And I wasn't about to go to the studio in my stocking feet. Eliot would enjoy that too much. He loves laughing at other people's misfortunes."

"Have you gone to a doctor, Lynn? That toe may be broken."

Lynn shivered in the chill, once more hearing the crashing of the waves and feeling the damp sea breeze whipping at the skirt of her flannel robe. "Come on in, Adam," she said, avoiding his question. "Have a cup of coffee with me."

"I don't have long," he said, stepping on past her. "I've got to get to the radio station. My office should be just about ready for me to move in."

Lynn closed the door and limped on back into the living room, eyeing Adam admiringly. "You look fit as a fiddle," she said. She liked his gray tweed sport coat paired with navy denim jeans, white oxford cloth dress shirt and red knit tie.

"You don't think I'm too old to show up for work in jeans?"

"Adam," Lynn sighed. "Age is all in the mind, didn't you know?" She went up to him and straightened his tie. "You look spiffy. Absolutely spiffy!"

Adam lowered a soft kiss to the tip of her nose. "You're good for the ego, kid," he chuckled. "I guess that's why we always got along so well."

Forgetting her toe, and putting her full weight on her foot, Lynn let out a loud yelp, edged her way to a chair and eased down into it.

"Lynn, for heaven's sake!" Adam said. "Did you go to the doctor?"

"No," she murmured. "And stop worrying. I'm going to be all right." She nodded toward the kitchen. "Adam, the coffee is in there. If you want a cup, I'm afraid you'll have to get it yourself."

"I've already had a half dozen cups this morning," he said, strolling to the wide, glass sliding door to gaze intently through it. Then he swung around. "I'll get you a cup if you'd like."

Lynn shook her hair back from her face and settled against the plump cushion of the chair. "No. I don't need any either," she said. "I'm filled to the brim with caffeine and jittery as all get-out!"

Adam went and leaned down over her. "Before I

leave, isn't there anything I can do for you?"

Reaching out a hand, she touched his cheek. "Nothing," she whispered. "Except . . ."

"Except what?"

"Go knock 'em dead on the radio!" she said, laughing softly.

"Oh, yeah!" he chuckled. "That would only be guaranteed if you were sitting at my side."

Lynn's hand dropped to her lap and she looked away. "You know those days are gone for good," she said.

"And there's no sense fighting it. Right?" Adam growled, straightening his back.

Meeting his steady gaze, Lynn said, "There is something you can do for me, Adam."

"Anything," he said.

"It's so cold in here," she said, shivering again. "Maybe you could start a fire in the fireplace?"

"Then you're planning to stay home the rest of the day?"

Lynn's eyes traveled to her foot. "Maybe for the rest of the week," she laughed. "And, Adam, I'm even kind of glad."

"You are? Why?"

"Because I'd hate having to run into Eliot Smith again for any reason, even if it means being edged out of the show!"

Adam began placing wood and wadded newspaper on the grate of the fireplace. He struck a match to it and stood back, watching the fire take hold, spreading from newspaper to newspaper. "I'm sorry, Lynn," he murmured. "None of this would've happened if I'd signed that damn contract."

"Adam!" she scolded. "What a thing to say. You

45

and I both know you did what you had to do. You were working your head off—and for what?"

Adam lifted another log in place, then wiped his hands on his Levi's as he walked toward her. "Yes, I know," he said. "But I'd hate to see that I've messed up your life."

"I'll be all right." She warmed inside as he took one of her hands and kissed it. "Just you run on to work. I'll relax today and clear my head of all questions and doubts."

"Sure?"

"Sure."

The ring of the doorbell drew Adam up, away from Lynn. "Are you expecting anyone?" he asked.

"It may be Cathy. She always watches 'Morning Magazine.' I'm sure she's as curious as you were about why I wasn't on." She looked up at Adam, pleading with her green eyes. "Would you go let her in? I think I'll just stay put. My darn toe just won't quit throbbing."

"Okay. And then I'll go ahead and leave." He leaned over and kissed her brow. "You sure you'll be all right?"

"Sure," she laughed. "Absolutely. Bye. You've got things on your mind more important than me. Go to it, Adam. Show 'em who's got the best voice in San Francisco!"

"Like I said," he laughed. "You're good for my ego."

With wide strides, he went to the door and opened it. Lynn turned around to see Eliot standing there, facing Adam with a dark frown etched across his handsome face. Her heart began a wild thumping. She was torn. A part of her was undeniably glad to see him and another part was angry, furious that he had the gall to invade her privacy again.

"Well," Eliot said, stepping into the room. "Isn't this cozy?" His eyes took in Lynn's casual attire and the romantic glow from the fireplace.

"What are you doing here?" Adam growled. "You should have your hands full at the station with Lynn not there."

"I wanted to check on Lynn first hand," Eliot said dryly. "I feel she's partly my responsibility since she's my co-host now."

With a low growl, Adam went to Lynn and touched her gently on one cheek. "I'm going," he said. "Will you be able to handle things?"

"Yes," Lynn whispered back. "Please do go on. I can take care of myself." Yet she silently wondered about that. Eliot did have a way about him, one she found hard to resist.

"I feel I'd better get out of here or I may do something quite out of character," Adam whispered, nodding toward Eliot. "There's something about him that sure doesn't tickle my funny bone."

Lynn giggled and blew Adam a kiss as he nodded toward her and quickly left the room. Then she turned her eyes accusingly to Eliot. "That was quite uncalled for," she said icily.

Eliot, dressed in beige slacks and matching V-neck sweater, kneeled down beside her. "I don't know what you're talking about," he said innocently. His dark eyes were wide and gleaming as he let his gaze move over her. His face was in shadow, as he wondered if Adam had spent the night. Jealousy tore at his insides. He was convinced that he had to win her over quickly before telling her the news that he had that very morning been put in charge of the programming for 'Morning Magazine,' Lynn's responsibility up until now.

"You were quite rude to Adam," she accused.

"And he wasn't to me?"

"What did you mean by that snide remark about coziness?" she further fumed.

"Did I say that?" he teased.

Lynn could smell a rich cologne emanating from his flesh and his dark eyes were turning her insides to mush. "Would you please . . . ?" she murmured, inching down in her chair, away from him.

"Please what?" he said huskily. "Kiss you?"

Lynn's eyes flashed, and she gave him a shove which sent him tumbling awkwardly to the floor. She covered her mouth with a hand when she saw him look up at her with astonishment. She couldn't help but break into a soft laugh as he pushed himself clumsily up from the floor.

"What's so damn funny?" he snarled, brushing his dark hair back into place.

"You," she said, unable to stop laughing.

"Touche," he said, chuckling. "I deserved that. I remember laughing at you yesterday when you hurt your toe." He quickly sobered, looking down at her bare foot. "And how is it? It still looks swollen."

Lynn wiped tears of laughter from the corners of her eyes. "Yes, it is," she said. "Or I would've made it in to work. I've never missed a day of work at the station. As far as that goes, while in school, I didn't miss a day there either."

Eliot settled down on a chair and leaned forward, resting his elbows on his knees. "Where did you go to school? I've been in Seattle most of my life, except . . ."

His hesitation caused Lynn's eyebrows to arch a bit. "Except?" she repeated.

"Except for 'Nam . . ." he finished, raking his fingers through his hair.

Lynn was taken aback at his mention of Vietnam. It was as though someone had thrown cold water against her face. "You were in 'Nam?" she whispered. Her fingers were digging into the arm of her chair and her throat had become dry. The mention of 'Nam brought with it too many lonely, bitter memories. Somehow she would have never associated him with the war, perhaps because of his age.

"I was there in '73," he said.

"Were you in DaNang?" she murmured, trembling, remembering where Randy had died.

"Yes," he said.

"And you made it back alive," she sighed. "You were one of the lucky ones."

"I didn't fight. I was a war correspondent," he told her.

"Oh," she said, eyes wide.

"I know about your husband."

"You do?"

"Yes. Taylor told me."

Lynn's face flushed. "He seems to have filled you in fairly completely about my life," she said coolly. "Perhaps he would do better, though, if he just got on the tube and shouted out my private life to everyone. Then I wouldn't have to be so darn surprised when I find out that they already know."

"He's only trying to help," Eliot argued.

"He's interfering," Lynn said, rising awkwardly

to her feet. She let out a soft moan when she felt the pain shoot from her toe up into her ankle. She stumbled a bit and then found Eliot suddenly there, catching her.

"Here. Let me help you," he said huskily.

His face so close to hers and his hands on her waist sent a sensuous thrill through Lynn's body. Her eyes wavered as she met the challenge of his gaze. When his lips moved slowly to hers, she closed her eyes in mindless rapture and slowly twined her arms about his neck, returning the kiss with a breathlessness she could not conceal. And when his hands slid upward, stopping at her breasts, an involuntary shiver traveled through her, accompanied by a low moan of building passion.

"Lynn . . ." Eliot whispered, drawing his lips momentarily away from hers. "I need you. God, I need you!"

"But . . ." she began to protest, and was stopped by the hot demand of another kiss. She welcomed his tongue separating her lips and his hands easing her robe open and then from her shoulders. She felt the robe slide slowly to the floor, where it lay crumpled at her feet. She wanted to cry out in protest but instead a pleasurable warmth spread through her as one of his hands found and fondled one of her breasts while the other traveled over the nude velvet of her back and on down where her waist flared out into the sensuous curve of her hips.

"Baby . . ." Eliot groaned, then once more searched inside her mouth with his hot spear of a tongue.

Lynn's head was becoming giddy, her senses clouded. The throbbing between her thighs was driving her wild with the need of him, yet she fought this need more strongly than she had ever fought anything else in her life. To give in to him in this was the same as relinquishing everything to him, and she had yet to prove her worth to him in all other ways of importance. Yet her heart and the treacherous body would not listen, sweeping her recklessly onward.

"You can't walk, so let me carry you," Eliot whispered, lifting her gently into his arms.

She placed her cheek against his chest, in a semidrunken stupor. "Where are you taking me?" she whispered back.

Eliot once more cupped a breast and bent a kiss to her lips, then murmured, "Where would you like to go? I'm hoping to hear only one answer. I'm sure you know what *that* is."

Lynn nodded toward the hallway. "That way . . ." she said, laughing softly. But when he began carrying her in that direction, she suddenly tensed, remembering who he was. He should be the last person to be invited into her bedroom. Just as he stepped through the bedroom door, she began to squirm and push at his chest.

"Eliot, put me down!" she ordered. "This is wrong. I don't know what I was thinking." She was overpoweringly aware of her nudity and ashamed for having let things get this far. Usually she had more control of her feelings. What was there about Eliot that made her behave so recklessly?

She was quickly reminded. As he placed her on the bed, he leaned down over her, swept her once more into his arms and gave her a burning, lingering kiss. His fingers twined through her hair then forced

51

her lips even closer and harder against his. Then he whispered, "*Now* tell me to leave. Go ahead. I'm waiting."

He lowered his lips to one breast and sucked the nipple into his mouth, lapping his tongue hungrily over it while his free hand traveled slowly downward, setting small, sensuous fires along her flesh. And when his fingers crept on downward to the furry vee between her legs and slowly entered her there, Lynn knew that she was lost, slowly drowning in an ecstasy that she had denied herself for much too long. Eliot seemed to be an artist and she the canvas, as he slowly painted this scene of consuming pleasure. Lynn wanted him to complete it, up to the final stroke.

Moaning, she lowered a hand to his Levi's. She searched and found his zipper and slowly lowered it, to give her freedom to place her fingers inside. But when she felt his ready hardness, she flinched and jerked her hand away, once more awakened to what she was allowing him to do to her.

But this time all struggle was impossible. His fingers and mouth were already sending her on a cloud of rapture. She felt as though she were floating and knew that she didn't want this to end, no matter how much she knew she should hate this man.

"Lynn, darling . . ." Eliot whispered, lowering his lips across her body, even lower, until his tongue slowly replaced his fingers and let it worship her in a way that sent spirals of many shades of color spinning through Lynn's consciousness. She placed her hands on his head and forced him closer. She opened herself more to him, moaning gutturally.

Then she felt herself too close to the brink and urged him back up.

"Please . . ." she whispered, seeing him through haze-filled eyes. "Now. Please do it now. I can't wait any longer."

The burning ache was fast consuming her. She watched as he quickly discarded his clothes and as he finally entered her fully and began his soft, sweet strokes inside her, Lynn closed her eyes and let herself enjoy fully the sweet pain of passion.

When it was over, and Lynn lay curved into his body, she felt an urge to cry. She had never experienced anything as exciting as her union with Eliot. Though she had known the danger of these intimate moments with him she had willingly participated. And now that she had, she knew that she was as hopelessly addicted as an alcoholic who couldn't stay away from the bottle. She knew that she would want more and then more, as though she had lost control of her very existence because she would have to depend on him to fulfill this shameful craving.

"What's the matter?" Eliot whispered, turning to frame her face between his hands. "You're awfully quiet, Lynn. Are you sorry we . . . ?"

Lynn raised a finger quickly to his lips, sealing them. "No," she said, smiling softly at him. "I'm not. It's just that . . . well . . . it's been so long, Eliot. I haven't been with a man in so many years."

Eliot's heart raced. Surely she had to mean that Adam hadn't been intimate with her. But then he decided that perhaps she was not telling the truth. A woman like this could not possibly have gone for years without making love. She must have been with Adam—but he would change that. He was quite aware of the power he had over her.

"I hope I'm not just *any* man," he said huskily.

"No. You're not," she confessed. Then she laughed softly. "I even forgot about my sore toe!" And she had, only now she was reminded of its renewed throbbing. Her eyes grew wide as Eliot scooted down on the bed and gently placed his lips to the toe.

"Let me kiss the pain away," he said. Once more he kissed it, then sensuously sucked it inside his mouth, curling his tongue softly around it.

An ocean of renewed desire arose inside Lynn. Her heart began to pound and her eyes took on that crazy haze again. "Eliot, what *are* you doing?" she asked, laughing nervously.

One of his hands crept upward and captured a breast. He kneaded it, then rose back on top of her and kissed her with such heated passion Lynn felt as though her body was fusing to his. Wrapping her legs around his waist she eagerly accepted him inside her again and met his quick, hard thrusts until they both shuddered against one another in another rapturous release of desire for one another.

Panting beneath him, Lynn laughed even more drunkenly. "I think I was wrong about you, Eliot Smith," she said. "I think we're going to make one hell of a team, both on the screen and off!"

Eliot leaned up on an elbow. "I'm glad to hear you say that," he sighed. "I was fearing stormy waters ahead. It would've been hard working under those conditions."

"I guess I was wrong about you from the beginning," Lynn said, tracing his facial features with a forefinger.

Eliot laughed. "It took a session in bed to prove my worth, did it?"

Lynn felt a slow blush rising. "No, silly," she said. "I'm just realizing how foolish I was to blame you for what happened to Adam. I guess I knew all along but just didn't want to give in. I was too angry about Adam's leaving, and I overreacted. I'm terribly fond of Adam."

Eliot rose from the bed and began stepping into his clothes. He didn't want to talk about Adam. He was too afraid of what such talk might uncover. He wanted to believe that now she could put Adam and all other worries behind her. "I'd like a cup of coffee," he said at last, avoiding her eyes. "It sure smells good."

Lynn sat up on the edge of the bed. "Eliot, did I say something wrong?" she asked softly. "I thought you would be happy that I had conceded. Instead, you look a bit ill at ease."

Eliot slipped his sweater over his head. "You're imagining things," he said, forcing a smile. "Come on. Let's get that cup of coffee and sit before the fire." A fire Adam probably built, he thought angrily to himself. Well, as far as Eliot was concerned, Adam wouldn't have the chance to start any more fires for Lynn. Not in her fireplace, nor in her heart!

But then Eliot suddenly remembered the chore ahead of him . . . that of telling Lynn the news that could possibly separate them again, and this time forever.

"Eliot, will you please go and rescue my robe from the living room floor?" she asked, crossing her arms over her breasts. She shivered a bit. "It's darn cold in here."

He leaned down over her, placing a hand on the bed on each side of her, and kissed her softly on the lips. "Do you want me, instead of the robe, to warm you up again, darling?" he teased.

Lifting a finger to his lips, she whispered, "I think a robe will do just fine for now."

Eliot's eyes brightened. "Ahha," he said. "For now? Does that mean a promise of something much more interesting later?"

"I guess it does," she laughed. "Are you game?"

"Just you name the time and place," he said huskily, "and I'll be there."

"Well, for now, Eliot, I prefer a robe over anything else," she said, pushing him gently away from her. "Or do I have to get it for myself?"

"I could carry you into the living room," he teased.

Lynn laughed nervously. "Heaven forbid!" she said. "That would be much too distracting, and then you'd never get that coffee." She nodded toward the bedroom door. "Just get my robe. Please?"

"If you insist," Eliot said, shrugging. He smiled over his shoulder at her as he made his way toward the bedroom door.

Lynn watched him, admiring the corded muscles at his shoulders and the sinuous grace with which he moved. She felt a renewed twinge of guilt for having fallen completely under this man's spell. Nothing like this had ever happened before. She had for so long dreaded meeting him. And now she had given herself fully to him and knew she would again whenever the opportunity arose. She was caught in a web of passion and could hardly believe the reality of it all.

"One robe coming up," Eliot said, moving back into the room. His dark eyes spoke of his feelings for her as he leaned down and wrapped it around her shoulders. His perfectly chiseled features took on an unfamiliar gentleness as his lips moved once more toward hers and captured her in a moment of unbelievable sweetness.

He gripped her arms, lifting her from the bed and close against his body as his lips devoured hers once more with even more passion and fire. Trembling with desire, she twined her arms about his neck and returned the kiss, then drew away from him, laughing weakly.

"Eliot, this has got to stop!" she said. She steadied herself against him as he helped her into her robe, then leaned into his embrace as he supported her on her way into the living room.

"I'll get the coffee if that's all right," he said, eyeing her questioningly. "A man is allowed in your kitchen, isn't he?" She smiled and nodded.

As Lynn eased down into a chair in front of the fireplace, she shook her head, still not believing any of this. What on earth was she doing, thinking, feeling? What had happened to the old self-sufficient Lynn? It was as though her body had been invaded by a sensual stranger, a woman whose only thought was of the man who had reawakened her to passion.

The thought of what might lie ahead for them sent goose pimples rippling across her flesh. Things would be so much easier this way. Oh, how she had dreaded having to face him each day while sitting in front of the camera.

But now, things were going to be all right! She

might even be falling in love with him . . .

"Coffee for my lady," Eliot said, offering her a steaming cup of coffee in a ceramic mug.

Before, his reference to 'my lady' had rubbed her the wrong way. But now, she gladly accepted it. "Thanks," she murmured, snuggling more deeply into her robe as she eased farther down into the chair. She stretched her feet out before her, feeling the warmth from the fire against their soles.

She felt crazily content as Eliot settled on the floor beside her, sipping his own cup of coffee. "I wonder what color the woolly-bear caterpillars are this autumn in Illinois?" she said, looking dreamy eyed into the flames.

Eliot's head turned with a start and his eyes showed a quiet amusement. "Woolly-bear caterpillars?" he chuckled. "What on earth are you talking about?"

"It's so cold out today," she laughed, glancing toward the glass sliding doors, seeing the gloomy gray of the sky, "I'm reminded of Septembers in Illinois."

"What on earth does that have to do with caterpillars?"

"Don't you know that some people forecast weather by woolly-bears?" she teased, taking a slow sip of her coffee.

"I've heard about many ways of predicting the weather, but that's not one of them," he said, once more chuckling. He placed an arm on her knee and rested his chin against it. "Tell me about woolly-bears, my dear."

A pleasureable glow rose inside her. She loved his voice. She had been wrong in thinking that

Adam had the best voice in San Francisco. She now knew that Eliot would be the winner if there were a contest between these two talented gentlemen. Eliot's voice continued to spin a web of rapture around her heart.

Shaking her head to clear her thoughts, she also cleared her throat, then said, "Mother and Father always went out to the garden and looked for the woolly-bear caterpillars when the leaves first began to change colors in the autumn," she said. "I remember the first time they brought one into the house and explained their prediction to me. The caterpillar was covered with a thick coal-black coat of fur. They said that this black caterpillar was a sure sign of an exceptionally bad winter ahead. And if it had been white, that would've meant the promise of a mild winter."

Eliot chuckled. "If I'd have been there, I would probably have dropped the caterpillar down the front of your blouse," he said, winking at her.

Lynn laughed. "Were you a naughty little boy?"

"I was always teasing my sister when we were small," he said, placing his coffee cup on the floor beside him. "I dropped a few worms down her neck just to hear her squeal."

"Why, that's horrible, Eliot!" Lynn said, then laughed softly, trying to envision him as a mischievous child. It wasn't all that hard to do.

"Did you have a brother to tease the daylights out of you?" he asked then.

"No. I was an only child."

"Then you missed a lot," he said.

"I know," she replied with a wry smile. "And it's made it all the harder for my parents, my leaving the nest and moving to San Francisco."

"You're not sorry you made the move, are you?"

"No," she said. "I get home as often as I can. My parents have learned to get along without me." Lynn placed her cup on the table next to her. She eyed Eliot cautiously. "I'd like to know a bit more about you," she said.

"Anything. Just ask."

"I heard that you're divorced. Do you have any children?"

Eliot rose from the floor and busied himself by placing a log on the fire. Then he poked at the logs with a poker, keeping his back to Lynn. "No. No children," he said.

Lynn could feel tension in the air. "I'm sorry if I've pried into a part of your past that you don't want to talk about," she said, rising and limping to his side. She lifted a forefinger to his chin and urged him to turn to face her. "I said I was sorry, Eliot," she whispered.

"You shouldn't be on your feet," he said thickly. "Do I have to stay here all day and supervise your every movement?" He tried to walk her back to the chair, but she stood her ground.

"Am I forgiven, Eliot?"

"For what?"

"For mentioning your divorce."

Eliot fell to one knee and began stirring the poker around in the ashes beneath the grate. "I'll tell you about Caroline, my ex-wife," he growled. "She wrote me a 'Dear John' letter while I was in 'Nam. By the time I returned to the states to see what it was all about she had divorced me and was living with a damn plumber!"

Eliot laughed throatily and placed the poker in its stand. Rising, he put his hands on Lynn's shoulder. "You're the first woman since then that I've allowed myself to feel anything for," he said huskily. "And, Lynn, that's been a damn long time between commitments."

Lynn swallowed hard and looked deeply into his dark pools of eyes, placing a hand on one of his cheeks. "Then we're even," she said. "I haven't allowed myself much in the way of feelings, either, since the death of my husband. And, Eliot, I would have never guessed that my heart would have chosen you."

"What about Ad . . . ?" he began, then quickly cut off his words, knowing that this wasn't the time to ask about Adam. Surely she hadn't said the same thing to him. Then other things entered his mind. It was time to tell her . . .

"What were you about to say, Eliot?" Lynn asked.

Eliot moved away from her, feeling like a heel about what he had to tell her concerning his new appointment at the station. She would probably hate him! But he had decided it was best that she hear it from him firsthand, rather than from someone else who might be thoughtless and blunt, and might hurt her even more deeply.

"I need something to drink," he mumbled, taking wide strides to the bar. Once there he helped himself to some wine.

"It's kind of early in the day to be drinking, isn't it, Eliot?" Lynn asked, limping across the room. She settled down onto a stool and rested her elbows on the bar, eyeing him quizzically.

"Just a glass of wine," he said, laughing awkwardly. He tipped the glass to his lips and swallowed the red liquid in one gulp. He cast her a sideways glance and motioned with the empty glass. "I didn't ask," he said. "Would you like one?"

Lynn shook her head slowly, feeling that something was amiss here. He was suddenly acting so darn peculiar, so sheepish, as though he had something to hide. But what?

"I never drink during the day," she said, "unless it's for a special occasion."

"And this isn't?" he laughed, pouring himself another glass.

"I feel that you're drinking for some reason other than the special occasion you are referring to, Eliot," she said, her voice strained. "What is it? What's the matter?"

Eliot placed the empty glass on the bar, then swung around and covered her hands with his. "I do have something to tell you," he said.

"Well? What?" she queried, lifting an eyebrow.

"You won't like it, Lynn."

"I won't know until you tell me," she said, already feeling a cold numbness circling her heart. It's something to do with the station, isn't it?"

"Yes," he admitted. His eyes seemed darker and small frown lines crinkled his face at his eyes and brow.

Lynn pulled her hands away from his and straightened her back. "What about the station?" she asked grimly. She flipped her hair back, eyeing him suspiciously.

"Well, it's like this . . ." Eliot said, walking away from her, raking his fingers nervously through his hair. He began pacing back and forth, occasionally giving her cautious glances.

"Eliot!" Lynn stated sharply. "What on earth is it that you're finding so hard to say?"

Eliot went to the sliding glass door and leaned his palms against it, watching the moods of the ocean. He was battling his own torn feelings, hating like hell to have to tell Lynn that he had taken over her position at the station. She wouldn't understand. He wouldn't understand either if it had happened to him!

Lynn sighed and slid from the stool, limping toward him. When she moved to his side, she looked into his eyes as he looked her way, and she realized all at once that their newly found happiness was already a thing of the past. Whatever he had to reveal to her, she knew, was not something she wanted to hear.

"Eliot, maybe it's best that you don't tell me," she murmured, turning away. She went and slouched down onto a chair in front of the low-burning embers of the fireplace.

"You have to know," he said, following her. He lifted a log on to the fire, then spun around and faced her. "Lynn, I've been appointed Program Director at the station," he said. He flinched when he saw the incredulity and anger rise into her eyes and across her usually soft features. He took a step toward her, but when he saw a blazing flush suffuse her cheeks, decided it best to keep his distance.

Lynn's heart plummeted. Her fingers clenched into tight fists at her sides. Slowly she pushed herself from the chair, forgetting any pain other than that of her heart. "You've *what?*" she whispered harshly. "What did you say?"

"You heard me," he replied. He reached out a hand but she slapped it away. "Lynn, I'm sorry," he quickly added. "Really. I'm damn sorry. It wasn't my idea, believe me."

"You get out of my house!" she hissed. "How could you? Was this charming seduction all planned to soften me up? Did you decide to make love to me, then casually tell me that you've taken over my position at the station? How could you?" She covered her face with her hands. "And how could Taylor?"

"I was Program Director at KMRK in Seattle," he told her. "I did one hell of a good job, if I say so myself. That was one of the reasons Taylor hired me."

Lynn wiped an angry tear from the corner of her eye. "And I *didn't* do a good job?" she hissed. "Is that what you're trying to tell me, Eliot?"

"I don't know what Taylor's reasons were for replacing you," he said thickly. "And, Lynn, damn it, I *am* sorry. I felt it was best to tell you myself before you heard it from someone else."

"And after making love to me, right?"

Eliot placed his hands on her arms and held her tightly in her seat. "You don't really believe that's the way it happened," he said huskily. "You *can't* think I planned it all this way. Lynn, I've fallen in love with you. I haven't felt this way about a woman since . . ."

"You release me this minute," she said in a low, threatening tone. "Or, so help me, I'll kick you again! Eliot, I don't care if I bust my *other* toe! It would be worth it—only this time I'd like to be wearing hobnailed boots!"

"Lynn . . ." he softly pleaded, "listen to me . . ."

She jerked herself free from him. "You listen," she stormed. "I want you out of my house and my life. Do you hear?"

"But, Lynn, you can't just walk out on 'Morning Magazine.'"

"I'll continue to do my job," she said hotly, "but only until my contract runs out. Then I'll be glad to say good-bye to both you and Taylor."

"Lynn . . ."

Lynn limped to her door and flung it open. "Get out, Eliot," she whispered. "Now. I don't want to be with you any more than I absolutely have to."

"Lynn, you must listen . . ."

"Eliot, so help me, if you don't leave this instant . . ."

Eliot's shoulders slumped as he moved slowly toward the door. "All right," he said. "But you *will* listen. Damn it, you *will* listen. After you cool down I'll convince you to hear what I have to say. I refuse to lose you after having just found you."

He stopped before her and looked down into her eyes. "I do love you, Lynn," he murmured. "And I wouldn't have purposely hurt you for the world. Believe me, I'm sorry."

"Sure you are," she fumed. She lowered her lashes and nodded toward the door. "Please, Eliot, just leave. At least show some respect for what we've just shared by leaving without anymore hassle."

"All right," he said. "I'll leave. But you'll listen, eventually, even if I have to quit my position at KSFC-TV to prove my love for you."

Lynn's eyes glanced quickly upward and her heart skipped a beat. She began to speak but he walked on past her and out into the gloomy mist of the morning. "Sure you will," she murmured to herself sarcastically, watching his car pull out of the drive.

The cold, damp wind whipped up inside her robe, chilling her to the bone. She shivered and closed the door behind her, leaning heavily against it as she tried to get all that had happened into proper perspective. She wouldn't let his last words throw her off guard. Nothing would erase the fact that she had just been used, and in the worst way possible. She'd get even with him—the only question was how.

# *Four*

THE FLOOR manager was standing behind the camera, giving Lynn and Eliot the hurry-up sign, moving his forefinger in a rapid, circular motion. Realizing this meant they were running behind time on the program, Lynn forced a smile toward the "one-eyed monster," her nickname for the camera, as Eliot gave the closing statement of the morning. It had been a full week and his having taken charge had been devastating to Lynn's ego. She had come to the conclusion that Taylor had deliberately done this to her first because she was a woman and secondly because she had so furiously defended Adam.

A discrimination case against the station had been considered but she had thought it best to wait, to see how things progressed, one way or another.

"Until tomorrow," Eliot was saying to the unseen audience, "Lynn and I will say good morning to you."

As the camera faded to black, Lynn kept smiling, but spoke to Eliot from the corner of her mouth. "Good morning, is it?" she hissed. "Depends on how you look at it."

Eliot continued smiling toward the camera. "You

look ravishing this morning, Lynn," he whispered back, also from the corner of his mouth. "And now that you're able to get into some shoes, how would you like to take a trip with me to Central America?"

"What?" she gasped, jerking her head around to question him the minute she saw the red light on the camera had blinked off. "What are you talking about?"

Her gaze took in his astonishing good looks, which constantly kept threatening to crumble her defenses against him. He was dressed impeccably in a wool, herringbone suit with a crisp white shirt and Pierre Cardin brown tie. The way he was looking back at her with those lazy dark eyes sent Lynn's heart into a sensuous flutter which she sternly attempted to repress.

"It's all set," he said. "While you've been out this past week recuperating, plans have been made for us to fly to Carmen Island."

"Eliot, you're not making any sense," Lynn said irritably. "Why on earth would you want to go to Central America? And why would you think I would go *with* you?"

"To film some ancient Mayan ruins that have just recently been uncovered not far from Leon, the capital city of Carmen Island."

"Sure," Lynn scoffed. "Taylor would okay a jaunt like that when apples grow on cherry trees!"

"Ever heard of grants?" Eliot asked with a grin. "It's all set—one of my new programming ideas. You like?"

Lynn eyed him speculatively, then rose quickly from her chair and marched off the set without a word, relieved her foot was well enough now to get her from place to place at a fast clip. She seemed always to be running away from Eliot for one reason or another.

"Carmen Island!" she fumed to herself. "We'll probably be killed! Talk about a newsworthy event!"

Glancing at the window next to her, she could see his reflection in the glass, following after her. Then she glanced surreptitiously at her own reflection, seeing her smart Castleberry white wool blend suit with red trim and matching red blouse. She hated herself for having thought of Eliot when choosing this particular outfit, having silently hoped he'd approve of her appearance. But when she slipped into her red heels, still feeling some lingering pain in her injured toe, she had been quickly reminded of why she should still hate him.

"Damn it, he's making a lot of changes, all right!" Taylor had never permitted her and Adam to go on location for any reason whatsoever, and now he had agreed to Eliot's plan to fly straight into a country that was seething with unrest. Mayan ruins, indeed! What a perfectly idiotic notion!

"Lynn, slow down," Eliot called after her. "I thought you'd enjoy traveling. There's a lot of action there right now. Aren't you tired of the same, boring routine here at the station?"

Coming to an abrupt halt, Lynn spun around and angrily faced him. "And, may I ask, who is going to cover for us while we're away?" she asked, crossing her arms defiantly across her chest.

Eliot's gaze traveled over her, aching to pull her into his arms. Her hair was twisted up on the top of her head in a swirl of gold, and her green eye shadow matched the color of her eyes, making them appear wider and more seductive. Her face was flushed with anger and annoyance, giving her the appearance of a delectably sulky child. But that figure didn't belong to a child—oh, no. Although she was wearing a suit, he could still see the curves of her breasts and the smallness of her waist, and his memory of the beauty of her naked body sent his heart racing almost uncontrollably.

It was taking all the willpower he could muster not to throw caution to the winds and draw her into his arms for the whole damn crew to see! Instead, he said, "We'll tape ahead. We'll interview our guests two weeks ahead of time."

"Our ratings will drop if we don't continue appearing live," she stated flatly.

Eliot rested his hands on her shoulders. "Don't you see this trip as the chance of a lifetime?" he asked, looking down into her angry eyes. "Lynn, surely you're not going to let your stubbornness ruin this for us."

"For you, you mean," she scoffed. "Eliot, I don't want to go to Central America with you or anybody. Are you deaf and blind? Haven't you been watching the news? There's a lot of trouble brewing there. It would be dangerous." She laughed sarcastically. "I do believe you've failed to do your homework this time, Eliot."

"We've been guaranteed a safe expedition," he said, dropping his hands to his sides.

"Expedition?" she murmured, taking a step backward. "Is an actual expedition already planned?"

"We will be members of an expedition of experts who will be touring the Mayan ruins," he said.

"There will be newspaper and magazine reporters, college professors, archaeologists and anthropologists. We will film the expedition and do extensive interviews with each person there."

Lynn permitted herself a wry smile. "I guess I was wrong," she murmured.

"About what?"

"You have done your homework," she said dryly. "In fact, you've got it planned every step of the way. I should have known better than to think you'd be unprepared."

Lifting her chin defiantly, she turned and began walking angrily away from him. She tensed when he moved to her side. "Damn it, Lynn," he growled. "Why are you acting like this? Can't you see the opportunities here? As far as I know we'll be the only television crew there. We will be the ones bringing back this once-in-a-lifetime story of a city that has been until very recently swallowed up by the jungle. The Meltonian Institute of Washington D.C. is restoring the city. Think of what we will see firsthand! How can you disagree on something so historically important?"

Lynn sighed. She knew when she was beaten.

"When are we going, Eliot?" she finally conceded.

"In two weeks," he said. "There will be three of us going from the station."

"I assume the third is Hank the cameraman."

"You assume correctly," he said, relieved to see her chin and jaw relax.

"I'm still not totally convinced about this, Eliot."

"Ah, but I am," he teased, reaching out to take her elbow in one hand. He whispered into her ear,

71

"Just as I was convinced by your behavior the other day that you don't dislike me as much as you'd have me believe. I think I understand your feelings pretty well."

Fearing the erratic pounding of her heart and the weakness of her knees that his breath on her cheek was causing, Lynn jerked away and glared at him. "Eliot, which feelings are you talking about?" she asked sweetly. "My feelings of contempt, or my feelings of mistrust?"

She could tell she'd struck home. He flinched as though she'd slapped him.

"Lynn," he grated, "I was referring to what began between us that day—how we both felt."

She laughed wryly. "Eliot, I'm quite aware of what you meant," she said. "But you must forgive my moment of madness when I shared my bed with you. I assure you it will never happen again."

Not wanting to see the hurt and surprise in his eyes, Lynn rushed away from him, even more weak-kneed than before. What had happened that short time together at her beach house had been undeniably beautiful. It was hard to believe that it could never be again—but no. He had used her, taken advantage of her. She could never trust him again.

"Lynn, for Christ's sake!" Eliot said, once more at her side. "You've got to stop this."

"Stop *what?*" she asked innocently, pushing her way into the elevator, flinching when Eliot moved to her side and his elbow grazed hers.

"Stop being such a pain in the ass," he said, leaning down and whispering into her ear, as the elevator doors slid silently shut. "We're going to be thrown together constantly on this expedition. Are you going to play Miss Iceberg for the entire time?"

"It's your expedition," she answered sharply. "Sure, I'll be with you. But you'll be in charge, just the way you planned it. Just don't expect me to like it!"

"It could be very romantic," he quietly teased.

"Oh!" she said, tossing her head in annoyance and glaring up at him. "You're impossible, Eliot Smith! Romance is the furthest thing from my mind where you're concerned."

As the elevator door slid open, Lynn rushed out into the hallway and on toward her office.

"What's the rush, Lynn?" Eliot questioned, easily keeping up with her, taking one stride to her two.

"I'm going to go get my purse from my office and then I'm going to go out and buy myself a new hat," she snapped.

Eliot scratched his brow quizzically. "A hat?" he repeated.

"Yes," she told him. "Suddenly I have an overpowering urge to buy *another* new hat!"

Eliot stopped at his office door. "Women!" he chuckled. "Who can figure them out . . . ?"

Lynn stood at a mirror in Maria's Millinery, trying on first one hat and then another. "The nerve of him!" she muttered to herself.

She slammed one hat down on the table and then slapped another on her head. "Who does he think he is? First he steals my job, and then he talks about romance!" The hat made her look like a mushroom, she decided, and tossed it aside,

73

picking up a third and trying it on. She glanced at her reflection and laughed, thinking how ironic it was that this particular hat was there, at this time, for the choosing. "Just what I need for my trip into the jungle," she whispered, tilting it jauntily over one eye. It was a Frank Olive felt 'bush' hat that suggested the lure of faraway places, with a wide brim and a snakeskin band.

"Yes. This ought to do quite well," she decided lifting it from her head.

As she stood before the mirror, rearranging her hair which had become quite mussed, she discovered another image in the mirror, standing behind her. She turned quickly with a pleased smile. "Adam!" she said. "What on earth are you doing here?"

He was dressed casually in pale blue velour pullover shirt and black slacks. His eyes had never seemed bluer nor his smile friendlier. "Checking up on you. Seeing if your toe is okay," he teased.

"Sure you were. You knew I'd be here, trying on hats. Right?"

"If you must know, I was just passing by and saw you trying on a whole army of hats," he chuckled. He leaned over to kiss her cheek. "And I detected a spark of anger in those gorgeous eyes. What's up, Lynn?"

"Only one person these days gets my dander up," she sighed. She placed her comb inside her purse, then clicked it shut. "I'm sure you know who I'm talking about."

"Eliot Smith, of course."

"You got it," she said flatly. She picked up the 'bush' hat, took it to the front of the store and

74

handed it and her charge card to the salesclerk.

"What's happened now?" Adam asked. He stepped aside and held the door open for Lynn as she carried the hatbox from the shop and out into the hustle and bustle of shoppers in one of the busiest malls of San Francisco.

"You won't believe it, Adam," Lynn sighed. "You just won't believe what Eliot's done now."

Adam took Lynn's arm and gave it a little squeeze. "Want to talk about it over a cup of coffee?"

"If you'll add a doughnut to that offer, kind sir," Lynn teased.

"As good as done," Adam said, whisking her into a coffee shop where the lighting was low and candles flickered on red-checkered tablecloths.

Settling down across from Adam, Lynn gladly accepted the cup of coffee and doughnut. After a few sips and bites, she reached over and patted Adam's hand. "It's good to see you again," she told him. "I've missed you."

"And I you."

"How's the family?"

"I'm the proud grandpa of yet another sturdy grandson."

"Really?"

"Just yesterday," Adam said proudly. "I came to the mall to buy a box of cigars to pass around to the guys at the station. Then I got sidetracked by seeing you trying on hats."

Lynn laughed. "Only *fathers* are supposed to hand out cigars," she said, stirring a spoonful of sugar into her coffee.

"And also grandpas," he chuckled.

"How are things at the radio station, Adam?"

"Going fine," he said. "But from the scowl on your face and seeing you buying another hat, I'd say things aren't so good for you. Want to tell me about it?"

"Eliot has taken over as Program Director," Lynn informed him, lowering her eyes.

"You're kidding!" Adam gasped.

"And he's made plans for us to go to Central America."

"You're kidding. What on earth for?"

"I am not kidding," she mumbled. "To film the uncovering of some supposedly fabulous Mayan ruins on Carmen Island."

"So ol' Taylor's finally loosening up on the purse strings, eh?" Adam mused. He toyed with a spoon, turning it over and over on the table. "He can spend money for some damn fool trip when he couldn't give me a measly raise. Yeah. Sounds like something ol' Taylor would pull."

"I'm sorry, Adam."

Adam reached over and took one of her hands in his. "I wonder if either Taylor or Eliot Smith realizes the dangers in Central America right now. They must have their heads in the sand if they don't. I know what's going on over there. Isn't either of them aware of what's happening?"

"They're wearing blinders, I guess." She shrugged.

"You could refuse to go, Lynn."

"The hell I will!" she said sharply. "I don't want to go, but I wouldn't give Taylor or Eliot Smith the satisfaction of saying I chickened out because I'm a poor, weak woman." She shook her head. "No, Adam. I can't do that. I've got to go, regardless."

"Then make the best of the situation, Lynn," Adam

said, squeezing her hand. "Show Eliot up. Do your damnedest to outdo him with your reporting of the story."

"I don't see how," she sighed. "I don't know the first thing about Central America, much less this dinky island."

"Then you're talking to the right man," Adam said, releasing her hand, and pouring them both another cup of coffee. "Let me give you a quick rundown on Carmen Island's history."

"How do you know so much about it?" asked Lynn.

"To broadcast the news accurately about a country, one must study every aspect of that country," he chuckled. "Hon, you know me. When I get involved in a story, I jump in with both feet. Just you listen and when the time comes, you'll knock Eliot Smith dead with all your knowledge."

Lynn leaned her elbows on the table, resting her chin on the palms of her hands. "Shoot," she said. "I'm all ears!"

Adam talked for a good half hour while Lynn listened intently. The sound of footsteps stopping beside her drew her head around, and her heart raced, as she saw Eliot there. He was glaring from Adam back to her. She stiffened and her eyes narrowed. "It seems you continue to invade my privacy," she said coolly. Yet a thrill of sorts trembled through her, enjoying his obvious pursuit of her. How wonderful it would be if he were chasing after her for herself alone, and not for "Morning Magazine" ratings—but she refused to think about that.

"I just stopped in for a cup of coffee," Eliot said,

equally coolly. "I had no idea you two were having a tete-a-tete. Sorry if I interrupted something. I'll be on my way."

Adam rose to his feet and grabbed Eliot by the arm. "What exactly are you implying?" he growled.

Eliot casually brushed Adam's hand away and smoothed imaginary wrinkles out of his sleeve. "Oh, was I implying something?" he said innocently. "Sorry about that."

Lynn's face grew hot as she glanced from Adam to Eliot. If she didn't know better, she'd say Eliot was acting like a jealous lover who had just discovered his beloved with another man. Was *this* the reason behind Eliot's dislike for Adam—the fact that he constantly found Adam with her alone together? Did Eliot really believe that she and Adam . . . ? Preposterous! And yet . . . a slow smile dawned on her face as she pursued this line of thought. Though of course she didn't care for him at all, she was beginning to believe that perhaps Eliot wasn't just interested in how a personal relationship with her could consolidate his position at the station.

"What's this about you going to Carmen Island?" Adam asked, scowling. "You have to know the danger involved. You have no right to involve Lynn in such a harebrained scheme."

"What gives you the right to say what Lynn should or shouldn't do?" Eliot asked.

"I'm her friend," Adam said flatly. "And what are you to her? Apparently you don't have her best interests at heart. Surely you've heard about the counterrevolutionaries springing up all over the place down there."

"Believe it or not, I do," Eliot said dryly. "*Contras.*

That's what they're called, I understand."

Adam paled. "And you still plan to travel there with Lynn?"

"Lynn will be quite safe," Eliot assured him, giving her a lingering look. "I won't let anything happen to her, you can be sure of that."

"And how do you propose to see to her safety, if I may ask?"

"Adam, lay off," Eliot suddenly fumed. "The *Contra* camps aren't on Carmen Island. They're deep inside Nicaragua. It's only rumored that some are on the island."

Lynn rose from her chair and placed a hand on Adam's arm, looking from him to Eliot. "Please," she murmured. "People are staring."

"Let them stare," Adam growled.

Eliot leaned closer to Lynn "I'd like to talk to you," he murmured. "That is, if you can break away from your friend here." He cast Adam a sour look.

"Eliot, we have nothing else to say to one another," Lynn said. "You got your way. You're now program director at KSFC-TV and now we're going to Carmen Island. What else is there to say?"

"I've upset you and I want to explain . . ."

"I have things to do," she said firmly.

"You always have things to do," he grumbled.

Her eyes widened. "Well, I do," she snapped. "I can't just set off for the jungle with no preparations!"

"Of course not," Eliot said. "But a few minutes of your precious time won't put you too far behind."

Lynn eyed Adam with a sideways glance.

"Want me to leave?" Adam asked.

"Not really," she admitted. "But I guess now's as

good a time as any to get this thing settled between me and Eliot. We'll be constantly thrown together while we're away."

"Hon, call me if you need me," Adam said. He winked at her, then walked casually away. "You know the number."

Lynn swung around and faced Eliot. "Well? What is it you want to talk about?" she asked dryly.

"Let's get out of here and go where we can talk in private," Eliot suggested.

"This will do perfectly well as far as I'm concerned."

"No. It won't," he said. He lifted her hatbox from the table, then cupped her elbow with a hand, urging her toward the door and on out into the mall. "There's a nice restaurant at the end of the mall. I'm going to buy your dinner and by damn you're going to listen to what I have to say, whether you like it or not."

Lynn jerked away from him and grabbed her hatbox. "Eliot, you continue to think you can force me to do whatever you like," she fumed. "When will you ever learn that a woman . . . particularly *this* woman . . . doesn't like to be bullied constantly? I've been my own boss for too long and I've gotten by quite well alone!"

Eliot's eyes were filled with brooding anger. "Alone except for Adam Lowenstein, don't you mean?" he growled. "Every time I turn around, you're with him. I wouldn't exactly call that 'being alone.'"

"Again you're drawing the wrong conclusions," she said hotly. "Adam is only a friend, a very old and dear friend."

"And you think I'm going to believe that?"

Lynn stopped and glared up at him. "Eliot Smith, I don't give a damn what you believe," she whispered harshly. Seeing the sudden hurt appear in his eyes made her pulse race a bit. If she had the power to wound this arrogant man, then it proved he must care for her. His pain hurt her, yet she knew that he needed a jolt to make him suffer as she was suffering—and all because of *him*.

She didn't like playing cat-and-mouse games with a man, but this man was different. Somehow she had known this from the very beginning.

"Lynn, for Christ's sake," Eliot pleaded.

"I've got to run," she said flatly. "I really do have things to do. If I'm going to Carmen Island, I have an entire new wardrobe to buy."

"But we didn't talk . . ."

"We'll talk," she said with a jerk of her head. "On Carmen Island."

She heard his groan of frustration as she walked quickly away from him, and was torn by conflicting feelings. But she wouldn't turn back. Oh, no! Not on her life!

# *Five*

"THAT'S AN unusual hat, Lynn," Eliot said as they settled into their airplane seats next to one another.

Feeling a bit more relaxed about the upcoming adventure, and having gotten her emotions fairly well under control, Lynn smiled back at him. "I'm glad you like it," she said. "It's my 'bush' hat. I bought it especially for the trip."

"And how do you feel about our expedition at this point?"

"I intend to do what has to be done," she said flatly. She lifted her hat from her head and placed it on her lap.

"So you still don't think this is a good idea, do you?" Eliot said, crossing his legs. He tapped his fingers nervously against the leather of his new boots which he had bought for the trip. He had read about the presence of poisonous snakes and had determined to be in some way prepared for them.

"What makes you think that?" Lynn said sarcastically.

"Your whole damn attitude stinks," Eliot growled. He leaned over and whispered into her ear. "If you'd let yourself, we could both enjoy this trip. It *could* be romantic, you know."

"With *you?*" she mocked. "Hah! Never." But when he reached over and took one of her hands in his, she felt the familiar stirrings of the feelings she'd attempted to repress, and quickly jerked her hand away.

"I would appreciate it if you'd keep your hands to yourself," she said icily. "I may be here with you, but *only* because it's a part of my job. Don't expect anything from me other than a strictly professional attitude. This is a business trip, nothing more."

"You'll change your mind when you get caught up in the exotic setting," he said. "It's supposed to be a tropical paradise."

Lynn straightened the lines of her white linen suit. "Sure. A paradise complete with armed *Contras* sneaking around all over the place," she scoffed.

"Your hat, Miss Stafford?" a gorgeous, redheaded flight attendant asked as she leaned down over Lynn, offering to remove it from her lap.

"Yes. Thank you," Lynn murmured, handing the hat to her.

"And please fasten your seat belts," the flight attendant further stated, flashing Eliot an alluring smile. "We should be cleared for takeoff soon."

Eliot winked and returned the flight attendant's wide, toothy smile, then pulled the seat belt around and fastened it. He unbuttoned the top button of his blue plaid cotton shirt, watching appreciatively as the flight attendant reached up to place Lynn's hat in the overhead compartment.

"You're impossible," Lynn whispered to him. "How could you expect *any* woman to take you seriously when you obviously flirt with them all?"

Chuckling beneath his breath, Eliot leaned comfortably back into his seat. "I'm glad you noticed," he whispered back, now watching the flight attendant walk on up the aisle, and through the open door that led into the cockpit of the plane. From this vantage point, in the first-class section, they could see the pilots and the control panel of the DC-10.

"What on earth are you talking about?" Lynn asked.

"Then you won't become too sure of your hold on my fickle affections," he said, a glint of wicked humor in his dark eyes.

Lynn scowled. "Really!" she snorted.

"And you'll quit playing this cat-and-mouse game with me," he said, pressing his elbow intimately against hers. "Lynn, hidden beneath that icy exterior are feelings that you can't deny. Darling, you couldn't have responded to me that day at your beach house if you hadn't felt something for me. You don't appear to be the type who lets herself go with just *any* man." Then shadows drew onto his face, as he remembered Adam.

"You can believe what you want," she said, shrugging. "It makes no difference, Eliot. No difference, at all. Call it a momentary aberration if you like. Whatever it was, it's over."

"We'll see about that," he said thickly.

Lynn fastened her seat belt and watched the flight attendant come into view again and shut the cockpit door. The plane began a slight vibrating as the engines began revving up.

The flight attendant once more bent over Lynn and Eliot. "You have time for one quick drink," she said sweetly, concentrating on Eliot. "Can I get you anything?"

Eliot gave her a warm smile. "We'd like a couple of glasses of champagne," he said, giving Lynn a sideways glance, and noting a look of surprise as she glanced quickly back at him.

"Oh?" the flight attendant said. "Are you celebrating something?" Her gaze moved to Lynn's ring finger. "Maybe an engagement?" she suggested, smiling knowingly from Eliot back to Lynn.

"Engagement?" Lynn echoed, astonished, then set her lips into a narrow line as she glared at Eliot. "*Darling,*" she purred mockingly, "tell the lady. What *are* we drinking to, darling?"

"Success," he chuckled.

The flight attendant's thinly plucked eyebrows lifted. "Success?" she repeated.

"Yes. Success in paradise," Eliot continued, with a bold look at Lynn. "And I don't mean on a purely professional level," he added.

Lynn's face turned a bright crimson. "Eliot, that's quite enough," she snapped. "Just drop it, okay?"

"Never," he said with a grin.

"Two glasses of champagne coming up," the flight attendant said, walking away.

Lynn crossed her arms angrily across her chest, scowling at Eliot. "Eliot, why on earth do you do these things?" she began. Then her attention was diverted from him to the glass of sparkling champagne being handed to her by the solicitous stewardess. The sun shone brightly through the small window at Eliot's side and played on the two glasses, as the golden liquid continued to bubble and fizz.

"You have just enough time to drink it down, then I must take the glasses before we taxi out to the runway," the flight attendant warned, seemingly unable to tear herself away from Eliot.

"We'll want another glass as soon as we get in the air," he said. "Maybe even two or three."

"You may want another glass," Lynn quickly interjected, "but I won't. And I'd like to point out that I can speak for myself whenever I do or don't want something. I've been doing it for years!"

Eliot's dark eyes gleamed with amusement as he looked into Lynn's flashing green ones. "To us," he said, ignoring her statement and clinking his glass against hers. "To our time together in paradise."

Lynn trembled inside, hearing the huskiness of his voice and seeing the desire in his dark eyes. She couldn't say anything, for fear that her own voice would reveal the strength of his attraction for her. She was beginning to wonder if she would be able to control her emotions while in constant proximity to him during the trip. He had a positively diabolical talent for tearing down her defenses. One look, one brief touch, and she felt as giddy as a foolish schoolgirl. While they were on location, these feelings posed even more of a threat to her than a dozen *Contras* hiding in the brush!

"I must have the glasses now," the flight attendant said, interrupting her thoughts. "We've finally been cleared for takeoff."

Lynn took a fast sip then relinquished her glass, as did Eliot. Then Lynn settled down for the takeoff, silent as the plane taxied onto the runway and paused for a brief moment before it swept quickly into the sky.

Eliot's left hand covered Lynn's right hand as the plane suddenly began its thrust forward and then its ascent. Lynn tried to move her hand away, but Eliot held it firmly in place. She circled her fingers tightly around the arm rest, attempting to ignore the heat of his flesh against hers, but unable to deny to herself that she enjoyed the clasp of his hand. She was very much aware of his shoulder touching hers as well. She closed her eyes, feeling a throbbing in her temples, realizing her emotions were battling inside her. She had known this would happen and now there was no stopping it. He was there. She was there. Their needs were the same and it seemed nature was once more going to take charge, whether she fought her instincts or simply, helplessly, gave in.

Feeling the plane leveling off, Lynn opened her eyes and saw the flight attendant moving toward her and Eliot with refilled glasses of champagne.

"Here we are," the woman said cheerfully. "Drink up. I'm saving the bottle just for the two of you."

Once more Lynn felt her face growing hot. "I told you I don't . . ." she began, shaking her head, but Eliot interrupted.

"Why, thank you," he chuckled. "You're right on the ball, aren't you?" He took both glasses, then held one before Lynn's nose. "Now you *know* you want this," he told her persuasively. "Don't be such a sourpuss, Lynn."

Lynn gave the flight attendant a wry, embarrassed look, then took the glass from Eliot.

"I'll be back soon," the flight attendant chirped. "But while I'm here I'll just go ahead and take your orders for dinner. Which would you prefer? Steak or chicken?"

"Steak," Eliot said at he same time Lynn said, "Chicken."

"One steak and one chicken," the flight attendant said. "And my name's Babette. Just ring if you need anything else."

"Will do," Eliot said, then winked as he added flirtatiously, "A very attractive name—Babette. Are you from France?"

"No," Babette said, leaning down, across Lynn in order to stage whisper into Eliot's ear. "Don't tell anyone, but I'm from Kentucky." She giggled and moved on down the aisle to the next seat, swinging her shapely hips.

"You're really going to enjoy this flight, aren't you?" Lynn said caustically, giving Eliot a cold stare.

Eliot lifted a brow. "Do I hear a tinge of jealousy in your dulcet tones, my darling?" He laughed.

"Don't call me darling!" she fumed. "As far as that goes, don't call me *anything*."

"Little Miss Nothing," he teased. "Somehow that doesn't fit you."

"Oh!" Lynn said, shaking her hair angrily back from her face. She was glad to see Babette moving toward them, two trays in her hands. At least while they were eating, Eliot would have something to occupy his attention other than herself. For the moment, at least.

But once the meal had been consumed and the movie was about to begin, Lynn was on her fourth glass of champagne, feeling warm, well-fed and crazily content. As the lights in the cabin were turned off and the blinds at the windows pulled shut, Lynn found the darkness a welcome reprieve from Eliot's steady, admiring glances. Eliot, however, seemed determined to take advantage of the situation, as indeed he did every situation, Lynn had learned by now. Yet she had to admit that the romantic atmosphere was heightened by the effects of the champagne, and when Eliot placed an arm about her shoulder and drew her close to him, Lynn felt herself relaxing against his shoulder, suddenly aglow inside.

"Lynn, I'm going to kiss you," Eliot whispered into her ear.

His hot breath against her cheek and the heady scent of him sent rapturous tremors through her, much as she hated to admit it. As though under a spell, she lifted her eyes to his as his lips moved slowly to hers.

"God . . . Lynn . . ." Eliot whispered huskily, then devoured her lips with his, twining his fingers through her hair, drawing her even closer to him.

Lynn entwined her arm about his neck and returned the kiss, caught up in the dizzying passion of the moment. In the darkness of the cabin, she allowed his free hand to roam beneath her suit jacket to find and caress one breast. A soft moan rose from deep inside her as his tongue plunged inside her mouth and teased her to an almost mindless state.

Then Eliot drew slowly away from her. "I need you," he whispered. "God, how I need you!"

Once more he kissed her, long and passionately, then appeared content to sit there at her side as she snuggled into his embrace to watch the movie, realizing that he had broken down her defenses. Surely once they reached their destination, she'd know that he expected to share more than kisses.

"I love you, Lynn," Eliot whispered, squeezing her shoulder.

Lynn tensed. Was it possible he really meant it? Or was he saying those tender words in order to weaken her defenses? A part of her was still rational and she was suddenly wary.

"Did you hear me?" he asked, forcing her face around as he placed a forefinger beneath her chin.

"Yes," she murmured.

"Well? What do you have to say?"

A slow smile curved Lynn's lips upward. "Don't you remember?" she teased. "I told you that I wasn't going to talk to you until we reached Carmen Island."

Eliot's eyebrows raised. "Huh?" he mumbled.

"That day in the restaurant, at the mall?"

"What about it?"

"I told you then—that I would only talk to you when I had to."

"But, Lynn, you already have spoken to me—and more than spoken!"

"I had forgotten I had said that until now," she said demurely. "So, please, let's just finish watching the movie. In silence if you please."

Eliot raked his fingers through his hair, groaning dejectedly. "Women! I'll never understand 'em," he grumbled.

Lynn giggled, then sighed deeply as she once more tried to get absorbed in the movie. Yet somehow she was only able to concentrate on Eliot and his nearness.

\*　　\*　　\*

As the plane started its descent to the airstrip, Lynn leaned over Eliot and looked out the window. The sun shone brightly on mile after mile of virgin forests cloaking the mountain slopes. It was quickly becoming a panorama of shapes and hues of towering, bold mountain peaks which suddenly would dip low to form lush green plateaus and rolling valleys dotted with blue, reflecting lakes.

From this vantage point in the sky, Lynn could see broad, unruffled rivers slowly meandering toward the blue waters of the Pacific and the Caribbean Sea. It was a breathtaking sight, one which Lynn would always remember.

A sudden sparkle among the trees in the distance caught Lynn's eye, and it turned into a spectacular view of the gleaming glass office buildings and hotels of downtown Leon.

"I see Leon!" she said, surprised at how modern it appeared to be. Somehow she had expected everything in this part of the world to be quaint and hundreds of years out of date. "It appears to be so *modern*."

"Well, don't look now, but I'm afraid the runway isn't quite up to the city's standards," Eliot said, flinching.

Lynn immediately saw what Eliot was talking about. She drew quickly away from the window, suddenly nervous. "I can't watch," she said, gripping hard to the arms of the seat. "It looks as though two mountains have been blasted out for the plane's approach. And it's so *narrow!*"

"Ha!" Eliot said, still looking out the window. "That's only the half of it. There's a sudden drop off at the end of the runway. If our pilot isn't quite skilled at what he does, we're taking our last breaths."

"Is your seat belt fastened, Eliot?" Lynn asked, swallowing hard.

"Yes. Is yours?"

"Yes," murmured Lynn. She reached for Eliot's hand. "Please hold my hand?"

Eliot chuckled. "Lynn, I was only kidding," he tried to reassure her. "Planes land and take off here every day. There's no danger, believe me."

Lynn glanced out the window again, and cringed. "Eliot, I have *eyes*. I can *see!*" she said. And as she saw trees suddenly outside the window, she jerked her head back against the seat, squeezed Eliot's hand and closed her eyes as the plane thumped and bumped noisily onto the runway. She was barely breathing as she waited anxiously for the plane to come to a halt. As the brakes screeched and the wheels skidded and smoked, she could almost see her entire life pass swiftly before her eyes.

"Stop, darn it," she whispered to the plane, then sighed with relief as she felt it make a sharp turn and begin slowing down as it headed toward the wide, low stucco airport terminal.

"I'm glad we didn't have to ride in coach with Hank," Lynn said, laughing nervously. "I bet the landing was even rougher for him."

"All peasants to the rear, including top-notch technicians," Eliot growled. "I'm beginning to see right through KSFC-TV's managing director."

"Well. *Really* now," Lynn said dryly. "I thought you and Taylor saw eye to eye on everything."

"I feel that the station's ace cameraman should

receive first class treatment," Eliot said. "I get the impression that Taylor is pretty close with a buck."

"I can't believe you actually said that," Lynn said, eyes wide. "You know Adam no longer has his job because of Taylor's refusal to raise his salary."

Eliot cast her a harried look. Why the hell did she have to bring Adam into the conversation? He'd thought that maybe for once, so many miles from San Francisco, no occasion would arise for the discussion of the peerless Adam Lowenstein.

"Must we talk about him?" he finally said, unfastening his seat belt as the plane came to a halt.

"Guilty, huh?" Lynn accused, also unfastening her seat belt.

"Your hat," Babette said, handing Lynn's bush hat down to her. "It's really stunning," she gushed.

Lynn smiled at Babette. "Thanks," she murmured. She took the hat and lifted it to her head.

"And how was your flight?" Babette purred, looking from Lynn to Eliot. "Everything satisfactory?"

"Fine," Eliot grumbled.

"Fine," Lynn echoed.

"And the champagne?" Babette persisted.

"Excellent," Eliot grumbled.

"Yes. Very good," Lynn agreed, reaching down for her purse which she'd rested on the floor at her feet.

"Good!" Babette said, beaming at the handsome couple. "Maybe we'll meet again on your return flight to the States."

Lynn smiled. "That would be nice."

"Yes. That would be nice," Eliot said.

"Till then," Babette said. She turned and undulated to the next seat and bent down to say her good-byes to the passengers there.

"Well? Shall we go?" Eliot said. "People are beginning to file out."

"Yes. Let's," Lynn said dryly. She moved out into the aisle, feeling the heat from the bodies crowding against her. She held on to her hat and moved on toward the door.

"Your flight bag," Eliot said, moving next to her. "You left it under the seat." He handed it to her and she slung it over her shoulder.

"Thanks, Eliot," she said. "That champagne seems to have clouded my senses."

But not enough to forget Adam, he thought angrily to himself. Determined to make her focus her entire attention on him, he placed an arm possessively about her waist and helped her down the steep flight of steps leading away from the plane to the asphalt-paved landing strip.

"You'd think they could have taxied in closer to the terminal," Lynn fussed, attempting to smooth the wrinkles out of her skirt as she eyed the terminal many hundreds of feet away. Then, holding onto her hat, she peered up into the sky, seeing a brilliant blue with no clouds in sight.

The blazing sun beat down harshly on her face, making her feel as though she were being scalded by the fiery heat of its rays. The breeze that was lifting her skirt away from her legs was hot and humid and everything within viewing range seemed to have a dancing haze of heat about it.

"Hey! Wait up!"

Lynn and Eliot turned and eyed the tall, lanky man

moving toward them. His dark beard hid most of his facial features except for his short, snub nose, gray eyes and narrow lips. His hair hung long and dark over his shoulders and he was dressed in a khaki shirt and pants.

"Hank," Eliot said, clasping the cameraman's hand with a friendly handshake. "How was your flight?"

"Hairy as hell," Hank laughed. He nodded toward Lynn. "See you made it okay, Lynn."

"Sure," she said, laughing softly. "But barely. That landing was something else."

"Well, guys, I'm going to go see to the camera equipment," he said. "Then I plan to take in the city once I'm settled at the hotel. Hope you don't mind if I don't see you 'til we're ready to leave for the ruins. I have a lot of sightseeing I want to do."

"Just be sure you register in the right hotel," Eliot joked. "It's best we stick pretty close together, you know."

"The Saint Francis?"

"Yes," Eliot said. Then he chuckled. "And no, it's not a church. It's really a hotel."

Hank gave Eliot a half salute. "I'll see you there," he said, then spun around and headed back toward the plane to supervise the unloading of his camera equipment.

Eliot took Lynn's elbow with one hand and hurried her on toward the terminal. "I hope our luggage gets to the right hotel," he said worriedly.

Lynn gave him a sideways glance. "Maybe we should see to it ourselves."

He shrugged. "Southern Airlines guaranteed safe

delivery to the hotel," he said. "So let's just not worry about it."

"Who's worried? Not me. Do you think we'll be able to get a rental car?"

"Avis is the only rental agency available," he said. "And I was told that with so few privately owned vehicles in Leon, the rent-a-cars are hard to come by."

"But weren't you able to reserve one?" Lynn asked.

"From San Francisco?" He laughed softly. "Lynn, this is Carmen Island, not America."

The humidity clung to Lynn's hair, causing it to curl rebelliously, and her hose clung moistly to her legs. "I wouldn't have guessed," she laughed back. "God! I thought summers were humid in Illinois. This climate puts Illinois summers in the shade— which is where I wish I were right now."

"The hotel should be air-conditioned."

"But the jungle won't be," she pointed out. "I'm going to die on this expedition, I know it. Jungle rot!"

Eliot leaned down close to her. "Then while there, we'll take a swim in a lagoon to cool ourselves off," he teased. "Just imagine, Lynn. Swimming in a lush, cool, exotic lagoon, all alone, like Adam and Eve . . ."

"Right—Adam and Eve," she said. "Do you perchance recall what else inhabited Paradise? A snake, that's what, and I'll bet there are plenty of them in your 'exotic lagoon'!"

Eliot chuckled beneath his breath, then guided her on inside the terminal. They pushed their way through a crowd of dark-skinned people, hearing the staccato chatter of Spanish being spoken on all sides.

Small, barefooted boys attired in ragged clothes were everywhere, begging. When one came up and stopped at Eliot's side and tugged at his elbow, Eliot and Lynn stopped and looked down at him.

*"Equipaje?"* the small boy asked, his eyes dark and wide.

Eliot patted the boy on the head, tousling the child's dark hair even more than it already was. "No. No, *equipaje*," he said, shrugging. *"Lo siento."*

The boy's expression saddened, then he held out a hand anyway. *"Dinero?"* he murmured. *"Por favor?"*

Eliot plunged one hand deeply into a pocket and pulled out some coins which he handed to the boy.

The boy's mouth dropped open as he stared at the money. Then his fingers clamped tightly over the coins as he began to run away. But suddenly he turned and yelled, *"Muchas gracias, gringo!"*

Eliot waved. *"Que le vaya bien,"* he called back. Then he once more took Lynn's arm and steered her on toward yellow lights that spelled out AVIS.

"What was that all about?" she asked.

"He wanted to carry our luggage and when I told him we had none, he wanted a handout."

"Which you graciously gave to him."

*"Sí,"* he chuckled.

"And you speak Spanish. How fortunate, since I don't speak one word of it."

*"Sí,"* he repeated.

"Well, sir, use your Spanish and see if you can

get us a rental car," Lynn laughed as they stepped up to the Avis counter.

"Sure. We'll be driving merrily down the streets of Leon before you can bat an eye," he assured her.

"I'm supposed to be happy about that?" she sighed. "I feel very much out of place here. Just look around, Eliot. Do you see any other Americans? When is the rest of our entourage arriving?"

"Some later today and some early tomorrow," he said. "Relax, Lynn. Try to enjoy it. Remember, we're the only TV team here. Our ratings will go sky high once they see the show on the screen back home."

"I hope you're right," she murmured. She straightened her hat and nodded toward the rental car attendant. "Go to it, Eliot." She eyed the Spanish woman carefully, noting her white, off-the-shoulder blouse and brightly colored gathered skirt. Her dark hair was pulled back behind her ears and held in place by colorful plastic combs. She was pretty, with her golden-brown skin and bright, brown eyes. A wide smile greeted Eliot as he stepped up to the counter.

"Do you have any available cars?" he asked, leaning against the counter.

"*Sí. Bastante.*"

"Good," Eliot said, removing his wallet from a rear pocket. "Then I need one, please. A compact, if you have one on hand."

"*Nada,*" she said, shaking her head slowly back and forth.

Eliot shrugged his shoulders. "Okay," he said. "Then how about a subcompact?"

Once more she shook her head back and forth. "*Nada,*" she said, frowning.

"What do you mean by saying you have nothing?" Eliot asked, lifting an eyebrow quizzically. "You just said you had rental cars. Do you, or don't you?"

"I have nothing left but a pickup truck," she replied in perfect English. "I assure you it has four-wheel drive, *essential* for the back country."

"But I don't want a truck," he argued. "I only want something small for a couple of days of sight-seeing."

"*Lo siento,*" she said with a shrug.

Eliot angrily thrust his wallet back inside his pocket. "Well, now what do we do?" he stormed.

Then he leaned over and once more spoke to the attendant. "You do have *automovile de alquilers* here, don't you?" he growled.

"*Si,*" she said calmly. "We have taxis." She pointed toward a wide glass door. "Out there on the street. You will find one, I am sure."

Eliot half saluted her mockingly. "*Gracias,*" he grated, then once more took Lynn by the elbow. "Come on, Lynn," he said. "Let's get this show on the road."

"I have a feeling that this is just the beginning of our problems," Lynn said dryly. And as they stepped out onto a flagstone walkway where the hustle and bustle of traffic and scurrying, chattering people were almost deafening to the ears, Lynn felt that her prediction would more than likely prove accurate.

"Did you say there were few privately owned vehicles?" she groaned, gesturing with a hand. "Then they must all be here, in this one street."

Horns continued to blare as the cars inched on past the terminal. Beggars added to the confusion as they clung to the doors of the slowed cars.

"Let's try to get out of this mess," Eliot growled. He eyed the cars at the curb, feeling less than confident that they would succeed. The cars were taxis, all right—the word *Taxi* was painted in bold red paint against the scratched and dented yellow bodies of the cars—but Eliot was hesitant to trust himself and Lynn inside one. The windows of most of the taxis were shattered, many of them lacked bumpers. The drivers were young and reckless-looking and spat constantly from their open windows.

"Well, there are our chariots," Eliot finally said, nodding toward them. "Take your pick, Lynn. Our lives are in your hands."

"You're kidding," Lynn said, laughing nervously. Something compelled her to cling to Eliot's arm.

"Wish I were," Eliot said. He urged Lynn toward the least disreputable-looking car and bent down to speak to the driver. "*Automovil de alquiler?*" he said, lifting an eyebrow as his eyes traveled over the car's interior. It was dust-laden and springs and foam rubber were protruding from the seats.

"*Sí,*" the young, dark-eyed driver said, indicating with a broad gesture that Eliot and Lynn should get into the car.

Eliot helped Lynn inside, groaning as he himself settled gingerly down onto the filthy, torn seats. When the driver turned and questioned Eliot with his dark eyes, Eliot said, "The Saint Francis Hotel."

Comparing the white of her suit against the filth of the car's interior, Lynn gave Eliot a harried look. "This is unbelievable," she whispered.

They were thrown back into their seats with a sudden jerk as the taxi sped away from the terminal, swerving dangerously in and out of the crowded streets, leaving everything and everyone else behind. Clinging to the seat, Eliot's eyes grew wide, and he winced as he listened to the taxi's brakes squeal and the tires spin as the driver stopped and started at the stop signs. "This *is* unbelievable," he gasped. "No wonder the taxis are so battered!"

Lynn placed a hand on Eliot's knee, amused at his discomfiture. "Relax," she teased. "Wasn't that your advice to me?"

"God . . ." Eliot gulped as the car suddenly seemed to go sideways. "Where is he taking us?"

"He's giving us our money's worth, Eliot," Lynn said with a mischievous grin, hanging onto her hat.

"He'll be lucky to get one damn penny out of *me*," Eliot grumbled. "If we reach the hotel alive, that is."

Lynn smiled to herself, glad to see Eliot unnerved for a change, and tried to take in the setting around her. The sun was shining on the white steeples of a cathedral and the glass office buildings were gleaming brightly, yet between these modern buildings were still signs of the past. Squat, slate-covered roofs supported by tapering pillars of masonry still stood with their barred windows and long, dark corridors.

The buildings were built flush with the sidewalks and the streets were narrow and uneven and covered with cobblestones. Then there were the private houses that stood proudly between the buildings of the city. Most had been built around open patios filled with flowers, plants and splashing fountains with solid doorways, iron balconies and window grilles.

Adam had told Lynn that there had once been silver mines in the surrounding hills, but the silver had all been mined long ago and now only an occasional nugget could be found to show around and brag about.

"I think we've finally arrived," Eliot said, leaning forward as the car came to a screeching halt.

"Well, pay the man and let's get out of here," Lynn said, brushing dust from her skirt and repositioning her hat.

"Only to get rid of him," Eliot growled. He pulled several dollars from his wallet and thrust them into the sweaty palm of the driver, then helped Lynn down onto the street.

Lynn once more held on to her hat as she leaned back and allowed her eyes to travel up the full height of the building. If she didn't know better, she would believe she was back in San Francisco, entering one of its plush hotels. It was made of all mirrored glass, and tropical plants decorated the grounds outside the entranceway.

Stone tables and umbrellas opened over them on a patio on one side of the building, offering a refuge from the sunbaked street, but Lynn was anxious to get out of the heat and urged Eliot on inside, where a delicious rush of air-conditioning met their quick entrance.

"Ah," Eliot said, running a finger around the inside of his collar. "At last."

"I do believe we are spoiled Americans," Lynn laughed, clinging to Eliot's arm.

"Well, *this* spoiled American wants a shower. Let's get our key."

"Don't you mean *keys,* Eliot?" Lynn said sharply, eyes narrowed.

"Oh, yes," he said, coughing nervously into a cupped fist. "*Keys.* Plural. Of course."

"Eliot Smith, if I hadn't said anything, would you have gone ahead and bullied me into sharing a room with you?"

"You can't blame me for trying," he laughed, winking at her.

"Oh, can't I?" Lynn snapped, yet knew that at this point, had he asked, she might have said yes.

# Six

WITH HER arm linked through Eliot's, Lynn tried to enjoy her outing with him, after having gotten settled into the hotel. The sun had dipped behind the distant mountains, making the temperature at least a bit more tolerable.

"I feel as though I'm being stared at constantly, Eliot," Lynn whispered. "Aren't these people used to foreigners?"

"*Gringos*, so they call us," he said, laughing softly.

"Well? Aren't they?" she said, nudging him in the side with her elbow. "Surely tourists arrive here every day. It is quite a unique city."

Eliot's gaze raked over her, appreciative of what he saw. "Maybe it's your shorts," he said, nodding toward women and children passing by, some with water jugs supported on their heads. "Do you see any women dressed in shorts, or even slacks? In many countries, it's considered very immodest for a woman to wear trousers of any kind, much less shorts. They are quite a religious people here. Maybe that's the reason behind their interest."

Lynn moved closer to Eliot, placing a hand over

her partially exposed cleavage. Yet her low-cut blouse didn't reveal any more of herself than the native women she was studying. All were wearing the same types of drawstring blouses and most were worn low, leaving nothing to the imagination. But she now wished she had on one of their brightly colored, gathered, street-length skirts. At least she'd feel less conspicuous and blend into the crowd.

"And then again, maybe it's your hair, Lynn," Eliot said, lifting some thick strands from her shoulders. "Maybe they've never seen such golden hair before or such big green eyes."

"Maybe so," Lynn murmured, still looking around her.

The people of Leon lived in a brilliant patchwork quilt pattern of pastel houses perched on narrow, winding streets that faced and dipped into little unexpected plazas at every turn. In its crowded streets, no two faces were alike in coloration or features. Lynn could see traces of all the various people who had mingled over the centuries, some with the high, aristocratic cheekbones of the Maya, others with Indian features and even some Africans, but hardly ever the light-skinned Caucasian.

"I wonder if the talk of *Contras* has frightened the tourists away," Lynn murmured. "Eliot, we may be in real danger here. Maybe we should return home on the next plane."

"Oh, no," Eliot groaned. "Don't start that again!" He stopped and turned to Lynn, clasping on to her shoulders with his hands. "Lynn, we're here. We've a job to do. Now please relax and let's enjoy ourselves before we get into the business end of this thing. Today we're tourists. Let's *act* like tourists. Let's go buy a souvenir or something. Anything to get your mind off all your worries."

His dark eyes and the passion in them that he did not attempt to conceal caused a familiar, dangerous weakness in Lynn's knees. His jaw was set with determination and his polo shirt revealed the tautness of his muscular body, so close to her own. Even in the midst of the hustle and bustle that surrounded them, Lynn was tinglingly aware of his masculinity, and desire surged through her. In this foreign country, far from civilization as she had always known it, she felt loose and free and even a bit reckless.

"All right," she said, tossing her head with a soft laugh. "Let's do our best to enjoy ourselves . . . I wonder where I might be able to buy a new hat."

A low rumble of laughter rose from inside Eliot. "A hat?" he said, dropping his hands to his side. "Lynn, what is this thing with you and hats? I bet you have a closet full."

She raised a hand to his cheek. "I'll let you in on my little secret," she said softly.

"Secret?"

"I usually buy a hat when I'm upset about something," she admitted.

He looked at her quizzically. "And you want to buy a hat now," he murmured. "What's upset you, to make you want to buy a hat *now?*"

Lynn swung herself next to him and linked an arm through his, urging him onward. "Silly," she giggled. "I don't *always* have to be upset to want to buy a hat."

"Oh? So I didn't upset you by scolding you?"

She gave him a sideways glance. "Naughty girls

need scolding sometimes," she teased. "Anyway, that's what my father always told me."

He bent and whispered into her ear, "And you're in a naughty mood?" he said. "Maybe we'd better return to the hotel. I want to take advantage of *that*."

"Eliot, get your mind out of the gutter," Lynn snapped, blushing. "That's not what I meant and you know it! Come on. Let's really do some window shopping. And who knows? Maybe I *will* find the ultimate hat!"

"I doubt if you will here," he said. "But we'll give it a try."

They wandered in and out of shops where brightly colored rolls of material were enticingly displayed for sale. There were no dress shops. The material was sold to the customer and if one wished a dress to be made, a seamstress measured and sewed it according to the design chosen from a large selection of pictures shown to the customer.

There were many other shops selling pieces of brass and hand-carved mahogany items such as tables, chairs, bowls and statues. Also there were duty-free shops which offered radios, china and cameras, which for a price could be delivered directly to the airport for the convenience of the tourist who didn't wish to be burdened by his purchases while continuing to shop from street to street.

There were many cantinas along the walk. Music blared noisily from them and the strong aroma of tortillas with *chorizos* and *arepas* floated temptingly out onto the street.

Elderly women with leatherlike faces and drawn

mouths sat along the walkway grinding maize between stones and baking their own types of tortilla cakes over small open fires, which they offered for sale. Wagons passed by, creaking under the weight of cabbage, carrots, lettuce and red, shining tomatoes, looking for a good spot in which to display their wares.

Lynn stared at a man passing by on the cobblestone street. He was leading a mule from which on braided grass rings hung live chickens, straw hats and fresh vegetables.

"There's a hat for you," Eliot teased, pointing to the straw hat on the mule. "It would be perfect to wear into the jungle."

"Not my style," Lynn replied. Then she spied another shop, one that featured an assortment of ladies' hats. She quickened her steps. "In here," she said firmly. "Surely I can find one in here. I *must* buy a hat in Leon to add to my collection. I'm anxious to show it off to my friend Cathy back home."

Eliot sighed wearily. "If you insist," he said. "But we'd better hurry. It's getting dark pretty rapidly. We don't want to be out on the streets after dark."

"Why, Eliot, do I detect a hint of cowardice?" Lynn said, stepping into the crowded shop.

"I'll just buy one of those *machetes* over there," he responded, pointing to a fancy leather case hanging from the wall with a *machete* gleaming over its edge. "That should serve well enough as protection."

Lynn laughed, then became absorbed in trying on hats while a short, dark-eyed clerk stood by, anxiously watching. "This one," Lynn decided at last. She smoothed her hair beneath the hat until only a few curls peeked out at her brow. It was a truly elegant concoction, and became her outrageously.

"Hey, I like it," Eliot said. "I'll let you buy it if you promise to wear it to dinner with me tonight with a daring black dress."

"You'll let me?" Lynn said, flashing her green eyes up at him, yet smiling provocatively. She knew that she surely looked seductive in the slinky, sexy hat, a black satin helmet overlaid with a frosting of jet beads.

"Yes," he said, kissing her gently on the cheek. "I'll let you. Does that annoy you, darling?"

Lynn warmed with the intimacy that was drawing them closer and closer together. She was beginning to fear that once they returned to the hotel, all else but their need for one another would be forgotten. Though they were in separate rooms, the rooms were connected by one flimsy door . . .

She refused to answer. Instead she removed the hat and handed it to the clerk. "Now, Eliot, use your skill in Spanish to tell the lady I'd like to purchase this hat," she said, reaching inside her purse for her billfold.

Eliot removed her hand from her purse. "This is my treat," he said. He transacted the deal expertly, then both hurried back to the hotel and into the elevator. A few minutes later, they stood outside Lynn's door.

"You *are* going to ask me in, aren't you?" Eliot asked huskily, placing a hand against the wall, leaning close to her.

"I need a shower, Eliot. Maybe later."

"There's room in the shower for two," he suggested, with an exaggerated leer.

"Not in my shower, there isn't!"

"Lynn, let me have your key."

The forcefulness of his voice unnerved Lynn a bit, but she clasped her fingers tightly about her key. "You *still* persist at ordering me around," she said dryly. "Eliot, I'm going to go in my room *alone*, take a shower *alone*, and then maybe, just maybe I'll invite you in for a drink."

"Got your dander up again, I see," he chuckled, searching in his pockets for his own key. "All right. Have it your own way."

He shrugged and walked away from her, tossing his key playfully up into the air.

"Well!" Lynn thought, a bit confused and maybe even a little disappointed. "He gave up much too easily. I wonder why?"

Feeling a bit dejected, she turned the key in the lock and pushed the door slowly open. Reaching around on the wall beside her in the dark, she finally found the light switch and flipped the light on, flooding the room with low, dramatic lights from indirect lighting above the drawn drapes.

Tossing her hatbox aside, Lynn turned on several more lights from lamps at various places in the room. Again she admired the suite that consisted of two large, airy rooms with high ceilings. In this outer room were two long chaises covered in white velour, with matching white ottomans, glass and brass triangular tables, plus thick cocoa-colored carpet and handprinted wallpaper. A mirrored bar was at the far end, and at the other was a door that led into the bedroom.

Already pulling her blouse over her head, Lynn hurried to the bedroom. She then stepped into the bathroom and turned the shower on, after which she moved back into the bedroom and finished undressing, letting her gaze languidly move around her.

The furniture was made from the finest pecan woods fashioned into two tier cabinets, a storage headboard and a queen-size platform bed. A large, glass sliding door led out onto a veranda that overlooked the city.

Another door drew Lynn's sudden attention as she saw the knob slowly turning.

Taking a step backward, Lynn felt her heart beginning to race from fear. She knew that the door led into Eliot's suite, but he hadn't asked for the key while in her presence. So who could it be? What if Eliot hadn't gone into his suite. What if he'd gone to the downstairs bar instead for a drink, leaving the way clear for someone to break into his room and hers as well.

All sorts of horrible thoughts raced through her mind—and then she gasped and began a slow boiling inside as Eliot opened the door and stepped casually into the room, smiling devilishly.

"Well, hello," he said huskily, letting his gaze slowly appreciate her nudity. "Fancy meeting you here. Small world, isn't it?"

"Eliot!" Lynn whispered harshly, crossing her arms over her breasts. "What do you think you're doing? Who do you think you are, coming in here like this? And when and how did you get the key?"

Her eyes searched frantically around the room for something to wrap around her. She was completely vulnerable, ravaged as she was by his eyes. But all her clothes had been placed neatly in the closet and drawers. A towel being the next best thing

111

to clothes, she reached quickly into the bathroom, jerked one from a towel rack and hurriedly draped it around her body. She knew she was blushing from head to toe.

"How did I get the key?" Eliot chuckled. "Just a few dollars, my rosy darling, in the proper hands. And when? Just now. All I had to say was that my fiancé wanted the door between our rooms unlocked because she was a bit afraid, being in a foreign country and all."

"You've got some nerve!" she hissed, taking a step backward. "Eliot, I never know what to expect from you next. Now will you please leave?"

His eyes swept over her anew, with a silent message that she could so very well decode. And her heart and body were sending messages as well, reminding her of her wants and needs, and she knew that one touch of his lips would cause her to respond in a blaze of uncontrollable passion.

Eliot closed the door behind him with the toe of his boot. He nodded toward the bathroom. "You've got the shower ready for us, I hear," he said, with passion-darkened eyes. He reached for Lynn, but she flinched and drew quickly away from him.

"Eliot, I don't . . ." she began weakly.

"You *do*," he said, reaching out again and this time obtaining his objective. He wrapped his fingers around her wrist and drew her slowly to him while his other hand unwound the towel from her rosy body.

"No . . ." she said throatily, barely recognizing her own voice, it was so desire-filled.

"Yes," he whispered, then bent his head and placed his hot lips over a breast, toying with the nipple until it became taut and throbbing between his teeth.

A moan rose from deep inside Lynn as her body arched backward and her hair hung in long, silken strands down her naked back. She placed her hands on his shoulders and dug her nails into his flesh as she closed her eyes to the building ecstasy, now feeling the flame of his tongue circling her other breast, then lower, to her navel.

"Oh, Eliot, why . . . ?" she whispered.

"Because you need me just as much as I need you," he whispered huskily.

His lips rained hot kisses upward, along her soft curves and crevices, seeking out all her pleasure points. Then he twined his fingers through her hair and forced her lips to meet the heat of his demanding kiss, causing Lynn's senses to drift slowly away into a void of timelessness.

Her fingers eagerly crept inside his shirt, feeling the crisp tendrils of hair along his sinewy chest and the tightness of his shoulder muscles as he drew her body next to the male strength of his.

"Let's take that shower together, darling," he whispered. "Undress me. Let's forget everything except each other. We're the only two people alive, the only inhabitants on this wide expanse of earth. Let's make love like there's no tomorrow for either of us!"

Obeying his words as though in a trance, Lynn leaned away from him in total surrender as his dark eyes burned into hers. With trembling fingers, she slowly pulled his shirt up and over his head. Wild desire flamed inside her as her trembling fingers touched his bare flesh.

She let a forefinger trace the muscle of one of his breasts, then ran her thumb across his taut, dark nipple. And as though ordered to, she lowered her lips to it and sank her teeth gently into it.

She enjoyed realizing the pleasure she was giving him which was evidenced by his low groan and the shudder that rippled through his entire body.

"Lower, darling..." Eliot whispered shakily. "Devour me with your kisses!"

As though in a drunken haze, Lynn unsnapped his Levi's, then lowered the zipper and eased his pants over his hips and then lower, surprised that he wore no shorts beneath them. She was suddenly face to face with his swollen need of her. Brazenly, she let her fingers play along his flesh and cup him there, as he helped her by sliding himself seductively up and down between her quivering fingers.

But when he reached out and urged her head downward, Lynn regained control of herself quickly and stepped, gasping, away from him. She covered her face with her hands and choked back her revulsion at herself and what she had almost let herself do.

"No..." she softly cried. "We must stop, Eliot."

But Eliot was not to be dissuaded. He pulled off his boots and socks, then lifted Lynn up into his arms and kissed her once again into a dizzy mindlessness. As he withdrew his lips from hers, he carried her into the bathroom and stepped slowly beneath the warm flow of the water.

"I love you, baby," he said huskily, then eased her from his arms, to stand before him. "Let me show you how *much* I love you."

As the water beat down on both their naked

bodies, Lynn watched in rapturous silence as Eliot began applying heated kisses first on her breasts, then lower until he bent to one knee and kissed her sweetly and gently where she ached so painfully with intense, building need of him.

Spreading her legs, she let his tongue send spirals of pleasure up and down her spine, drowning her senses in wild delight. Then she welcomed him into her arms as he rose to slowly place himself inside her. Wrapping one leg around his body, she met his eager thrusts, closing her eyes as his lips once more sought hers out in a meltingly hot kiss.

Her arms twined about his neck, her fingers curled into his hair and she leaned ever closer to him as the water lubricated their movements, rippling sensuously over their entwined bodies.

The thrill of the moment was heightened by the sound of their bodies moving against one another. It was as though they were beneath a tropical waterfall on a deserted island, clinging, mating, threatened by drowning—but only in the dangerous crests and tides of their desire for one another.

Lynn's body ached—her mind swirled. They were as one, thigh to thigh, breast to breast. It was as though one flame consumed them both, burning brighter and brighter, a flame that no amount of water could ever extinguish.

His male strength continued its love play, lifting her higher and higher. The hungry pressure of his mouth gave rise to soft moans surfacing from inside Lynn. She clung, she arched, she was fast becoming breathless with his endless, powerful surges inside her. Yet she never wanted it to end.

His fingers stroked her velvet back, his mouth

moved to the hollow of her throat and as Lynn felt spasms of joy engulf her, she also felt his release as it surged warmly and powerfully within her.

Lynn eased away from him, yet touching him still, wanting this moment to last forever. She shivered as his hands cupped her breasts. His eyes were soft and peaceful with his love for her. "I *do* love you, Lynn," he said huskily.

One of his hands traced a seductive line downward and brushed against her tender love mound. He stroked it gently, taking her breath momentarily away. She closed her eyes drunkenly and thrilled even more when she felt the love-play of his tongue once more on her most sensitive love point and gave way to more rapture as he gave her a long, lingering kiss there, then rose back to his feet.

"Darling, I feel as though I'm turning into one large prune," he teased, brushing her wet hair back from her eyes as she slowly opened them to his boyish, charming grin.

"Oh, you mean the shower," she laughed. She reached over and turned the water off, then eased back into his arms, trembling at the exquisite feel of him against her own sensitive body.

"Yes, the shower," he said.

"Well, you *asked* for it," she murmured, flicking her tongue hungrily over one of his taut, wet nipples. "Are you sorry, my love?"

Eliot lifted her chin with a forefinger and implored her with his haze-filled eyes. "And are you sorry that I got hold of that key?" he asked thickly.

"You really shouldn't have," she pouted.

"Are you *sorry?*" he persisted.

Lynn giggled, snuggling once more into his arms,

not caring that his hair was dripping water onto her cheeks. "Not really," she murmured. "But, Eliot, we really must talk these things over in the future. I'm not used to such surprises. That could've been anyone coming through that door. It *did* frighten me."

"I'm sorry, baby . . ."

"Well, truthfully, I'm not," she murmured. "After all, once we're in the jungle with the rest of the expedition, we won't even be able to *kiss.*"

"Oh? You've thought that far ahead, have you?"

"Truth?"

"Yes."

"Well, then, yes," she said. "Eliot, I've so wanted to dislike you. I even wanted to *hate* you when you took over as Program Director. But, damn it, I just couldn't!"

"I'm glad," he whispered huskily. "For a while I thought your feelings for Adam . . ."

He quickly withdrew his further words, thinking it best not to question her about her ex-co-host. Surely such feelings were a thing of the past.

"What about Adam?" she asked, reaching for a towel. Something inside her rebelled, wishing he hadn't reminded her just why she should still dislike him. For a moment there she had forgotten all about Adam!

She eyed him questioningly. Why did Eliot persist in bringing Adam's name into the conversation? Did he want to upset her? Actually, it should have been Adam with her filming the ruins, not Eliot. It wasn't fair, no matter how one looked at it.

"Nothing," Eliot said, taking the towel from her. He began rubbing it gently over her body.

Lynn grabbed the towel back away from him.

"Eliot, I can dry myself," she said coldly.

Eliot framed her face between his hands. "Lynn, what's the matter?" he said thickly. "You're placing that damn wall between us again."

"Am I?" she said, avoiding his eyes, her emotions already aroused by the touch of his hands.

"You know you are."

"It's just that I'm cold."

"I can take care of *that*," he said huskily, drawing her gently into his arms.

Lynn shoved him away and rushed into the bedroom. She went to the closet, pulled a pale blue satin robe from a hanger and slipped quickly into it. She tied its belt snugly in front as she turned around to forestall Eliot's approach. Her eyes wavered, not wanting to let his nudity unnerve her all over again.

"Lynn, I'm not going to let you do this to us," he growled, clasping his fingers on her shoulders. He jerked her roughly to him and gave her a fierce, demanding kiss. Her defenses began to crumble. Her insides were warming, her pulse racing.

Eliot whispered in her ear, "Let's step out on the terrace and take a look at the jungle. We can see it between the buildings, you know."

"I'll be seeing the jungle soon enough," she argued.

"Lynn, come on. Look at that gorgeous sunset. Surely you can't resist *that*."

"And are you planning to let everyone see your gorgeous body?" she said, forgetting why she had gotten mad at him.

Eliot glanced quickly down at himself and a rumble of laughter rose to the surface. "You see what you do to me?" he said. "You scramble my brains, pretty lady."

Lynn stooped and picked up his Levi's and tossed them at him. "I imagine we'll both have scrambled brains after being out in that jungle for a full day. The heat will probably be unbearable."

"Let's hope we can get to the ruins and back in one day," Eliot said, stepping into his pants.

"You said the ruins aren't too far from Leon," she said. "Didn't you?"

He shrugged, then slipped his shirt over his head. "That's what I was told," he said.

"I hope we won't have to spend a night there," she said. "Not in the jungle . . . with all those wild animals and snakes!" She shuddered.

Eliot leaned down and winked at her. "I'll be there," he said. "I'll protect you."

"Sure," she said, laughing softly. "You and your machete."

"Yes. Me and my machete," he said, brushing a soft kiss against her lips. Then he nodded toward the terrace. "Shall we?"

Lynn's gaze traveled over him. "Yes—now that you've hidden your tantalizing body beneath your clothes," she teased. "I wouldn't want to cause a worse traffic jam below in the streets."

"Heaven forbid," Eliot laughed. He draped an arm about her waist and guided her out on the terrace, then gestured with an arm. "Just look," he said. "Now tell me, can anything possibly happen to us out there in all the beautiful greenery?"

Lynn eyed him with a skeptical glance, then let herself get absorbed in the setting. Beyond the buildings were rolling hills of green and outlines of towering mountains even farther in the distance. The sun had set behind the mountains, leaving crimson streaks in the sky which were quickly becoming consumed by the fast approaching black velvet curtain of night.

"It looks almost too peaceful," Lynn murmured apprehensively.

Eliot placed a hand to his ear. "Listen," he whispered.

"To what?" Lynn asked.

"Do you hear the marimba band?" he said. "Let's go dancing. There's supposed to be quite a floor show downstairs in the lounge."

"Yes, let's," Lynn said, hurrying back inside. "I want to be a part of civilization as long as possible before we get lost out there in that mess of trees and creeping vines."

"Lost?" Eliot said, laughing. "Darling, one thing you *don't* have to worry about is getting lost."

Lynn certainly hoped he was right.

# *Seven*

"I THOUGHT you were kidding when you said you were going to wear the bush hat on the expedition," Eliot said, looking amusedly at Lynn's hat as she desperately held onto it. The taxi lunged forward through the narrow streets of Leon.

"Would you rather I'd purchased one of those straw hats we saw on that mule the day before yesterday?" Lynn asked, taking a quick intake of breath as a chicken scuttled out of the taxi's path squawking fiercely. "Eliot, *you* will wish for a hat of any make and design when this sun begins beating down on your bare head."

"Darling, we'll be in the jungle," he laughed. "We may not see the sun for hours at a time."

"Then I will use my hat for a fan," Lynn said stubbornly.

"You may have to fight off snakes with it instead," Eliot teased, watching the sun reflect from the car window onto Lynn's face, making her skin take on a rosy sort of glow. Her green eyes were enhanced by pale green eyeshadow and the soft contours of her nose and chin made his fingers itch to reach out and caress them. The seductive curve of her lips caused

121

an ache to gnaw at his groin as he remembered the magic those lips had spun across his flesh.

Lynn shuddered visibily at the mere mention of snakes. "What do you mean, Eliot?" she said, wide-eyed. "Why on earth would I have to fight off snakes?"

"One of them might try to mate with your hat."

"What . . . ?"

"The band of your hat. The snake skin!"

Lynn sighed heavily. "Good grief, Eliot," she said. "Your sense of humor leaves a great deal to be desired!"

"So does this taxi," he laughed, thrown off balance with the quick turn of the taxi as it began traveling down an even narrower street.

"Seems as though we're quickly leaving civilization behind," Lynn said, looking through the shattered pane of the window. The tall buildings of downtown Leon were no longer in sight and even the smaller houses that had led to the edge of the city had disappeared. The cobblestone road had changed into a rut-filled dirt path where tangled undergrowth extended its feelers daringly from the dense jungle on either side, as though trying to ensnare the wheels of passing vehicles in its green tendrils.

"We should be there soon," Eliot reassured. He crossed his legs and began tapping his fingers on the leather of his boot.

"Why couldn't we have all met at the hotel?"

"Too much confusion, I suppose," Eliot said, shrugging.

"Hank should have come with us."

"He can find his own way. Don't worry about him."

Lynn gave Eliot a withering look. "Eliot, without him and the camera, we're out of luck," she sighed. "We'd *better* worry about him."

"He was given the same directions as everyone else on the expedition. He'll make it. You'll see," Eliot said. Then he leaned close to Lynn's ear. "And, darling, if you must know, Hank had a little . . . uh . . . something delaying him this morning, if you know what I mean."

Lynn shot Eliot a quick, unbelieving glance. "You mean a *woman?*" she whispered.

"Exactly," Eliot chuckled. "Seems he got a bit looped last night at the bar. When he woke up, he found some beautiful chick in bed with him."

Lynn laughed a bit, then pulled at her clinging, damp Levi's and wiped beads of perspiration from her brow. Her long-sleeved, brown-plaid shirt also clung to her arms, and her hair had kinked from the humidity as though it had been permanent waved.

She spread her legs out in front of her and began fanning herself with her hat. "Hank would be the smart one if he got conveniently lost and had to stay behind in the cool, air-conditioned hotel," she grumbled.

"But as you said, without him, there would be no point in our going either," Eliot interjected.

"That's the idea," Lynn said, laughing softly. She scooted forward on the seat, as the taxi came to a sudden halt. Placing her hat back on her head, she rolled the side window down and leaned her head out. "We're here," she stated. "Or should I say I *think* we're here."

"What do you mean you think we're here?" Eliot said, leaning in front of her to gaze slowly around him. "If we aren't here, where are we?"

"Where is the tourist bus?" Lynn asked. She saw only a few distinguished-appearing people, several mules, and two natives. Just then Hank stepped into view from behind a tree, carrying his camera equipment packed securely in two leather bags. Lynn breathed a sigh of relief.

"Damned if I know," Eliot said. He slid across the seat and out of the taxi, waving to Hank. "Hank! Hey, buddy. Over here," he called. He thrust some money into the outstretched hand of the taxi driver, then helped Lynn out and placed an arm securely about her waist.

Lynn clung to her large, leather shoulder bag and looked toward Hank, not liking his scowl. It was obvious that he was quite annoyed about something. The weight of his camera cases was causing his shoulders to slump, and his khaki shirt showed sweat stains beneath both arms.

He had tucked his pant legs into the tops of his high leather boots and had tied a bandana around his head to hold his long, black hair out of his eyes and to soak up the perspiration on his forehead.

His long, dark beard made him look the complete adventurer, but it was the anger in his eyes that attracted Lynn's keenest attention.

As Hank came to a stomping halt beside them, Eliot placed a hand heavily on his shoulder. "Hey, man, what's up?" he said. "You look madder than a wet hen."

"Did you know that we'd be travelin' on *mules* into this jungle?" Hank growled, glaring from Lynn to Eliot.

Lynn blanched. Her gaze went quickly to the

mules and she now noticed the packs secured to their backs. "You've got to be kidding," she gasped. "Mules? We're actually going to travel on mule back?"

"I was told that mules can travel much easier over the jungle paths," Hank grumbled.

"Well, you'd think a jeep could at least be tried," Eliot said, silently amused by Lynn's horrified reaction.

"No jeep, no tourist bus, not even a damn *horse!*" Hank said, turning to glower toward the two dark-skinned guides. "And to top it off, those two barely speak English. You'd think the Meltonian Institute could at least supply American guides or someone who could speak English."

"The Institute is working on a low budget," Eliot explained, then added, "but no sweat, man. I speak Spanish quite fluently. And just remember how lucky we are that the Institute chose 'Morning Magazine' for this expedition. It could've been any other program in any other city. But they selected us."

"No matter what you say, I *knew* we shouldn't have tried this," Lynn sighed, once more fanning herself with her hat. "If our ratings improve with this film footage, I'll be surprised. What it will probably do is make us the laughingstock of the TV industry."

"Both of you just don't have faith," Eliot chuckled. He gestured with a wide sweep of his arm, looking up into the sky. "I can see it now, everyone envying us our adventure by mule. We'll start a trend. Anybody remember that old song, 'Mule Train'?"

Lynn gave him a shove. "Will you shut up?" she

said hotly. "You are impossible!"

Eliot chuckled a bit, trying to see the amusing side of what could in truth be a fiasco. "Well, Hank," he said, patting Hank on the back. "What are you waiting for? We want to get this on film from the very outset."

"You're serious, aren't you?" Hank grumbled.

"Very," Eliot said flatly, quickly sobering and realizing the necessity of looking totally professional as the group of people moved his way. "Get the camera out. Fast, man," Eliot whispered harshly to Hank. Then he smiled broadly as he extended a friendly hand to the first arrivals and began introducing himself and Lynn to everyone.

There were two magazine journalists, three newspaper reporters, several college professors, three archaeologists and two anthropologists—all male. Lynn felt a bit out of place, discovering she was to be the only woman on the expedition.

Once all the instructions were made and the two guides had assured everyone in halting English that they would lead them safely to the Mayan ruins and that there were plenty of canteens of water and food to pass around, everyone gingerly climbed aboard the mule of his choice and began the slow journey.

Lynn and Eliot, seated awkwardly on their own mules, dropped back from the rest. Hank was mingling with the others, filming while balancing himself astride his mule.

"What a story I'll have to tell my grandchildren," Lynn groaned. The muscles in her back began a slow, agonizing ache and her inner thighs felt bruised as they rubbed continuously against the saddle of her mule.

"At this pace, we'll get there sometime next week," Eliot grumbled, as he squirmed restlessly in his saddle.

The sound of machetes chopping away at the thick brush ahead was steady as the guides cleared the way for the group.

"One thing's for sure," Eliot said, "We're the first people to travel this route."

"How can you be so sure?"

"The guides are having to cut a path."

"Only here," Lynn argued. "There could be other paths only a few feet away."

"If there were, we would be taking *that* route," Eliot argued back.

"Not if the guides had been instructed to make this as authentic appearing as humanly possible, for effect."

Eliot chuckled. "Lynn, not everyone does everything for 'effect.' Only we in the so-called entertainment industry continuously have that on our minds."

Lynn gave him an exasperated look. "Eliot, we're not the first to be taken to the ruins," she said. "There's so much excitement about the discovery that I'm sure others have gone before us. And if that's true, there have to be paths cut elsewhere."

Eliot threw a hand up into the air, in defeat. "Okay, okay," he said. "I just wanted to ease your mind about the *Contras*. I didn't want you worrying about them."

Lynn unfastened the three top buttons of her shirt, held the fabric away from her and blew down its front, glad that she had chosen to leave her bra off. "My main concern of the moment is this darn heat," she grumbled. "I feel as though I'm going to melt right down into my boots." She removed her hat and once more began fanning herself with it.

"But you have to admit," Eliot said, "it's damn pretty here."

"Yes, I guess you're right," Lynn said, replacing her hat on her head. "Everywhere I look is a feast for the eyes."

Ferns grew thickly everywhere and giant trees supported masses of tangled vines that partially concealed the shapes of the trees themselves. Underneath the mule's hooves, the floor of the jungle was covered with rotting vegetation. Lynn had never seen such lush greenery.

Small creeks and waterfalls occasionally sparkled in shafts of intermittent sunlight. All around them was a steady cacophony of sound as macaws moved in flocks, splashing the jungle with vivid explosions of color and boisterous squawking. Spider monkeys danced through the branches above the travelers' heads and peccary snorted and rooted in the undergrowth.

Epiphytes, air plants, which grew upon but did not draw nourishment from other plants, were suspended high in the air, and large, beautiful orchids, begonias and many other varieties of flowering plants provided a pageant of brilliance, piled up in vibrant masses upon the trees, crowding the leaves from tip to tip, and emitting a fragrance even more heavenly to Lynn's nostrils than the most expensive French perfume.

Suddenly an arc of flame soared through the air right above Lynn's head, causing her to catch her breath and almost lose her seat on the mule's back.

"That was a quetzal bird," Eliot said, grabbing for Lynn. He helped her regain her seat and watched with amusement as she arranged her hat more firmly on her head.

"It frightened me," Lynn laughed nervously. "Imagine being scared by an overgrown parrot. I must be losing my grip."

"It's to be expected," Eliot said, removing his canteen from his saddlebag. He unscrewed the lid and handed it to Lynn. "Here—take a swig of water. You'll feel better."

"Thanks," Lynn sighed. She lifted the canteen to her lips and let the wetness trickle down her parched throat, gulping thirstily.

"Hey! Enough," Eliot said, leaning to reach for the canteen. "Too much at once might make you sick. You're not used to this heat."

"You're telling me," Lynn said, wiping her mouth with the back of her hand. She handed the canteen back to Eliot. "When are we going to stop and stretch our legs?"

Eliot screwed the lid back on the canteen and replaced it in the saddlebag. Then he leaned over, trying to relax his back muscles. "The guides know what's best," he said gruffly.

His eyes rose to the trees, seeing only glimpses of sunshine through the thick branches. "I imagine we're working against time on these mules. There's just so much light in one day."

"I don't want to hear about it," Lynn said, shaking her head. "I don't even want to think about it. I don't want to spend even one night in here. Pretty or not, I'm sure it's quite different at night."

"Yes. Instead of flowers gleaming back at you, there'd be a thousand eyes," Eliot teased.

Lynn shuddered. "Will you shut up?" she hissed. "Please don't make this any worse than it already is."

Leaning closer to her, Eliot pinched a buttock playfully. "Now, darling," he said, also playfully, "wouldn't it be fun to be lost out here, just the two of us? Think of all the things we could do and nobody would be the wiser."

Blushing, checking to see if anyone had seen him pinching her, Lynn angrily brushed Eliot's hand aside. "Quit that!" she whispered. "We're not alone. Or have you forgotten?"

"I wish we were," he said huskily, glancing at her open shirt and appreciating the outline of her bare breasts beneath the cloth.

"Well, we're *not*," she said stubbornly. "So get your mind back on business. That *is* why we're here, if you recall."

"I'm afraid you're not going to let me forget."

"Darn right!"

Hours passed, filled with their constant bantering, when suddenly a break ahead in the tangle of brush and trees gave Lynn her first glimpse of what they had traveled so far to see.

"I think we're here," she said, feeling her first shimmering of true excitement since the day she heard of the expedition. Now that she could see the first signs of ancient temples rising into the sky, she knew it was right that it was to be put on film, for posterity.

She watched as Hank jumped from his mule and began running toward the ruins with his camera.

He too had apparently decided that the trip had not been made in vain.

"Now our true job begins," Eliot said, climbing from his mule. He lifted his arms to Lynn and helped her to the ground.

"Eliot, don't you see?" she said, nodding toward the carved figures and crumbling pyramids. "This is no longer just a job. This is educationally *fun*."

Eliot laughed. "Educationally fun?" he said. "That's the first time I've heard that expression!"

Lynn quickly buttoned her shirt and rushed toward Hank, leaving Eliot behind. "Hank, film every last inch of this," she said, breathless. "Then we'll interview everyone, with the ruins as a backdrop."

She placed her hands on her hips and spread her legs. "And, Hank, talk as you film. Get your gut feelings into this." She eyed him warmly. "It's in your eyes, Hank. You're as caught up in this as I am."

"It's incredible, isn't it, Lynn?"

"Yes. Quite."

Workers were picking gently at tall, stone carvings. Plastic was spread across others, preserving what had already been uncovered. A tall, thin, aging man moved toward Lynn. He pushed his gold-framed glasses back on his bent nose and his face was flushed from the heat. His brown shirt and workpants were covered with dust and his balding head was beaded with perspiration.

Smiling, he offered Lynn a frail, bony hand. "I'm Glenn South," he said in a deep voice. "I'm from the Meltonian Institute. I'm glad you've come. You are Lynn Stafford, aren't you?"

"Why, yes," Lynn said, laughing softly. His firm handshake belied his frail appearance.

"I've admired your work," Glenn said. "I'm glad you're the one who has been given this assignment."

Shadows raced across Lynn's face. She knew she should not be receiving all the credit; and Eliot stepping to her side was a quick reminder that she certainly wouldn't be the recipient of such an honor.

She linked an arm through Eliot's and drew him closer to her side, trying to remove the rising bitterness from her mind. "Mr. South, this is Eliot Smith," she said. "He is now KSFC-TV's Program Director. He's the one who is actually responsible for our being here."

Glenn's eyes wavered as he questioned Lynn with a lengthy stare, then looked toward Eliot and offered him his hand. "My pleasure, Mr. Smith," he murmured. "If I can help you with anything, just let me know."

"We'll be filming a lot," Eliot said, glancing eagerly all around him. "I'd like to just get into it—film it with a natural ease."

"It's all yours," Glenn said. "I'm glad for the publicity. Maybe we'll get more funding from the government. These are valuable discoveries, not only to the people of Carmen Island, but to all civilization. A lack of funds has hampered the restoration project, I'm sorry to say."

"I hope we *can* be of some help," Eliot said. "Now, Glenn, we'll use several different camera angles . . ."

Lynn moved away from Eliot and Glenn while

they continued to talk technical details, and she let herself become absorbed in a lost civilization. It was a bit sad to see that what had once been a bustling ceremonial center, with its richly carved stone monuments and temples, was now home only to wild animals and the brightly colored birds that continuously darted through the tall jungle trees.

During her studies of the Mayan Indians, Lynn had discovered that their cities were primarily ceremonial complexes controlled by priests and the nobility. The priests supervised the complex carvings of faces, figures and animals onto stelae, ten-foot columns of stone on which the passage of time had been recorded. Mayan art had been mathematical. Each temple, stairway, animal, column or figure represented a date or a time relationship.

Lynn moved about, gingerly touching the carved stones in the shapes of animals. She knew that the ancient Mayans had believed that their world was supported on the backs of two alligators. Their gods had been the animals or forces of nature, such as the rain or sun, which controlled their lives.

"Well now, are you sorry I became Program Director?" Eliot said, coming up next to Lynn and placing his arm about her waist.

"Eliot, that's a dumb question," she said dryly.

"Oh? You're not pleased with the ruins?"

"You know that's not what I mean."

"You're still sore with me because I took your job," he said.

"Exactly."

"Lady, you sure know how to prolong a grudge," Eliot sighed.

Lynn said nothing, only raising a quizzical eyebrow.

"Well, what do you say we get Hank over here and get the two of us on film and forget I reminded you what a rat I am, okay?"

"Fine," she said, fanning herself with her hat.

Hank moved in with his camera and Lynn repositioned the hat on her head. She licked her lips and smiled into the camera, gesturing with an arm. "Most of these temples, buildings and monuments that have been uncovered here are grouped around a central courtyard," she said into the microphone in her most professional manner.

Eliot moved in next to her, smiling too. "And as you see," he said, "outside the main area are piles of moss-covered stones among the creepers of the jungle floor waiting to be restored to their former glory."

Lynn began moving as Hank focused the camera on her. "One of the most important monuments that has been discovered to date is an altar with etchings of sixteen human figures, each sitting cross-legged on a hieroglyph," she said. "As you can see, all the dignitaries are finely dressed, with jade and snail-shell necklaces, and have documents in their hands. The top of the altar is divided into thirty-six squares of hieroglyphs that represent the Mayan calendar."

Eliot stepped into view of the camera. "The human figures are thought to represent envoys who came to Carmen Island for a scientific congress to devise a calendar for the entire Mayan empire. The hieroglyphs name the city-states, or regions, that the envoys represented. Because this altar is so valuable, workers place plastic sheets over it each night to protect it from the elements."

Lynn added, "Although controversy exists about why the Mayan civilization disappeared, it is generally thought that the common people revolted against the nobility and priesthood. All we know for sure is that this city was abandoned and the great monuments and temples were quickly reclaimed by the jungle."

Eliot nodded toward Hank. "That ought to do it for this segment," he said. "Let's wrap it up."

Lynn and Eliot then became deeply engrossed in interviewing everyone, not realizing that the sky was losing its blue brilliance. Only when the crimson blaze of sunset became evident through a break of the trees did Lynn become aware of how late it had gotten. Her heart began to race as she moved quickly to Eliot's side. She grabbed his arm.

"Eliot, we're not going to be able to get back to Leon before dark," she said. "Why didn't you notice the time?"

"Why didn't you?" he argued. "I've been busy."

Lynn crossed her arms angrily. "And I haven't been?" she said sharply.

Eliot chuckled and placed a forefinger beneath her chin. "Darling," he murmured, "getting angry won't change a thing."

"What are we going to do?"

Eliot looked around him, seeing pup tents being set up in the clearing. "I think that's your answer," he said, nodding toward the tents.

"Why weren't we told?" Lynn fretted.

"I imagine they thought we knew."

"So we're the dummies of the group, huh?"

"Now, I wouldn't say that," Eliot said, laughing. "What's the matter, Lynn? Afraid of roughing it?"

Lynn clenched her fingers into tight fists at her sides. "Of course not! But I'm going to find out why we weren't told," she said, whirling around and angrily marching toward Glenn South, who met her approach with a raised eyebrow.

"Sir," Lynn said dryly. "Why did you allow the time to get away from us? You know the ways of the jungle. Why didn't you tell us how suddenly night comes? We should have been told so we could have started back to Leon by now."

Lynn noticed a quizzical questioning in the man's deep-set gray eyes. She followed his gaze which had moved to Eliot as Eliot came to Lynn's side. Lynn realized that there was something about the exchanged glances between Eliot and Glenn that indicated she had been left out of something.

"Eliot . . ." she murmured, touching his arm.

"Didn't you tell Lynn that everyone would be spending a night here at the ruins?" Glenn asked, scowling at Eliot. "If you're the one in charge, you should have shared this knowledge with Lynn."

Eliot laughed a low, nervous sort of chuckle, giving Lynn a wry look. "Slipped my mind," he said.

Color rose to Lynn's face as her back stiffened in anger. She took a step toward Eliot and frowned up at him. "Eliot, did you know about this all along?" she hissed.

"Yes," he said, sheepishly smiling. "It's a feature of the expedition to spend one night here."

"And you just took it upon yourself not to tell me!" she fumed.

"I didn't see why I should worry you."

"Worry?" she echoed. "Eliot, do you think I'm a child? Or some weak, addlepated female who'd pass out at the thought of sleeping in a tent?"

Eliot leaned down, giving her his most charming smile. "You said it," he murmured. "I didn't."

"Oh!" she said, turning to storm away from him.

Glenn moved quickly to her side. "I'm sorry about this," he said. "I just thought everyone knew."

Lynn gave him a sideways glance, embarrassed. "Everyone but me," she said irritably.

"The tents are being prepared," Glenn added. "You'll be comfortable enough. There are plenty of blankets in the mule packs."

Lynn tossed her hair from across her shoulders. "I had wondered why the packs were so fat," she said. "Now I know."

"If there is anything I can do to make you more comfortable, please don't hesitate to ask," Glenn said. "I'm truly sorry about the misunderstanding."

Lynn sighed and shrugged. "No sorrier than I am," she said. Then, seeing his concern, she placed a hand on his arm. "And I'm sorry I've been behaving like a spoiled brat. What can I do to help prepare things for our night here?"

Glenn nodded toward a campfire that was already being built. "Just don't worry about a thing," he said. "Everything will be done for you. Our main concern is to make you and your crew as comfortable as possible. We would like this to be an unforgettable experience for you."

Amused, Lynn laughed acidly. "Believe me, it will be," she said.

She glanced around and found Eliot watching her,

smiling in his idiotic, good-humored way. This made her even angrier at him. He was enjoying this, and now she knew why. He hadn't neglected to tell her because of concern for her, but because he wanted to enjoy seeing her reaction. He'd probably worn that same mischievous grin as a nasty little child when he'd dropped worms down his sister's back. And since he didn't have his sister available to tease and torment, he had chosen Lynn as a substitute. What nerve!

She silently mouthed the words "You devil" at him, then turned and let Glenn direct her to the tent that would be hers for the night.

"And Eliot Smith will have the tent right next to yours," Glenn said, gesturing with his hand. "I'm sure that will make you feel more comfortable with this arrangement, won't it?"

Lynn gave Glenn a look that said more plainly than words, "you've got to be kidding!" then fell to her hands and knees and crawled inside the tiny tent. A thick layer of blankets had been placed on an air mattress on the ground and next to this a Coleman lantern was burning dimly. It gave her a glimpse back into the past when she had occasionally acted like the son her father had longed for and never had. She had gone on camping trips with him even though she'd hated the cold, dark nights in the tent and the scary night sounds all around outside. She didn't like it then and she knew she'd dislike this even more. This campsite wasn't beside a tame, meandering river. Instead, it was miles away from any kind of civilization as Lynn had always known it.

"Darling, am I forgiven?"

Lynn tensed, then gave Eliot her sourest look over her shoulder as his face appeared at the lifted entrance flap of the tent. She scooted farther into the tent as he edged his way inside.

"Lynn, let's make the best of the situation," Eliot said, settling down at the back of the tent, his back bent to keep his head from scraping the top of the tent.

"I can just guess what you have on your filthy mind," Lynn said, jerking her hat from her head. She tossed it aside and wrapped her arms about her knees.

"And that is . . . ?" Eliot teased.

"You don't plan for us to sleep in separate tents," she said scarcastically. "But Eliot Smith, you've got another think coming. You're not sleeping in my tent with me!"

"I could protect you from all those snakes who'll want to curl up in your hat," he suggested.

"I am capable of fending for myself, thank you," she said icily.

The aroma of coffee wafted enticingly into the tent, making Lynn's stomach growl.

Eliot stretched out a hand. "Coffee awaits, my lady," he said. "Unless you can perform the magical feat of making your own coffee, perhaps over the fire in the lantern, I think we ought to join the others. All the comforts of home, wouldn't you say?"

Lynn gave Eliot a withering look, then crawled out of the tent, backside first. She rose to her feet and went to the campfire, which everyone else was already circled close around, and settled down on a blanket spread before the fire. Immediately Eliot sank down beside her.

He whispered into her ear, "It gets cold in the jungle at night. You'll need me to keep you warm."

Clenching her teeth, she forced a half smile as a tin cup of coffee was handed her way, then leaned closer to Eliot. "I have my bush hat," she whispered back. "Remember? With all the snakes you tell me it will attract, I certainly won't need one more!"

Eliot broke into a soft laugh as a tray of assorted fruits and cheeses was passed to them. Then everyone relaxed and ate by the light of the fire as Glenn South rose and towered over them.

"I thought you might like a bit more insight into the Maya's way of life," he said, looking almost ghostly against the backdrop of the dark mass of the jungle behind him. "I would like to explain the sacred connections between the crops, the earth, the Mayan family and the gods. Corn, for example, was the umbilical cord of their world. It connected sun to earth, man to woman and humanity to the gods.

"One of the ceremonies has been described as follows: Within a dark hut a Mayan man takes an ear of corn off a pole that is adorned with a toucan breast. As he shells the corn he explains, 'The first thing that my child touched after leaving his mother's womb was this ear of corn, over which his umbilical cord was cut. This bloodstained corn was hung upon this pole to protect my child from the Lord of Death. Each kernel is a warrior guarding my child.'

"The man is surrounded by smoke, with flames leaping from the heads of his ceramic god pots. He is chanting in the godhouse, passing his hand through the flames. This is the umbilical corn of his child. If the child lives through the planting and harvesting of this corn, the first fruits will be offered to his god. But if his child dies, this umbilical corn will be fed to the chickens instead of to the god."

Glenn shifted weight from one foot to other, then continued, "And these people believed that all trees had souls," he said. "Before they cut down a sacred mahogany tree, they informed Hachakyum, the true Lord . . ."

Glenn continued to talk for way over an hour, then in conclusion sent a bottle of wine around the circle of onlookers. He rejoined the group himself as the wine was consumed to the last drop from the bottle.

Feeling tired and relaxed from the warm, toasty fire, the effects of the long talk and two cups of wine, Lynn rose slowly to her feet. She excused herself and began walking toward her tent, flinching when she felt hands suddenly grasp her around the waist. She glowered up at Eliot as he spun her around to meet his lingering, passion-filled gaze.

"You aren't really going to refuse me your company tonight, are you?" he whispered, glancing over his shoulder as everyone else crept into their tents and lowered their lanterns' lights.

"Eliot, please just run along like a good boy and get into your own tent," Lynn whispered back, afraid of being overheard. Out of the corner of her eye she saw Hank crawl into his tent. "We're the only ones left standing out here in the open. We're awfully conspicuous."

"I can't force you, Lynn," Eliot growled beneath his breath.

She laughed softly. "Well, at least I have *that* to be thankful for," she said.

She eased away from him and strolled on to her tent. She crawled into it, trembling both from fear and the sudden chill that was encompassing her. Away from the fire she was just finding out how cold it actually was. It seemed to be getting even more so as the minutes passed. She knew that the best thing to do was to try to get settled beneath a pile of blankets and go to sleep.

Grumbling to herself, Lynn pulled her boots off and tossed them on the other side of the tent, then rubbed her sore toes. They were aching from the tight boots which she had not had an opportunity to break in before having to wear them on the expedition.

When she felt a familiar ache in one big toe, she was reminded of the day she had kicked Eliot, and why. She grumbled a bit more to herself. She knew that if he were here now she just might be tempted to repeat her action. He deserved a swift kick in a vulnerable spot for getting her into a situation like this. She hated tents, hated camping out! What she wouldn't give to be back in her nice, civilized hotel room!

When a loud screech resounded through the trees overhead, Lynn froze. Her eyes darted wildly around, hoping that she was sealed well enough inside her tent. She could imagine many nasty things that might try to crawl in with her . . .

The screech seemed closer the next time it broke the silence of the jungle making Lynn dive quickly beneath her blankets, even using them to cover up her head.

Trembling, she lay there for a while, then let one eye slowly peek out from under the blanket. She sighed with relief when all seemed to be calm and peaceful again—except for the high whine of a mosquito circling around overhead. Smacking away at the devilish creature, she knocked the lantern over.

With a pounding heart, Lynn reached for the lantern—and felt a sudden stinging and smelled the aroma of hot kerosene. She'd burned her fingers while putting the lantern back in place.

Tears glistened at the corners of her eyes as she held her throbbing hand, rocking back and forth on her knees, clenching her teeth to keep from crying out. And then Eliot was there, suddenly pulling the entrance flap open, peering inside at her. She felt a joyous warming of her heart.

"Eliot, please come on in," she murmured tearfully.

"I thought I heard you let out a little squawk," he said, scrambling inside. Then he saw the redness of her fingers and reached for her hand. "God, Lynn, what happened?" he asked anxiously.

"I knocked the lantern over," she said. "And when I tried to pick it up, I burned my fingers." She laughed a bit awkwardly. "Pretty clumsy, huh?" she added.

Eliot settled down next to her and moved her hand closer to the lantern which he relit, examining the damage. "Looks like you won't get any blisters," he encouraged.

His dark eyes sought hers as he slowly lifted the hand to his lips. With great gentleness he kissed the enflamed fingers. "I'll kiss the pain away," he said huskily.

Once more he placed his lips there, then let his

tongue move slowly and sensuously from one finger to the other.

Lynn gasped quietly as he sucked one fingertip between his lips, then another. She closed her eyes and held her head back, wanting to fight the rapture building inside her. But she knew that more than anything else she wanted him and could not deny her desire anymore than she could deny herself food if she were starving.

"I'd like to stay, Lynn," Eliot whispered. "I hope you've changed your mind."

Lynn cast him a languid glance, then reached out and extinguished the flame of the lantern. She eased into his arms and let her lips be consumed by his. After a blissful moment, he drew away from her.

"Is it because you're afraid to be alone . . . or because of your need of me that you want me to stay?" he asked huskily, twining his fingers sensuously in her hair.

Lynn laughed softly. "Both," she said. "Maybe a little more of one than the other—but I won't say which!"

"You she-devil!" He laughed. Then his fingers busied themselves unbuttoning her blouse and lifting it away from her. When he could see the well-defined shape of her full breasts silhouetted against the wall of the tent, he lowered his mouth to one and playfully ran his tongue about the nipple.

Gasping with pleasure, Lynn reached her fingers to his shirt and quickly unbuttoned it. Reaching inside, she searched then found one of his nipples and squeezed and played with it in return.

Eliot moaned with building passion, then lowered his tongue to explore the dimpled sweetness of her navel. While worshipping her there he unsnapped her Levi's. The noise her zipper made being lowered sounded loud in the silence of the night and Lynn giggled drunkenly.

"Someone might hear us, Eliot," she whispered.

"Who gives a damn?" he chuckled, easing her Levi's from her legs, and then removing her panties, revealing the softness of the pleasure patch between her thighs to the skill of both his fingers and tongue.

"I feel so utterly wicked," Lynn whispered. "We're surrounded by tents filled with people and here we are . . ."

"Making passionate love," Eliot finished for her.

She eased his shirt from his shoulders, nuzzling her nose into the crispness of his chest hair. She began showering his flesh with fiery kisses as her fingers worked with the snap of his Levi's. Soon a scraping noise inside the tent was evidence of another zipper being lowered.

As Eliot lifted his hips and struggled out of his pants, Lynn's kisses began anew, starting at his abdomen. She placed her fingers around on the smoothness of his buttocks and urged him even closer to her face. Taking a deep breath, drunk with ecstasy, she kissed his hardness and flicked her tongue teasingly around his velvet tip. When he moaned and shuddered against her playful lips, she began the slow ascent back up his body, feeling victorious in her assault as his lips hungrily possessed her mouth.

"Take me, Eliot," she whispered, lacing her arms about his neck, leaning sensuously into the urgent, hard line of his body. Feeling the strength of his maleness throbbing against her thigh, she reached down and stroked it. Funny—the pain in her hand seemed to have disappeared.

"Enough," Eliot said, laughing throatily. "You know there are dangers in such actions, baby."

"Then my love, don't make me wait any longer," she begged. "Let's share the danger! Make me a *part* of the danger!"

Eliot cupped a breast and kissed its taut nipple tenderly, then eased her down and stretched out on top of her. The pressure of his muscular chest against her tender breasts evoked a quivering sigh from Lynn. Then as he entered her, filling her with his powerful hardness, she gasped ecstactically, raising her hips to his.

Lynn's thighs trembled as Eliot thrust within her. She sought his mouth. They kissed wildly, passionately. Their hearts beat out their passion against one another's breasts as Eliot's arms engulfed her in a searing embrace.

His lips devoured her mouth. His tongue speared her lips open and as the effervescence blossomed, closer to the completeness of their union, Lynn threw her head back with an ardent, ecstatic sigh of absorbing, breathless release . . .

Afterward, Lynn snuggled contentedly into his embrace. The shadows of the campfire outside made patterns against the tent's walls and the occasional call of a distant wild animal filled the dark void of the jungle night.

Lynn traced Eliot's chiseled features, not seeing, but loving the touch of him. Everything about him embodied masculine strength. She trembled as she felt his hand stroke her inner thigh where she was still so exquisitely sensitive.

"Eliot, I don't know how you do it," Lynn said at last.

"Do what?" he asked, amused.

"Always make me forget why I'm mad at you," she murmured.

"A combination of skill and perserverance, my proud beauty," Eliot teased.

"Eliot?"

Silence. Then, "Hmm?"

"Please no more white lies," she said. "Be up front with me at all times. Okay?"

"Why, sure, baby. Anything you say."

"And, Eliot . . ."

"Hmm?"

"Please get us back to civilization tomorrow!"

"Sure," he said. "Your wish is my command."

Lynn brushed a kiss against his lips. "I do have to admit this has been fun."

Eliot's voice brightened. "Oh?" he said. "Then I'll have to arrange it so we can get lost out here in the jungle. Think of all the exotic nights of sensual love we could share!"

Lynn scooted up on an elbow. "That's not the first time you've made reference to getting lost," she accused. "Surely you don't have any more tricks up your sleeve!"

Eliot's fingers slipped around to the back of her head and eased her lips to his. "Now, darling, what are you trying to say?"

"You *wouldn't* . . ."

He laughed softly and said, "You think I'm crazy or something? Believe me, I'm as eager to get out of the jungle as you are."

Lynn once more snuggled against him, closing her eyes sleepily. "Just testing," she teased. Then she yawned. "I'm so sleepy . . ." she murmured.

Eliot rested his cheek on her head, smiling, yet sad. Tonight their lovemaking had had a special, primitive thrill to it. He didn't look forward to returning to the faster pace of all the tomorrows . . .

# *Eight*

"WHY ON earth aren't the guides taking us back the way we came?" Lynn grumbled, brushing scratchy leaves back from her face as her mule sauntered onward. She and Eliot were the last of the procession, lingering farther behind for a bit of privacy.

"Well, at least they're not having to cut our way back with machetes," Eliot said, leaning down to mop his beaded brow with his shirt tail.

"But there's no path," Lynn argued. "How do they know which way to go?"

"I imagine those guides could be blindfolded and get anywhere they pleased," Eliot said. "Remember, they're part Indian. Indians are always the best trackers."

A hummingbird scarcely larger than a man's thumb fluttered around an orchid close to where Lynn's mule stepped. Lynn silently watched it, then saw it disappear into the profusion of tangled undergrowth and dense thickets. Thick, lush creepers covered the ground, reaching out in all directions, and screeching monkeys screamed and played overhead.

"Well, I hope they get us back to Leon soon,"

149

Lynn said. She removed her hat and began fanning herself with it. "I believe it's even hotter today than yesterday."

A shimmering through the lush greens to the left of her drew Lynn's attention. She saw that it was the brilliant blue of a lagoon edged with beautiful, open-mouthed orchids. The thought of splashing some of that water on her face to refresh her made her grab at Eliot's arm.

"Eliot, over here!" she gestured at the lagoon. "Let's stop for a moment."

"What?" he said, lifting his eyebrows. "Why?"

"I'm hot," she complained, feeling almost limp. The oppressive humidity was sapping her of her usual vitality and strength. "I'd like to splash some water on my face."

Eliot could see her discomfort in the droop of her shoulders and the heaviness of her eyelids. Perspiration streamed down her face and her face was flushed and blotchy. She definitely looked like a prime candidate for a heat stroke.

Lifting a hand to her head, a tremor coursed through Eliot as Lynn relaxed her face into the curve of his palm. "Yes. We'll stop," he said firmly. He looked toward the rest of the expedition. "But not for long. We don't want to fall too far behind the rest."

"And you're the one who's always joking about how great it would be to be lost out here in the jungle," she teased.

"Now you know. I'm a devout coward," he said, chuckling.

Pulling his mule to a stop, Eliot jumped from his, then went and helped Lynn get down from hers. Placing an arm about Lynn's waist, Eliot helped her through scrub brush, avoiding thorns and vines. The broadleafed trees towering overhead were a mixture of mahogany, Spanish cedar, balsa and rosewood. Exotic red, yellow and blue macaws and green toucans fluttered in and out and from limb to limb, their screeches echoing on into the distance.

The lagoon sparkled more clearly now, looking like a sea of glittering diamonds as the afternoon sun beat down on it. Lynn moved away from Eliot and hastened toward low-hanging mangrove trees that ringed the water, then dropped to her knees and eagerly began splashing the water on her face.

"Watch out for that crocodile!" Eliot warned, coming up next to her and touching her lightly on the arm. When she jumped back with a shriek of alarm, he rocked with laughter.

With a pounding heart, Lynn eyed him angrily. She pulled her hat from her head and hit him with it. "You just love to aggravate me, don't you? That was a dirty trick, Eliot! There *are* crocodiles in this region, you know."

"And also snakes," Eliot said, pointing upward into a tree.

"Yes. And snakes," Lynn said flatly.

"Lynn, there is a snake up there in the tree," Eliot said quietly, still pointing. "He's coiled around a limb, soaking up the sun."

"Eliot, you just never give up!" Lynn said, glowering at him. "I know there's no snake there any more than there was a crocodile."

Eliot held her face between his hands and gently forced her around. He watched her color quickly

151

fade as she spied the huge boa constrictor resting peacefully overhead.

Lynn's pulse raced and her knees weakened. "Good Lord!" she gasped.

"Just don't move," Eliot said softly as the snake awakened and began slithering down the tree. Jokes were the farthest thing from Eliot's mind; this was no longer fun and games.

"Eliot, what if . . . ?"

"Just keep still," Eliot whispered, still holding her face between his hands, afraid to move.

The grass separated as the snake began moving from the tree's trunk in a different direction from where Lynn and Eliot still stood, frozen to the spot.

"It's moving away from us," Lynn shakily whispered.

Eliot breathed easier. He dropped his hands to his side and resumed his usual jovial, lighthearted teasing. "I guess he just wasn't hungry," he said, shrugging.

Lynn gave Eliot an exasperated look, then dropped her hat to the ground as he drew her quickly into his arms.

"I can't resist this dangerous, exotic setting, darling," he said huskily, devouring her with his dark eyes. His lips bore suddenly down upon hers and kissed her long and hard.

Still fearing the snake, Lynn shoved against Eliot's chest, protesting against his sudden ardor. But as his hand crept up the front of her shirt and cupped one breast, the swooning sensation inside her took over, making her throw caution to the wind.

Twining her arms about his neck, Lynn clung to

him. She emitted a soft moan as his fingers caressed her nipple, then lowered and unsnapped her Levi's, to slide his hand down inside them. As the warmth of his fingers traveled over her flesh, small flames ignited, threatening to set her completely afire. Yet she leaned away from him.

"Eliot, we must get back . . ." she whispered.

"You're too tempting, darling," he said. "How can I think of anything else when I'm here with you? This is more interesting than climbing back on that mule, wouldn't you say?"

"Yes, but . . ." she protested. She closed her eyes and arched her neck as Eliot lifted her shirt and tenderly kissed the flesh of her breast.

"As soft as a marshmallow," he whispered huskily.

"A marshmallow you're scorching with your tongue," Lynn whispered back.

"It even tastes as sweet," Eliot continued. His fingers circled her breast and gently squeezed it, forcing the hardened nipple between his teeth. He nibbled on it and once more let his fingers explore beneath the enclosure of the Levi's.

Lynn could feel the flush of her face and the erratic pounding of her heart. But a movement in the brush behind her drew her quickly to her senses. She withdrew from Eliot and swung around, eyeing the movement of the brush—then gasped when she saw a scaly four-legged reptilian creature half wobble, half slither away.

Eliot laughed. "That was only an iguana," he said. "They're not dangerous."

Lynn buttoned her Levi's and straightened her shirt. "We must catch up with the others, Eliot," she said. She picked up her hat and brushed it off, then let her gaze settle on some beautiful clusters of pale-colored orchids only footsteps away.

"All right," Eliot grumbled. "If you insist."

"But first, let's take time to pick a few orchids," Lynn said, already walking toward them.

"Anything for my lady," Eliot said, moving on ahead of her. He plucked a few and handed them to her. "I only wish I had some champagne to go with them," he said gallantly.

"We should be back at the hotel before night falls," Lynn said, sniffing the flowers. "Then we can bathe in champagne! We'll deserve it, making it safely in and out of this jungle."

"Ready to go on?"

"Yes. We had better get moving," she murmured. "As much as I hate those mules, they're our only means back to civilization."

Eliot draped an arm about her waist and drew her snugly next to him and began walking away from the lagoon. "It would've been fun to swim in the lagoon with you, darling," he said, leaning to brush a soft kiss on the tip of her nose.

Only half hearing him, Lynn began looking desperately around her. She could feel the sudden rapid beating of her heart in the hollow of her throat and an iciness filled her veins. "Eliot . . ." she said in a strained whisper. "Where are the mules?"

He laughed. "Probably wandered off a bit," he said. "Don't look so worried. They couldn't have gone far."

Lynn looked cautiously in all directions. "Eliot, where is everyone?" she said. "I see no signs of the rest of the expedition."

She looked closely at the ground. "I can't even

see where they *were*. There are no signs of trampled grass. Which way did they go? I'm suddenly so disoriented!"

Eliot's smile faded as he looked into the distance, in all four directions. There were no signs of mules nor people. He looked down at the ground, agreeing with Lynn. There were no telltale signs of anyone having passed along this way. He moved away from Lynn, kneading his chin.

"Eliot, say something!" Lynn shouted, moving to his side. "It's as though they've disappeared off the face of the earth! That can only mean one thing . . ."

"That we're lost," he said grimly.

"Yes . . ."

Eliot began to tear through the brush, taking giant leaps over fallen trees and tangled tendrils of weeds. "Those mules have to be here somewhere," he growled. His face grew hot, his hands were torn from briars, and his breathing became shallow as he rushed around, searching wildly.

Lynn threw the orchids to the ground and joined him in his search. Then, panting, she dropped to her knees and buried her face in her hands. "Eliot, those damn mules have deserted us!" she cried. "They aren't anywhere to be found!"

Eliot stooped and rested one knee on the ground. He broke a twig from a tree and began snapping it nervously into smaller pieces. "Not only have the mules deserted us, but also the whole damn expedition of *people*," he growled.

He threw the twig fragments to the ground and rose angrily to his feet, placing his hands on his hips. "Surely someone saw us stop at the lagoon."

"Maybe Hank did," Lynn suggested.

"I doubt it," Eliot grumbled. "If he had, he wouldn't have allowed the rest of them to go on without us."

Lynn once more felt the burden of the humidity pressing in on her, and began fanning herself again with her hat. "What are we going to do, Eliot?" she asked in a small voice.

"We'd better figure out which way to go."

"But how?"

Eliot scratched his brow absently, tilting an eyebrow. "I'll be damned if I can tell which way they went," he grumbled. "Everything looks the same—thick and green."

"I know," Lynn said, shaking her head. "I'm still totally disoriented."

"Well, we can't stay here," Eliot said flatly. "Let's try our luck and go *that* way," he added, with a nod of his head.

"Maybe we'd just better stay put," Lynn argued. "Maybe they'll come back for us."

"Darling, they won't even know at which point we strayed if it takes them so long to *miss* us."

"But the guides . . ."

Eliot clasped his fingers on her shoulders. "Yes, they will find us," he reassured her. "You'll see. But let's also try to find *them*. We can't just sit idly by waiting for them."

"We're really lost, aren't we?" Lynn whispered, blinking her thick lashes nervously.

"Yes. Seems that way," he said briskly.

"Now that it's truly happened, it's not as romantic as you had imagined, is it, Eliot?"

A scowl shadowed his face. "If you want to know,

it's damn terrifying," he blurted out. Seeing the frightened look on her face, he quickly drew her into his arms. "But, darling, it won't be for long," he murmured. "They'll find us. You'll see."

"Without the mules, we have no food," she wailed. "We'll starve to death!"

"Lynn, for God's sake," Eliot said. "Please stop it! We'll be found. Will you stop worrying?"

Lynn linked her arm into the curve of Eliot's, placed her hat on her head and trotted alongside him. The tangled brush grabbed at her boots, the low limbs of the trees scratched at her face and the ever-present humidity clung to her body, making her feel clammy and exhausted.

"Do you see anything yet?" she asked, panting for breath.

"Birds and more birds," Eliot said, laughing nervously. "We have our own private menagerie, darling."

"With a few coiled snakes for added attraction," she fussed, trembling as she caught sight of a coral snake wrapped about a tree's limb on one side of her.

"Just keep moving," Eliot warned. "If you ignore the snakes, maybe they won't see you as a threat and they'll return the favor."

"Sure," Lynn whispered, forcing a strained laugh. "Famous last words!"

"We mustn't stop now," Eliot warned. "Not for anything."

"And what if we're headed in the wrong direction?"

"God only knows. Right?" he said.

"I wish He'd tell us," Lynn sighed. "I don't like

this, Eliot, not one bit. If I had guessed for one minute that this could've happened, I would've said to heck with 'Morning Magazine' and joined Adam at KEZ-90 Radio."

Eliot's gut twisted at the mention of Adam. Lynn could think about Adam Lowenstein at the strangest, most inopportune times! And each time she did and spoke of him aloud, it ate even more of Eliot's heart away. "It would've been that easy, huh?" he growled, casting her a hurt look.

"Anything would be easy compared to this," Lynn said, stopping to get her wind. She unbuttoned her shirt and blew down its front, then removed her hat and combed her fingers through wet tendrils of hair.

"We've got to make the best of the situation," Eliot said, taking her hand in his. "Keep your chin up, baby. That's the best advice I can give you."

Lynn flashed him an angry, sour look. She jerked her hand from his. "Adam gave me the best advice of all and I didn't listen," she said dryly.

Eliot's anger caused his eyes to narrow. "And what advice was that?" he growled.

"To join him at the radio station," she said.

Eliot placed his hands angrily on his hips. "And what made you decide not to take his advice?" he growled.

"I had something to prove . . ."

"Like what?"

"Like showing you that I would not be pushed around by you or anyone!"

"And what made you think I'd do that?"

"Eliot," Lynn said with wide eyes. "You did exactly

that! You took over my position as Program Director, didn't you? You did just what I so desperately wanted you not to do."

"Okay. So I did," he agreed. "You could have called it quits then and you didn't." He clasped his fingers on her shoulders. "Why not, Lynn? No one was tying your hands at the time."

Lynn wriggled herself free. She turned her back to him, refusing to answer.

"We both know the answer to that one," Eliot said softly. "You stayed on because of me. Why can't you forget about Adam Lowenstein and his damn job offer?"

Lynn spun around on a heel. "Eliot, why on earth are we going over this now, of all times?" she sighed. "We've got to find the expedition or do you realize we'll be out here, all alone, without any protection for a full night?"

Eliot avoided the pleading look in her eyes, now knowing they were indeed lost and maybe for more than just one night. He had a sudden feeling that he had taken the wrong route, innocently guiding Lynn farther and farther away from safety. If not, he knew they would have joined the expedition by now, for he knew that he and Lynn had been traveling at a much faster rate of speed than the mules.

"And, Eliot, I just remembered something," Lynn said, covering her mouth with a hand. "I don't know how I could have forgotten."

Eliot heard the fear in her voice. He noticed the pallor of her cheeks, though it was even hotter now than before, and realized that she should instead have been flushed from the heat.

Feeling responsible for her discomfort, he took

her hand in his. "What's that, Lynn?" he asked softly.

"The *Contras*," she said, even more wide-eyed. "What if we run into one of them?"

Eliot drew her to his side and forced her onward. "Lynn, you're letting your imagination run away with you," he said firmly. "Don't you remember? They haven't infiltrated Carmen Island."

"The peasants interviewed for a recent newscast said differently," she softed argued.

"What newscast are you referring to?"

"Adam's."

Eliot stiffened. "Adam's," he repeated. "And Adam never makes mistakes, right?"

Lynn gave Eliot a harried look. "Let's not get started on that again, Eliot," she said. "It seems that every time I bring Adam into the conversation . . ."

Eliot interrupted. "Lynn," he said, quickly changing the subject.

"Yes?"

"Have you noticed something?"

"What?"

"It seems the sky is losing its luster," he pointed out. "I think we've walked much longer than you or I realized."

"Do you mean it will be dark soon?" she asked, trembling at the thought.

"Exactly."

"God!" Lynn whispered.

She locked her arm even more securely through his and clung to him as they continued to make their way through the scratching, twining brush. Then Eliot grabbed at Lynn and quickly stopped her.

Lynn's breath caught in her throat. She glanced

up at Eliot. "What is it?" she whispered.

"I see a clearing ahead," he said.

Lynn squinted her eyes, shading them with her hand. Her heart began to race. "A hut," she said. "I see the roof of a hut! Maybe the people who live there can lead us safely back to Leon!"

"I certainly hope so," Eliot said, sighing heavily with relief. He squeezed Lynn's hand, then urged her onward.

Lynn's eyes were wide with excitement. She could see more and more of the hut as they moved closer to the clearing. But as the trees thinned and she got a full view of the entire hut, her hopes were quickly shattered. The small building made from roughly hewn, unpainted boards with a palm-leaf roof had apparently been ravaged by a storm. Some of its boards were splintered and torn away, hanging awkwardly to the ground. Only part of the roof remained intact. And as Lynn and Eliot drew closer, a flock of birds flew upward through the hole in the roof and out in all directions.

Lynn jumped, startled. Then she placed a hand to her throat, feeling a lump tightening there as she realized that they weren't to be rescued all that easily after all. This house held no occupants now and probably hadn't for many months past.

"Well, one thing's for sure," Eliot said as he stepped into the hut. "At least we won't be sleeping out in the open tonight."

Lynn inched inside beside him. Her gaze moved slowly around her. The floor was nothing but bare earth and a crude stone fireplace filled one whole wall. Beside it sat pottery bowls, most of which were cracked and some broken beyond repair. A blackened coffeepot lay on its side on gray ashes in the fireplace.

As her eyes became accustomed to the dimness, Lynn saw the remains of what had once been someone's living quarters. A rickety wooden table stood in the middle of the room with two spindly unpainted chairs leaning awkwardly against it. A rusty metal cabinet stood beneath a window with more odds and ends of pottery dishes and mugs on its warped shelves.

A makeshift bed had been made from piles of palm leaves intermingled with plaited coconut fronds. The loosened boards that composed the walls permitted light to filter through the cracks, casting strange, dancing shadows on a smaller table beside the bed, where a kerosene lamp with a smoke-blackened and cracked chimney stood, still partially filled with fuel.

A low, mournful sound made the hair raise at Lynn's neck. She grabbed Eliot's arm and glanced quickly up at him.

Eliot laughed and nodded toward the roof. "It's the wind," he said. "Blowing through the holes in the roof."

"Thank heavens," Lynn whispered.

"Well, what do you think?" Eliot said, gesturing with an arm to the shabby room. "Do you think we can make it livable until someone comes and rescues us?"

Lynn blanched. "Eliot, you can't be serious," she murmured.

"Darling, I've never been more serious," he said, moving away from her. He went to the fireplace and picked up the coffeepot shaking the ashes from it.

"Coffee, anyone?" he chuckled. When he received no reaction from Lynn, he left the coffeepot behind and went over to the table and brushed layers of dirt and dried palm leaves from atop it.

"How can you joke at a time like this?" Lynn fumed. She jerked a chair around and dropped her full weight onto it, exhausted, hot, hungry, and annoyed. And when she felt the chair legs buckle beneath her and land her unceremoniously on the dirt floor at Eliot's feet, she had one more word to add to her list of grievances—she was *embarrassed*. His low chuckle drew her smoldering gaze to the boyish grin that split his handsome face.

"Eliot, will you just shut up!" she hissed. Ignoring his proffered hand, she got up from the floor, brushing dirt from her elbows and Levi's.

Eliot went to the fireplace and knelt down on one knee before it as he began clearing debris from inside. "Time to get down to business," he said seriously. "The first thing we must do is get a fire started. It's the best way to keep wild animals away through the night."

Lynn visibly shuddered. She took her hat from her head and placed it on the table. She had never felt as dirty nor as unnerved in her entire life, even though being around Eliot always seemed to be cause for the latter.

Then his words soaked in and became reality. "Animals?" she barely murmured. "You don't really think we could be in some danger?"

"Grr," he teased. "You're always in mortal danger. Of me!"

Lynn formed her hands into tight fists at her sides.

"Eliot, for once, be serious!" she cried. "What are we going to do?"

Eliot rose to his feet, wiped his hands on his Levi's, then went to Lynn and tenderly drew her into his arms. "Lynn, I'm sorry," he murmured. "I just want to try to make you look on the bright side."

"I'll only look on the bright side when I'm back in my own house in San Francisco," she said, "and have left all of this behind me!"

"Behind us," he corrected. "Darling, we're in this thing together. And I'm no happier about it than you are."

"I know," she whispered, resting her cheek on his chest. "I'm sorry."

He leaned away from her and eyed her warmly. "Then let's get that fire started," he said. "That's the first order of business at the moment."

He glanced toward the hole in the roof, seeing the gathering darkness beginning to envelop the sky.

"If you'll give me a match, I'll light the kerosene lamp," Lynn offered, eager to banish the shadows.

Eliot's eyes widened. "Match?" he repeated. "God, Lynn, I don't have any matches."

Lynn groaned, then shook her head in disbelief. She smiled grimly. "Then I hope you were a skilled Boy Scout when you were a kid," she said, "because you're going to have to start rubbing two sticks together. It may take a very long time!"

# *Nine*

LYNN AWAKENED with an ache in her bones and an extreme dryness in her mouth. She reached sleepily around her and paused when she felt Eliot there, snuggled against her back.

With a start, Lynn sat up and looked anxiously about her. She and Eliot had slept fully clothed. For a moment there she had forgotten where she was. But now with the almost deafening chatterings in the trees outside the hut and the pungent smell of damp palm fronds beneath her and from the roof above her, she knew that she was still living in the nightmare that had begun by their getting lost in the jungle.

Running her tongue over her parched lips and combing her fingers through her tangled hair, Lynn let her gaze move slowly around her. There was no door and the windows had no glass in them. The morning sun pouring through the gap in the roof and the cracks in the walls made Lynn feel much too vulnerable, though she was thankful that she and Eliot had made it safely through the night without having been devoured by wild, hungry beasts searching for food.

An involuntary shiver ran through her as she looked toward the fireplace. Only a few coals glowed orange through a layer of gray ashes. Feeling frantic for fear of losing the fire completely, Lynn jumped from the makeshift bed of palm leaves and hurried to the fireplace.

Placing some dried twigs next to the live coals, she blew on them, relieved when a small flame ignited. She settled to her knees and began feeding wood into the flames, remembering Eliot's struggles at getting the fire started the previous evening. In the end he had proved that his years in the Boy Scouts had been fruitful. But still, she doubted if he could do it again and was afraid to let the fire go all the way out. She had found out pretty quickly that fire was good for more than heating and preparing one's food. It was a key to safety.

"Lynn . . . ?" Eliot mumbled from the bed. "Where are you?"

Lynn rose up on her knees and peered over the table at him. "The fire was just about out," she said. "I've got it started again."

Eliot yawned sleepily and rose languidly from the bed. "That's not necessary," he grumbled. "Lynn, it's going to be hot enough in here soon enough."

"What about those animals you were talking about last night?"

"We'll be safe through the day," he assured her. "At this point, we have a lot more to worry about than animals."

Lynn welcomed him at her side as he dropped to his knees next to her. Sleep was still heavy in his dark eyes and there were wrinkles on his right cheek from having slept with his cheek against a palm frond. Lynn giggled in spite of herself. His cheek had the look of a fossilized stone.

But as he awakened more, and the worry in his eyes became more evident, Lynn's laughter quickly changed to a deep sigh of concern.

"What are we going to do, Eliot?" she asked. "I'm so hungry and thirsty."

"I'm going to take a look outside," he said. He rose to his feet and straightened his pants, tucking his shirt as neatly as possible inside them.

As far as Lynn was concerned, this automatic gesture added a bit of humor to the moment. She rose to her feet, laughing again. "Do you think you'll find a camera outside our humble abode, ready to film you?" she teased.

Eliot raised his eyebrows. "What are you talking about?"

Lynn's fingers went to his collar and smoothed it down in place against his chest. "The way you're primping," she said. "You know—tucking your shirt so neatly inside your pants. It's as though you expect to find your devoted public outside, waiting to see you."

Eliot's lips curved upward in a wry smile. He drew Lynn into his arms and looked affectionately down into her eyes. "Why, darling, I'm just trying to make myself more presentable for you," he said cheerfully. He brushed a kiss across her lips. "Only you. You're the only public I care about."

Lynn's lashes lowered. "I wish I could return the favor, but it's hopeless," she said.

Eliot placed a forefinger beneath her chin, forcing her gaze back upward. "Why hopeless?" he asked.

"My hair," she said, reaching to run her fingers

through the tangles. "I don't even have a comb!"

She eased from his arms and went to the door and looked into the jungle surrounding them on all sides. "We're stranded out here without any modern conveniences at all," she sighed, leaning against the frame of the door. "Not even the smallest items."

She swung around and faced him with tear-filled eyes. "Not even a damn comb!" she wailed.

She flung her arms into the air in despair, pacing back and forth in front of the hut. "Why, oh why, didn't I at least think to bring my bag with me when we stopped by that lagoon?" she fumed.

Eliot grabbed her wrist and gently pulled her close to him. He ran his fingers through her touseled hair, lifting it from her shoulders. "To hell with a comb," he said, then crushed her mouth against his. He whispered into her ear, "We don't need anything but each other. Just think about it, Lynn—this is our own private paradise. It's truly a blessing in disguise. Imagine—alone! Completely alone, away from the business of the civilized world. A lot of people would give their right arm to trade places with us, Lynn."

Lynn pushed away from his chest and broke free from him. She shook her hair back from her eyes, giving Eliot a stormy look. "You must be crazy!" she said hotly. "Don't you think for one minute that I want to be here! A person would have to be out of his mind to enjoy being miles from anywhere, lost in this foul jungle!"

"Then I guess I'm nuts," Eliot said cheerfully. He dropped to one knee and stirred the fire with a stick. "We'll be found. There's no doubt about that. And probably even too soon. I'm suddenly kind of enjoying this."

"Well, while you're enjoying it, think of something for us to eat," Lynn said, crossing her arms angrily across her chest. "And something to drink might not be a bad idea either."

Eliot threw the stick into the fire and once more rose to his feet. "All right," he said with a scowl. "I know you're right. I'll go on outside and scout around and meanwhile, you take a look inside that cabinet over there and see what you can find."

Lynn nodded her head in agreement and watched him as he walked outside, then looked slowly around her at what was obviously to be their home for God only knew how long. Paradise, Eliot had said. If this was paradise, she'd settle for the other place!

Shrugging, she went to the rusty metal cabinet and opened its door cautiously, expecting possibly a rat, a scorpion, or some other devilish creature to pounce out at her. But something much more welcome met her eyes. It was a coffee can and it didn't even appear to be very old.

"I wonder if there's coffee inside," she thought, eagerly reaching for the can.

The plastic lid flipped open easily and to Lynn's delighted surprise, there was some coffee at the bottom of the can, possibly enough for at least six cups. But then she frowned as she turned to place it on the table. Who could have been there so recently to have left fresh coffee behind? Her thoughts traveled to the fear that was always lurking in the back of her mind—Maybe a *Contra* had been there. Maybe he would return . . .

Lynn hurried toward the door, then turned and fled from the hut to Eliot's side. "Eliot, I'm afraid," she murmured, visibly shaken.

"What on earth happened?"

"I found some coffee . . ." she whispered, looking cautiously about, watching for any movement in the brush.

Eliot laughed and took her hands in his. "Hey," he said. "What is this? You *are* afraid. I can see it in your eyes. And why on earth would finding coffee frighten you? You should be happy. You were the one grumbling about the lack of modern conveniences. You can't get much more modern than a can of coffee."

"But, Eliot, don't you see?" she said. "The coffee is *fresh*, Eliot, do you hear me? *Fresh coffee*. Where there's fresh coffee there must have been someone to drink it. And from the looks of the hut, it wasn't someone who stayed long, probably someone just passing by. Possibly a guerilla!"

He framed her face between his hands. "There you go again," he said. "Letting your imagination run wild. Will you just relax?"

"How can I?" she argued. "And how can you?"

"Because I *have* to," he said calmly. "That's why."

His face was shadowed as he said, "Lynn, I ran into much worse than this while in 'Nam and I survived. You've got to trust me. Everything will be all right."

Lynn's gaze moved slowly around her. It was such a beautiful, exotic place, with the lush green trees and vines and flowers. Even the birds and spider monkeys moving from tree to tree were things she had previously seen only in the movies. It did seem peaceful enough, yet she couldn't shake the feeling of impending doom that seemed to cling like a constant shroud about her.

She forced her eyes back to Eliot. "So have you found anything of interest out here?" she asked, trying to pull herself together, to appear as relaxed and as confident as he did. She wouldn't let him think she was a helpless ninny. She still had some things to prove to him.

Eliot urged her around. He nodded toward another clearing ahead, some distance from the one they had already found. "Look," he said. "What do you see?"

The sun was so intense, Lynn had to squint her eyes. She cupped a hand over them and then felt a sudden surge of hope rippling through her. "Is that water?" she asked incredulously.

"Yes. Give the little lady a great big hand," he chuckled.

But then Lynn's lips curved downward into a pout. "But it will probably be too filthy to drink," she said.

"Darling, any water is welcome to these old eyes," Eliot said, laughing. "Come on. Let's check it out. Maybe we can have that cup of coffee for breakfast."

"Sure. That will stick to our ribs," she snapped.

"How do you think the natives survived before the white man came to Carmen Island?" Eliot asked, taking her by the elbow to guide her along through the tangled brush.

"The white man never really settled in here," she argued. "You know that. Sometimes I even feel as though we are the first and only ones on the entire island!"

Eliot chuckled. "Okay, okay," he said. "So I worded the question wrong. I'll try again. What do you think was eaten before modern civilization took hold?"

"They were cannibals?" she suggested. "They ate each other?" She gave Eliot a half smile. "Hmm. I wonder how you would taste, my love? If I get any hungrier . . ."

"Before this day's over I'm going to give you the chance to find out," he said, giving her a meaningful look. "Then in turn I'm going to savor *your* flesh with my lips and tongue."

"Promises, promises," she said teasingly. She clung to his arm, smiling up at him. "But back to the serious side of life. What do you plan for us to eat, Eliot?"

"We'll live off the fat of the land," Eliot said, holding limbs aside for Lynn to pass by them. "If not fish, then fruit. We certainly won't starve."

"That sounds easy," she scoffed. "But first you've got to find the fruit or catch the fish."

"It's there. The jungle is full of fruit and there has to be an abundance of fish in the streams and lagoons."

The edge of the lagoon was reached and was a quick disappointment to both Lynn and Eliot. It was small in circumference and not very deep. Through its brilliant blue, pebbles of all colors and sizes shone through and an occasional quick darting, tiny fish raced from beneath thick lily pads.

Lynn emitted a soft giggle. "Is that the fish we're supposed to eat?" she said.

Eliot shrugged. "All right," he grumbled. "So I was wrong." His gaze followed the outline of the lagoon and saw where a small, meandering stream led away from it in another direction. "But I bet if we followed that stream, we'd find a larger body of water probably teeming with fish."

"Ha!" Lynn said with a jerk of her head. "You'd probably have to follow it clear to the Atlantic to get what you're after."

Eliot chuckled. "Have you forgotten something?" he said, nudging Lynn playfully in the side.

"Like what?"

"I thought you were thirsty?"

Lynn ran her tongue over her parched lips. "Yes, I am," she murmured.

"Well?" Eliot said, pointing down at the water. "Water. W-A-T-E-R. There's at least enough here to drink. Be my guest."

Lynn's face reddened. "You want me to drink water while those *fish* are swimming around in it?" She gasped.

"Those little fishies aren't drinking very much," Eliot teased. "They won't mind sharing with you."

"Oh, Eliot!" Lynn said, then watched as he fell to his knees, cupped water into his hands and took several swallows.

He glanced over his shoulder at her and motioned with his head. "Come on, Lynn," he said. "You'll have to give in sooner or later because this is the best I can do right now."

Dropping to her knees beside him, Lynn reached her hands into the water, relishing the coolness of it against her skin. Then she cupped her hands and drank eagerly until finally her thirst was slaked for the first time in what seemed like days.

Sighing heavily, she splashed some of the water onto her face. "It feels so good," she murmured. "I'd never even dreamed of what it might be like to have to do without water for drinking and bathing."

Eliot rose to his feet. "I'm going to go back to the hut and bring as many bowls as possible. We'll fill them with water and take them back to the hut," he said, already walking away from her. "You'll be safe. I'll be within yelling range."

"Bring the coffeepot," she yelled after him. "I can't wait to get coffee in me. Maybe that will perk me up a bit."

"As good as done," Eliot said.

The feel of the water was still on her face. Lynn looked down at herself, seeing her disarray and the dust that covered her Levi's. Then she looked back at the lagoon. She knew that it wasn't deep enough to submerge herself completely, but she at least could take a sponge bath until other means were figured out.

With eager fingers, she unbuttoned her shirt and slipped it off. Then she stepped out of her Levi's and panties and began splashing the water all over her body. Her skin tingled as the cold water caressed her flesh. Then she stooped even lower and bent over so that her hair could hang down into the water.

"Ah," she sighed happily. She scrubbed her hair and body as best she could, then scooted away from the lagoon and tossed her hair back from her eyes to hang in glossy, wet ringlets down her back. Leaning back against the trunk of a tree, she closed her eyes and let her whole body relax, enjoying the freedom of her nudity and the peacefulness that was settling inside her.

The sounds of the jungle were a serenade to her ears and the aroma from the flowers was tantalizingly sweet, evoking a sense of headiness inside Lynn's brain. When hands suddenly clasped around her waist, she jumped and let out a scream and quickly opened her eyes. But as Eliot moved on around her and settled down on the ground beside her to draw her into his arms, Lynn let herself melt against him in sensuous delight.

"I didn't mean to frighten you, darling," he said huskily. "But you looked so damn seductive. What are you trying to do? Make all the animals in the jungle go wild with the want of you?"

"No," she purred, sinking more deeply into his embrace. "Only you, my love. Only the animal in *you!*"

"Grr," he teased, nuzzling her neck. "Is that animal enough?"

"Not quite," she teased back. Then she traced his facial features with a forefinger. "I thought you were going to go get some bowls."

"I didn't get very far when I happened to glance back and see you undressing."

"I'm sorry if I disturbed your train of thought," she said, unbuttoning his shirt.

"I'm not," Eliot said huskily, welcoming her fingers lowering to the snap of his Levi's. Lifting his hips, he helped her remove them from his legs, then eased his hard, muscular body against her creamy skin.

A thick growth of moss became their bed of love. Lynn welcomed its softness beneath her, gripped by a burning ache that threatened to engulf her in flames as Eliot's mouth scorched her lips and his hands moved with a blaze of urgency over her.

Excitement surged through Lynn as his legs held

hers in bondage. Passionately, hungrily, she surrendered herself totally to him.

"Love me, Eliot," she whispered, twining her arms about his neck. She pressed her lips against the bare flesh of his shoulder, tasting the manliness of him. She savored this wild, free moment, as though she were one of the creatures of the jungle herself. And as he slowly entered her, she writhed beneath him and slowly sank her teeth into his shoulder.

His eyes sought hers and revealed a lust-filled haziness beneath the drowsy droop of his lashes. "Darling, give me your all," he said thickly.

The huskiness of his voice made Lynn lose all inhibitions. She felt as though intoxicated as his hair-roughened chest made contact with the softness of her love-swollen, aching breasts. She arched her neck backwards, sighing.

His hands moved seductively over her back, down her tiny, tapered waist, then to her buttocks. He fitted the palms of his hands beneath each round, soft globe and urged her even closer to him as he began his slow, enticing thrusts inside her.

"That's the way," Eliot crooned, as he rained kisses on her face. "You're all mine—every inch of you . . ."

His fingers kneaded into her flesh. Lynn's heart was racing frantically. She lifted her legs about his waist, giving him easier access to her. Tossing her head from side to side, she closed her eyes as his teeth teased and nipped at the nipple of one of her breasts. Wild shivers of delight washed through her and as his hands reached and guided her head to stop so that his lips could once more hold hers in bondage, she let out a soft sigh of complete rapture.

His tongue softly coaxed her lips apart. She let it coil around hers. Her fingers weaved through his hair. Then she seemed to experience a dazzling splash of color exploding inside her brain as his even more eager thrusts touched the depths of her inner being, to capture her soul in a total, sweet release . . .

Together they lay, clinging, eyes closed, breathing deeply against one another's shoulder.

Lynn broke the silence at last. "Eliot, isn't this a bit foolish?" she whispered tremulously.

Eliot's fingers renewed ardor through her heart as they worked through the soft tendrils of hair between her thighs. "How could something this spectacular ever be foolish?" he asked hoarsely.

Forcing her mind to focus on other things than his skills at making her lose her senses, she pulled away from him. She pushed herself up to a sitting position and slipped her arms into her shirt. "Eliot," she murmured. "We're lost, we have no food, and we've just made love as though we've no cares in the world."

She gave him a lingering look, wishing the sight of his naked body wouldn't make her heart race so. But there was no denying his handsomeness or the overpowering attraction he exerted on her.

His dark, tousled hair, the chiseled features of his tanned face, the corded muscles of his shoulders, and his torso sculpted to manly perfection made her want to reach her fingers out and touch him again. She loved the straight line of his nose, his high cheekbones and his seductively formed lips. But most of all she loved his dark brown eyes which were even now once more threatening to drown her in pools of passion.

Turning her gaze away from him, Lynn swallowed hard. She knew that they were influenced by the exotic lushness of this lost paradise. It was easy to forget the cares of the world in such a habitat. But the life they had left behind—the eight-hour day at work . . . the rush of San Francisco traffic . . . the people who depended on them each day to be on "Morning Magazine"—kept nagging away at Lynn, constantly reminding her that this moment shared with Eliot could be nothing more than a dream. And how quickly a dream could turn into a nightmare . . .

A hungry gnawing at Lynn's stomach drew her quickly up. She stepped hurriedly into the rest of her clothes and placed her hands on her hips. "Eliot Smith, get up and get moving," she ordered. "We've got to find something to eat."

He crawled toward her and teasingly grabbed an ankle. "You're all I need," he said, grinning devilishly up at her. "Come on, Lynn. Don't spoil this by turning into a damn drill sergeant."

He forced her down on the ground beside him. Reaching inside her shirt, he cupped a breast and caressed it.

"Eliot . . ." Lynn whispered, closing her eyes. As he lifted the shirt and gently eased his mouth over her breast, circling its nipple with the hot wetness of his tongue, Lynn arched her neck backward and rested her fingers to his shoulders. Her fingernails sank into his flesh as his lips tantalizingly moved over her abdomen—but the snap of her Levi's being unfastened brought her out of her mindless sensual stupor.

178

With flashing green eyes, she looked down at him where he continued to taste her flesh with his tongue. "Eliot, please," she said angrily, shoving his head away.

Nervously combing her fingers through her hair she managed once more to get to her feet.

"Please what?" he teased. He pushed himself lazily up from the ground and stepped into his Levi's, then slung his shirt over his shoulders, deciding to not wear it just yet. He could already feel the dampness of the jungle's humidity rising from the floor of the jungle. The thought of a comfortable air-conditioned room formed a clear, inviting picture inside his brain.

"We can't depend on our bodies for everything," Lynn murmured, blushing slightly. "We *must* start thinking about how we're going to survive. Eliot, for once quit thinking of ways to seduce me. Think *food*. God, think *food! I'm starving!*"

Eliot placed a hand gently on her cheek. "Okay," he said. "I get the message. We'll have to work together on this thing, though. Okay?"

"Anything," she murmured. "Let's just *do* it!"

"First, let's bring some water to the hut," he said, placing an arm about her waist, urging her toward the hut. "You get some coffee brewing and I'll go in search of fruit."

"You won't be far, will you?"

"Now don't you worry about a thing," he said, brushing a soft kiss on her cheek. He left her at the door of the hut. "You go back to the lagoon and fill the coffeepot and I'll be back before the coffee's boiling."

Lynn fell into his arms and hugged him tightly.

"Please be careful," she whispered.

Eliot emitted a low chuckle. "Well, I'll be damned," he said, burrowing his nose into the thickness of her hair. "I do believe you care what happens to me!"

Lynn laughed softly and stepped away from him, clasping her hands together behind her. "Yes, I do," she admitted. "Surely that doesn't come as a surprise to you."

He smiled at her. "I'll remember you said that," he said. He gave her a mock salute. "I'll be back in a jiff, baby."

Lynn's heart followed him as he started off into the jungle, leaving her alone. She turned and let her gaze move slowly around the inside of the hut. If this was to be their home away from home until someone finally found them, then she had to do something about the filth. Even if Eliot *did* find something to eat, how could they possibly enjoy it in such surroundings?

"I guess there's only one thing to do," she sighed. "Clean it up as though it were my own."

Having a purpose now, she went to the fire and placed more wood in the blaze, then walked to the lagoon and filled both the pottery bowl and the coffeepot with water. Once back at the hut, she got the coffee boiling and used a palm leaf to begin sweeping debris from the dirt floor.

Lynn wrinkled her nose in distaste as she began scrubbing the tabletop, using another palm leaf as a cleaning cloth. When she had gotten it as clean as she possibly could, she turned and studied at length the makeshift bed. The leaves that were spread there were dry and crumbling and she knew that if they were to spend another night there, she would also have to do something about that.

"Food for my lady," Eliot said suddenly from behind her.

Lynn turned with a start and felt a renewed aching and gnawing at her stomach when she saw Eliot standing there with a coconut in one hand and a pineapple in the other.

"Eliot, you *did* find food!" she cried excitedly. She hurried to the table and splashed water around inside two bowls and then rinsed out the two tiny cups she had found for the coffee. Another leaf was called into service as a cloth to dry these utensils.

As Eliot placed the fruit on the table, Lynn's heart suddenly sank. "Eliot, we don't have any knives, or a hammer," she said. "How on earth are we going to cut the pineapple and open the coconut?"

Without a word, Eliot stepped back outside and a moment later came back inside the hut, holding something behind his back and smiling devilishly at Lynn. "I found something else besides fruit," he said.

"What?" Lynn asked, inching her way around him, trying to see what he was concealing. Then she gasped. "My Lord, Eliot. A machete! Where did you find it?"

Eliot drew the machete in front of him and looked at it with interest. "I found it beneath a tangle of undergrowth," he said. He ran a finger over its edge. "It's not the sharpest but at least it'll do the job."

Lynn covered her mouth with her hand and frowned. "But it's so *rusty*," she murmured.

"A little rust won't hurt us," he said. He took the machete outside and poured water from the bowl

181

over it, then wiped it dry with a leaf. "That's about the best I can do."

Lynn pulled out the tail of her shirt and used it for a potholder as she lifted the coffeepot from the fire. The aroma almost sent her senses reeling and gave her a pang of homesickness. As she poured coffee into the cups, her eyes took on a dreamy, faraway look. "I wonder if anyone is looking for us right now," she said softly.

Eliot placed the coconut on the floor of the hut and swung the machete down on it, splitting the hard outer shell neatly in two. Then he split the inner shell. Its white milk splashed in all directions. "Sure they are," he said, giving Lynn a quick glance. "I'm sure we've even made the news back home. You know—two television personalities lost in the wilds of the jungle." He chuckled as he placed the machete in a corner and handed Lynn one half of the coconut.

"If they only knew," he added, with a wry smile.

Lynn picked up the coconut shell and started to pick out its sweet, white meat. Looking at Eliot with a raised eyebrow, she said as she worked, "If they only knew what?"

"That we've created our own luxurious love nest here, where we're enjoying a gourmet feast." He took a sip of coffee, then sank his teeth into the coconut meat which he had pried loose from its shell.

"I'm sure that possibility won't enter any of their minds," she replied. "The world probably thinks we're gone forever."

She placed the coconut back on the table and sipped from the tin cup, savoring the taste of the coffee. Nothing had ever tasted better.

"I'm worried about my parents," she said softly. "I'm sure they're worried sick about me."

Her voice quivered as she added beneath her breath, "And Adam. I'm sure he's absolutely frantic."

Eliot's expression became grim, as it always did when he heard her mention Adam's name. "What did you just say?" he asked.

Lynn's eyes moved quickly upward. "What?" she said, not really remembering where her worries had just taken her.

Eliot wiped coffee from his lips and moved quickly across the room to stand before the fire, glaring down into the ambers. "You were talking about Adam and his worries about you," he said irritably. "Even now you can't forget about that damn Adam Lowenstein." His words were barely audible.

Lynn strained her ears, trying to hear what he was mumbling, but unable to. She went to his side and linked an arm through one of his. "Darling, what did you say?" she asked. "You suddenly seem so withdrawn. Did I say something to upset you?"

Eliot's gaze slowly met hers, jealously apparent in his eyes. Then he reached a hand out and touched her cheek, once more astonished by her loveliness. Her eyes were the softest shade of green . . . the rosy glow of her flawless complexion . . . the gentle curve of her jawline . . . and her tiny, pert nose. She was the picture of innocence, and so damn beautiful he couldn't resist her, not for long. He twined his fingers through her golden, tangled hair and drew her lips to his.

"I love you, Lynn," he whispered. "Oh, God, how I love you! I only wish you loved me as much . . ."

Lynn laced her arms about his neck, savoring his closeness. "Eliot, I do love you," she whispered. "You know that. Don't you realize how I feel? I thought I'd made it pretty clear. Darling, I love only you. Forever!"

Eliot was filled with exaltation, wanting to make love to her again, this very moment, as they were exchanging such promises that most surely one day would be broken. But he realized that, when she was once more in San Francisco, she would more than likely rush right back into Adam Lowenstein's arms.

# *Ten*

BAREFOOT, HAIR braided and Levi's rolled up to just below her knees, Lynn was arranging fresh coconut and palm leaves on the floor, preparing a more comfortable bed, when Eliot sneaked up behind her and gripped her about the waist, pulling her up against his body. She gasped in surprise.

Placing her hands on his arms that were locked about her, she recovered herself and sighed, "Eliot, what are you up to now?" she said. "We've slept two nights here in this miserable hovel and I *still* can't get comfortable on this layer of leaves that's supposed to serve as a mattress. Let me go! I'm going to work on it until I can make it comfortable."

Eliot turned her around, cupping her face with his hands. "Let's go exploring," he suggested. "What do you say? We can work later. Let's play, okay?"

"Eliot, we shouldn't leave the clearing," she protested. "If anyone is looking for us, this would surely catch his eye faster than anything else."

"Lynn, I don't know about you but I'd like to find a place for a swim," he grumbled, releasing his hold on her. He swung around and raked his fingers through his hair. "If we follow the stream that leads from the lagoon, we'll probably find something larger."

Lynn looked up into his eyes. "At least we have shelter here," she said softly. "If we get lost again, it may be for good. We mustn't leave here. I'm afraid to."

"We'll follow the stream on the way back," he argued. "We won't get lost again, I assure you. Once is enough for me. Trust me." He kissed her softly on the lips. "Okay? Will you just trust me? We can't just sit around day after day twiddling our thumbs," he added.

Lynn giggled. "Is that what you call what we've been doing?" she asked. "Is that a new term for making love?"

"You know what I mean," Eliot said, smiling. "Now are you going with me or do I have to go alone?"

"You're serious, aren't you?"

"As serious as hell."

Lynn sat down on a chair and began pulling on her socks and then her boots. "Then we'll go," she said. She laughed, eyeing him warmly. "I'd like a swim, too."

"Let's just hope we find a lake," Eliot said, leaning against the door frame, looking out into the jungle.

"Let's just hope we can find our way back here," Lynn said, rolling the legs of her Levi's back down. "We did lose our way once, Eliot. It could easily be done again."

He turned and faced her. "Lynn, I said trust me," he said.

Her eyes wavered a bit as she rose to her feet.

"Darling, I really don't have much choice, do I?" she murmured.

"Ready?" he said, picking up the machete, offering his free hand to Lynn.

"As ready as I'll ever be," she said, taking a last glance backward at the room, hoping to see it again. Though she detested everything about it, she knew that it was at least a shelter that they could not do without.

"Then let's hop to it," Eliot said with a chuckle as he guided her on to the lagoon, and then along the bed of the stream that led away from it.

"Eliot, the undergrowth is so tangled, how do you expect to get anywhere?" Lynn argued, stopping and wiping beads of perspiration from her brow. "Everything is practically strangled by those blasted creepers."

"Just step back and watch," Eliot said. He was already swinging away with the machete, making a path wide enough for them to pass through.

Seeing a snake slither away in another direction, Lynn trembled and chewed nervously on her lower lip, but she buttoned her shirt up around her neck and proceeded to move obediently behind Eliot as he continued to clear the way.

Spider monkeys swung from tree to tree, chattering angrily at the intrusion into their privacy, and birds of all brilliant colors flapped and called noisily overhead. The jungle floor and the leaves above seemed a solid mass of intense green and only a speck of blue sky could occasionally be seen overhead.

The humidity caused droplets of moisture to hang diamondlike from the leaves of the trees and a damp pungency emitting from the profusion of growth stung Lynn's nose and eyes. She slapped mosquitoes away from her face and brushed strands of hair out of her eyes as her braids began to become undone. But she kept doggedly following Eliot, only an arm's length behind him.

The sound of the machete continuously chopping away at the underbrush mingled with the other jungle noises. The path Eliot was making was very narrow. Everything seemed so close and threatening, and the humidity seemed even more oppressive the deeper they penetrated into the denseness of the jungle.

"Eliot, just how far do you plan to go before giving up?" Lynn sighed, scratching at a mosquito bite on her cheek. "I'm getting eaten alive!"

Eliot peered ahead, barely able to see the curve of the stream through the trees, but determination led him onward. "A little farther," he said. "We have to try. Maybe we might even run into some signs of civilization along the way."

Lynn grimaced. "Sure," she said. "People would choose to live where the jungle is thickest and filled with man-eating mosquitoes!"

"Just stop grousing," Eliot snapped. He, too was hot and bitten, and his patience was wearing thin.

"And what if we run into a *Contra?*" she persisted. "This would make a perfect hideout for rebel soldiers. Nobody else would be dumb enough to come this far into the jungle. No one but us, that is."

"There will be no *Contras,*" Eliot said, sighing heavily. "Adam Lowenstein sure did put a scare into you, didn't he? He'd have been a damn sight smarter if he had kept his fool mouth shut!"

Lynn's shoulders straightened in anger. "Must you always talk about Adam that way?" she fumed. "He's never done anything to you. You were the one who changed *his* lifestyle, Eliot. If you hadn't taken his job at the station . . ."

Lynn stopped and covered her mouth with her hands, realizing just what she had said. And when he swung around with a set jaw and anger in the hard stare of his eyes, she knew just how he had taken it.

"So the truth is out!" he said dryly. "You'd rather we had never met. Is that what you're trying to say, Lynn? Because if I hadn't taken the job at KSFC-TV we *wouldn't* have met and we wouldn't have found what I had begun to think was special!"

Lynn lowered her lashes and swallowed hard. "Eliot . . ." she murmured.

"That's okay," he said, swinging back around, thrashing the machete even harder against the trangled brush. "Now I know. So much for love that lasts forever."

Lynn stumbled over the broken stubs at her feet and reached for his arm. "Eliot, I didn't mean . . ." she began again, flinching when he jerked away from her.

"Lynn, I know exactly what you meant," he growled. He turned his back to her and wiped his brow with the back of his hand, then let out a loud, sudden yell which scared the life out of her.

"Lynn," he cried. "I believe I see a waterfall ahead!"

He spun around and eyed Lynn with a renewed

smile. "We've done it," he said. "We've found even more than a large body of water—we've found a waterfall!"

Lynn smiled nervously up at him, not knowing how he truly felt about her now. But it seemed that his discovery had made him forget for the moment what they had been discussing, and she was glad. She would not hurt him for the world.

She smiled back at him and linked her arm through his. "So? Shall we go and take a shower?" she murmured.

Eliot moved away from her. "We haven't reached it yet," he said. "I've a bit more chopping to do wouldn't you say? You keep behind me. But it won't be long, darling."

Hearing him calling her 'darling' again made tears rush to Lynn's eyes. Relieved that he had apparently overcome his anger toward her, she followed on along behind him and then rushed by his side to the large body of water that stretched out before them, taking in the beauty of the waterfall and the profusion of flowers hanging lusciously from tree to tree on all sides of them.

"It's absolutely gorgeous!" Lynn sighed, resting a hand on her throat. She gazed transfixed at the waterfall cascading over a ledge, plummeting down in a steady stream onto outcroppings of rock. A soft spraylike mist seemed to hang low over the water, and a hazy rainbow glowed through the mist as the sun's rays struck it.

Exotic orchids hanging from the trees danced in the breeze emitted from the steady movement of the falling water as it rushed downward into the lagoon. Lynn inched closer to the edge to take a better look, then felt Eliot's hand around her waist as he lifted her into the water.

A muffled scream escaped Lynn's lips. Then she found herself falling. She closed her eyes and held her breath. She plunged into the cool, crystal clear water, then paddled with her arms and legs until she finally bobbed back to the surface.

Treading water, Lynn looked angrily about her. "Eliot!" she shouted. "Why, you . . . !"

Her eyes grew wide and then she closed them as she saw Eliot make a mad dash and dive into the water next to her. As his head emerged, Lynn reached out and ducked him. "You stinker," she cried. "You could at least have waited until I had my clothes off!"

But he had disappeared again. Feeling hands about her ankles, Lynn let out a shrill scream and felt herself being pulled beneath the water and into Eliot's embrace. She pushed at his chest and kicked at him, but his lips were suddenly pressed against hers, taking all the fight out of her, weakening her defenses as only he had the power to do.

The urgency of his lips and the sensation of the water making her clothes cling sensuously to her body made Lynn wrap her arms about Eliot's neck and ardently return his kiss. When his fingers worked up into her shirt and found her breasts, she gasped and struggled to the surface in need of renewed breath.

With Eliot's arm still about her waist, she floated upward. When her head finally emerged from the water, she began choking and laughing at the same time. "I never know—what to expect of you next,

Eliot Smith . . ." she sputtered. "Is this what you mean by a *bath*?"

"Not quite," he chuckled, brushing his wet hair back from his face. "But I just couldn't resist throwing you in. The water looked so enticing." He drew her closer to him. "And you do too, darling."

"Eliot, my boots are weighing me down," she worried. "I've got to get to shore and remove them."

"We'll undress together," he said huskily, swimming beside her. When they reached the shore, Lynn quickly disrobed, then without looking toward Eliot, dove headfirst into the refreshing, caressing clarity of the water. When she reached the bottom, she began swimming, opening her eyes to the wonder of the different colored rocks lining the sandy bed of the lagoon. She saw a bright red, transparent stone glistening like some rare underwater jewel and she plucked it up from the ones surrounding it and swam back up to the surface.

Once more treading water, she studied the stone. Suddenly her heart began to pound. This wasn't an ordinary rock. It appeared as though it were indeed a type of rare gem.

With anxious eyes, Lynn looked toward the shore. Eliot was now completely naked and poised on a large rock, ready to dive in next to her. Her sudden shouts brought his movements to a quick halt.

"Eliot, I think I've found something valuable," she called, holding the stone in the air. "It looks like some rare gemstone. Here—take a look."

She swam to the shore and clung to the bank, handing the stone up to Eliot. Her eyes grew anxiously wide as she watched him examining it.

"I believe you've found yourself a garnet," he said at last.

"Is it worth a lot of money?" she asked eagerly.

"It's a semi-precious stone. I'm not sure of its worth."

"I think there may be more on the bottom," Lynn said, looking back across her shoulder.

Eliot dove into the water and swam to the bottom with Lynn at his side. Together they picked through the stones, only finding a few more, then rose once more to the surface when their breath gave out and climbed out onto shore.

"They're beautiful," Lynn whispered as she rolled them around in her hand. The sun cast a shimmering light onto them, making the deep red brilliance of the stones take on an almost dancing effect as they glistened and shone in her palm.

"I believe these are often passed off as rubies," Eliot said, taking them gently from Lynn, and looking more closely at the stones. "They aren't the genuine article, but the next best thing. Not nearly as valuable, though."

"I want to take them back with us to the States," Lynn said. As Eliot handed them back to her, she reached for her Levi's and placed the garnets securely inside a pocket. "I'd love to find some more!"

The next hour was spent diving and hunting for more stones from the lagoon bed with no more luck. As Lynn began to swim back to the shore she looked around for Eliot, but he seemed to have disappeared in the blink of an eye. Then a small smile lifted the corner of her mouth when she felt his hands exploring her flesh beneath the water.

She began to swim hurriedly away, watching over her shoulder for him to surface. But when he didn't, Lynn turned with a start, afraid that maybe something had happened to him. Perhaps he'd gotten a cramp . . . Then she felt water being splashed on the back of her head and knew that he had come up behind her.

Slowly turning, she smiled seductively and met his approach with open arms. Their lips met in a passionate frenzy as Lynn moved into his embrace. The water was slippery cool and seemed to make her body even more responsive as Eliot eased himself inside her.

Feeling his powerful thrusts, Lynn grew breathless and let her head float back in the water, relishing the warm glow of the sun on her face as the heat inside her built to a greater and greater intensity.

"Eliot . . ." she whispered, trembling as his lips kissed the hollow of her throat. Then, "We're going to sink, Eliot!" she shrieked, realizing that he had lost his ability to tread water as he continued to make love to her.

Giggling, Lynn let the water slowly cover her head but was quickly brought back to the surface as Eliot slid out of her and began to swim at her side. With one hand he touched a breast then let it slide lower to where, despite the water's chill, she was hot and pulsating.

"Darling, let's go to shore," Eliot said huskily. "That was an interesting experiment, but now I'd like to continue it on dry land."

"I thought you'd never ask," Lynn purred, swimming closer to him and brushing her naked body against his.

Eliot placed an arm about her waist and eased her closer to him as they swam back to shore. Once there he helped her from the water, covering her with urgent kisses that set her blood on fire, then slowly lowered her to the ground. In one sweeping movement, he had her in his arms and had plunged inside her again, thrusting, groaning, while her hands worked magic across his back, down to his taut buttocks.

"I love you . . ." she whispered. "I'll never forget these moments, never . . ."

Eliot framed her face between his hands and kissed her long and hard, increasing the momentum of his eager thrusts. She lifted her hips and wrapped her legs about his waist. She felt the heat within her rising to feverish pitch, and welcomed his shuddering release in perfect unison with her own thrilling climax.

"Now is this paradise, or isn't it?" Eliot said softly, looking deeply into her eyes.

Lynn let out a trembling sigh as he lowered a sweet kiss to her lips. She reached a hand to the back of his neck and tangled her fingers in his damp hair, pressing him closer to her. "*Our* paradise, my darling," she murmured. "Only ours."

A sudden delicious scent washed over her and she looked up as Eliot placed a white blossom behind her ear. She smiled languidly at him, feeling like the princess of some fairy-tale tropical kingdom, accepting the homage of her handsome prince.

Eliot leaned up on an elbow and let his eyes wander over the soft curves of her body. He plucked another flower and tucked it in the soft vee of hair between her legs, then placed another at her navel.

When he tried to balance one on the swollen nipple of one rosy breast, only to have it topple off, Lynn laughed gently.

"That's not going to work," she told him. Her gaze drank in his massive chest covered with dark curling hair. Her lids grew heavy with renewed desire. As her fingers moved delicately over his flesh, she could feel his muscles tense under her light, sensuous touches.

"Then I'll remove them one by one," said Eliot. "I'm about to pluck flowers from my private garden of love."

Lynn's eyes widened, feeling a shudder go through her as his head bent and his teeth captured the flower from her navel and dropped it gently on the ground. While steadying himself over her, he moved his head lower and removed the orchid from between her legs with his lips. Then he moved his lips even closer and Lynn felt the sweet touch of his tongue exploring where the flower had been before, causing a tremulous sigh to escape from between her lips.

"I'll never get enough of you," Eliot said, lifting himself up over her and slipping inside her once more.

Lynn's lips parted seductively as he held her pinioned under him, so close she could feel every hard line of his body. She twined her arms about his neck and traced the sinewy sleekness of his back then nibbled at his neck as he buried his face into her shoulder.

His movements inside her were slow and deep this time, and Lynn felt the power of her love for him surge in a euphoric mindlessness, feeling the effervescence of rapture, as though her veins were filled with a very fine champagne.

"Lynn . . ." Eliot whispered against her flesh as he once more trembled inside her. After she had also reached completion, Eliot rolled away from her and lay on his back, breathing hard.

Lynn leaned over and kissed him on his heaving chest, then giggled as his chest hairs tickled her lips and nose. "I've never felt to wicked," she said, curving her body so that it fit against his side. "Eliot, how many times do you think we've made love these past two days?"

Eliot reached an arm about her shoulder and draped one hand over her breast. "Not nearly enough times to suit me," he chuckled.

"I am not a love machine," she said, laughing.

Eliot propped himself up on one elbow and his lips curved into an amused, affectionate smile. "Oh? You could have fooled me," he said. He kissed her nose softly.

Lynn rose quickly to her feet as she saw a brilliantly colored bird sweep by overhead. "How beautiful . . ." she whispered. She watched its rainbow-hued body as it fluttered behind the waterfall.

Eliot reached for his jeans and slipped into them, eyeing Lynn quizzically. "What's beautiful?" he asked. "What did you see?"

"A perfectly marvellous bird," Lynn said. She began to get dressed too, pulling on her Levi's. "It disappeared behind the waterfall. I'll bet there's a cave somewhere."

Zipping her pants, she looked eagerly up at Eliot. "Let's go see," she said.

"Ah, so you're the one wanting to explore now." He chuckled.

Lynn twined her arms about his neck and teased him with soft, feathery kisses across his face. She was keenly aware that neither had yet put a shirt on as her breasts felt the sensation of his coarse hair against her tender flesh. She moved seductively against him, loving this new-found freedom to make love when and wherever they chose without worrying about intruders. Never in her life could she have imagined herself being so carefree, so wild. Did the jungle always do this to a person? Did it automatically bring out the untamed animal in one's soul?

"Yes," she finally murmured. "Let's follow that bird. Let's see what else we might discover."

"You're not worrying about *Contras* anymore?"

Lynn saw a shadow flit across his face. "No," she whispered, placing a forefinger against his lips. "I'm not worrying about anything. You seem to have found a way to erase everything from my mind but you."

The shadows faded into a tender smile. He kissed her softly, then said, "That's what I like to hear."

He held her gently away from him, his eyes hazing over with renewed ardor as he looked at her breasts, so ripe for kissing. "But I suggest you get your shirt on or we won't get another damn thing done today but making love!"

Lynn reached out and tweaked one of his nipples between thumb and forefinger. "Is that a threat or a promise, my love?" she asked, giving him a seductive smile.

Eliot tilted his head sideways, lost once again in

contemplation of her nakedness. "Baby, you just don't know . . ." he said beneath his breath.

Then he bent and retrieved her shirt from the ground and handed it to her. "Here. Get dressed," he said firmly. "I'm serious as hell about not getting enough of you."

Feeling a slow blush rising, Lynn slipped the shirt on, watching him buttoning his own across his virile chest. Then, sitting down on the ground, she pulled her wet socks on, then struggled into her soaked leather boots.

She gave him a frown. "I sure wish you hadn't thrown me in the lagoon with all my clothes on! These boots are hell to get on and these wet things itch even worse than my mosquito bites."

"Sorry about that," he chuckled, pulling on his own boots. Then he rose to his feet and offered her a hand. "Ready?"

Flipping her pigtails back across her shoulders, Lynn rose to her feet and readily accepted the warmth of his hand in hers. "For you?" she said, laughing softly. "Always."

Pushing their way through the clinging vines and lush tangles of flowers, they finally reached the path that led to the waterfall. A light spray continuously filled the air as they moved carefully onto the moss-covered, slippery ledge of rock behind the curtain of water.

Lynn laughed as she wiped the moisture from her face. "Maybe we ought to set up housekeeping here," she said. "At least the continuing cool mist would make us more comfortable. Natural air-conditioning!"

"We'd soon look like prunes," Eliot laughed, taking a stronger grip of her elbow. "Watch it, darling. It's pretty slippery here. I don't think you want to take another swim so soon, do you?"

"Not quite," she laughed, awkwardly leaning her back against the cliff as she followed alongside Eliot until a wide opening was finally reached and they both edged inside, breathing hard.

Lynn turned and looked around her, smelling the sweet scent of flowers intermingled with the damp pungency of the rock walls. "It *is* a cave," she murmured.

As her eyes grew used to the semidarkness, she soon saw more wonders. She grabbed Eliot's arm. "Look," she gasped. "My lord, Eliot, it's even more beautiful than anything we've come across yet in the jungle."

Stalagmites rose up from the floor of the cave in many different colorful formations looking like icicles turned upside down and similar formations hung from the roof, some joining to form columns that appeared like stone curtains against the walls of the cave.

"Stalagmites and stalactites," Eliot said, moving on into the cave, running his fingers over the smoothness of one jutting up from the floor. "They've been formed by limestone dissolved in water dripping on the floor from the roof of the cave. It's probably taken thousands of years for these to form."

"When I was a little girl, my parents used to take me to a cave in southern Illinois," Lynn said. "It was called Cave-In-Rock. My parents and I used to take picnic lunches there on a Sunday afternoon and talk about the Kaskaskia Indians who had been known to hide there during the early 1700s."

She took a step and stood next to Eliot. "But that cave wasn't nearly as lovely as this," she added.

The rays of the sun filtered through the waterfall, casting an almost magical glow onto the colorful formations.

"I believe I saw some banana clusters on the other side of the entrance," Eliot said. "I'll go and get some for our lunch."

"Sounds marvelous," Lynn said. She laughed happily. "God, this is all so primitive! I love it!"

"I'll be back in a jiff," Eliot said, moving quickly away from her.

Lynn strolled around inside the cave, marveling still at the magnificence of it all, then searched for a spot to rest. She found a bed of thick moss near the cave's entrance. Settling down onto it, she welcomed Eliot once more at her side, hungrily eyeing a nice-sized bunch of ripe yellow bananas resting in the crook of his left arm.

"Shall we temporarily pretend we are monkeys?" he laughed, putting the bananas gently down on the floor of the cave.

"I'm beginning to feel anything but human," Lynn sighed, accepting a peeled banana from Eliot. "Humans never have so much fun!"

"And all because I had the good sense to get us lost in the jungle," Eliot teased, resting back on an elbow as he slowly consumed a banana.

"Good sense, huh?" Lynn laughed, enjoying the sweet taste of the banana between her teeth and on her tongue. "Tell me about it!"

Content, Lynn eased down closer to Eliot, and let

her gaze once more move about her. Suddenly she rose quickly to her feet and dropped the banana peel when a black bird flapped close overhead, flying in circles, as though seducing Lynn with its loveliness. Its warble was like an American robin, as if it was singing, "Cheerily, cheerily cheerily."

"Birds are known to return to the same place each year to build their nests," Eliot said, also rising, watching the robin swooping and fluttering overhead. "Maybe it resents our invading its privacy. Perhaps the bird has a nest of babies in here away from the heat."

"I don't want to leave, Eliot," Lynn whispered. "I want to see where it goes. It's so unusual, quite different from the red breasted robins I'm used to seeing back in the States."

"I just happen to be a bird-watcher in my spare time," Eliot said, rather pompously, she thought, amused.

Lynn's eyes widened. "You are?" she murmured. There was so much she didn't know about him. It was hard to picture this handsome, usually so sophisticated man peering at birds through a pair of binoculars.

"Do you know the legend about the robins?" he asked, obviously anticipating she'd say no.

She obliged. "No," she said obediently.

"In my studies of birds I discovered a number of interesting stories about the robin," he said, once more watching the bird now fluttering almost frantically above their heads. "According to an old English legend, the 'pious bird with the scarlet breast' plucked a thorn from the crown of Christ as He was on His way to Calvary. As the bird carried the thorn in its beak, a drop of blood fell from the thorn to its breast, dyeing it red."

"How interesting," Lynn sighed.

"And all the birds that do not have a red breast are said to have been left out because they had hidden from the dark, ominous clouds on that day when Christ was crucified."

"Yet this one is as beautiful as our robins back home," Lynn whispered. "Even without a red breast, it's really quite lovely." She quickly placed a hand over her mouth as she saw another bird join the first one. Both seemed to be building up to a frenzy.

"We'd better leave," Eliot said, taking Lynn by the elbow. "This is their home, I'm sure. And we must give them back their privacy to love and raise their families in peace."

"Yes. You're right," Lynn whispered. She followed Eliot until they reached the ledge once more and carefully edged their way along its slippery surface to the hot and humid jungle. Once outside she leaned heavily into Eliot's embrace.

"Tired?" he asked, leaning down to press his lips against the sweetness of her neck.

"Yes, I really am," she sighed. Then she glanced up at the sky. "Eliot, the day seems to have gotten away from us. The sun is setting."

Dark streaks of purple and crimson stretched across the brilliant orange sky as the sun was slowly sinking down behind the treetops.

"Talk about *beautiful*," Eliot said softly. "That sky is so beautiful, it makes me feel as though I want to reach out and touch it."

"I know," Lynn murmured, almost mesmerized by the serenity and beauty of all that surrounded her.

The bird songs were quieting and all that could be heard was the steady rumble of the waterfall as it cascaded into the brilliant blue-green of the lagoon beneath.

Eliot bent and picked up the machete from where he had left it. "But we must get back," he said. "This place is wonderful in the daylight, but imagine what must roam about after dark."

Lynn shuddered, then followed closely alongside Eliot as they began following the path that had led them to the lagoon. "Eliot, I love you so," she whispered suddenly, seizing his arm. "I wish this never had to end."

Eliot chuckled—a bit nervously, Lynn thought. "Darling, the way things are going, you just may get your wish."

Lynn felt a constriction in her throat and she gave him a quick, questioning glance. He hadn't been serious, had he?

# *Eleven*

THE EARLY morning light trickled in through the holes in the dilapidated roof, awakening Lynn from her deep, sound sleep. She yawned drowsily, stretching her arms above her head, remembering the excitement of yesterday's adventure. She reached a hand out to Eliot and touched his cheek, feeling the stubble there. A beard, she decided, would be very attractive.

She turned on her side and ran her fingers over the scratchiness of his whiskers, smiling to herself. Even hidden partially behind a beard, he was handsome. She loved looking at him while he slept—he looked so gentle, so defenseless.

A low snore rising from deep inside him made Lynn giggle and lower a soft kiss to his lips. "I love you, Eliot Smith," she whispered. "How did I ever survive before I met you? And to think I couldn't stand you at first!"

She ran her fingers down his furry chest, then further to where his sex lay limp between his legs. Something compelled her to lower her mouth and kiss him gently there. She was taken completely by surprise when Eliot's hands circled about her head and held her tightly in place, laughing throatily at her startled exclamation.

"Eliot . . ." Lynn laughed, struggling, pushing at his bare legs. One of her breasts tingled as it swayed against the male strength of him, his desire for her beginning to rise meaningfully right before her eyes.

"Eliot," she cried. "Let me go! I thought you were asleep."

Eliot lifted her away from his body, then raised her face upward until their lips met and ignited flames of rapture. His strong arms held her a willing prisoner above him and her breasts hung enticingly close to his chest where he could reach and tenderly cup each one as he reluctantly parted his lips from hers for a brief moment.

"How could I be expected to sleep with a seductress like you doing those wonderful things to me?" he whispered huskily.

His fingers traced a sensuous line across her abdomen, then paused when they reached the throbbing of her swollen love mound.

"Making love is supposed to be best in the morning, or so I've heard," he said, his lips curved in a lazy smile.

"We certainly have plenty of grounds for comparison," Lynn purred, raining kisses across his face, onto his eyelids, which closed under her lips, then across the straight, bold line of his nose and the firm set of his jaw just below his left ear.

Slowly she worked her way back to his lips and forced them gently apart with the soft probing of her tongue. With a spinning inside her head she found his tongue waiting to make contact with hers and the soft wetness sent added spirals of ecstasy through her tingling body.

Eliot's hands felt like hot coals, scorching her flesh as he let his fingers explore all her pleasure points, teasing, tormenting, causing her to writhe with the intensity of her need for him.

She trembled, poised above him, as he guided his hardness inside her. Easing her lips from his, she placed her head against his chest. She closed her eyes and began lifting, then lowering her hips, working with him, feeling the thundering of his heart against her cheek. She smiled, feeling her own heart beating in unison with his, then let out a soft moan as she was slowly engulfed in the warm, building glow of passion that suddenly became volcanic, erupting over and over again, until she collapsed against him, drained by the force of her powerful sensations.

Later, lying there, peacefully content in the aftermath of their lovemaking, Lynn lowered her lips to one of his nipples. Tenderly kissing it, she could hear a heavy sigh emitting from between his lips.

"You're the best thing that ever happened to me, Lynn," Eliot whispered. "When we get back to civilization, let's rush right off to a justice of the peace."

"*If* we ever get back, don't you mean?" she said, laughing softly.

"Lynn, you didn't answer . . ." Eliot grumbled. But a low rumble of thunder in the far distance diverted his attention to the hole in the roof and further upward, outside to the sky. Dark, rolling clouds were slowly building overhead.

"God!" he said, rising quickly from their makeshift

bed. "If it's going to storm, we'd better try to batten down the hatches. One puff of wind could blow this shack away, you know."

Lynn rose leisurely from the bed, like a contented cat, stretching. "I haven't seen any rain yet," she scoffed. "The clouds will pass. Let's eat some breakfast before we do anything else. Making love sure does increase my appetite!"

Eliot slipped into his jeans. "Maybe you're right about the rain," he said. "Sure—let's eat. We've got plenty of fruit on hand. You make some coffee and I'll cut up the fruit."

"It's a deal," Lynn laughed. She slipped quickly into her clothes, tossing her tangled blonde hair back from her face and over her shoulders. Barefoot, she went to the table, opened the coffee can and looked inside. She shook the coffee grounds at the bottom, frowning.

"This is the last of our coffee," she sighed. "We better enjoy it while we can."

She poured some water from a bowl into the coffeepot, then tossed in the coffee grounds and placed the pot over the hot coals of the fire. Then adding some small twigs, she blew on them and watched as the fire slowly took hold and flames began dancing around the pot.

"We can have fruit juice from now on instead of coffee," Eliot said, placing slices of bananas, pineapple, mangoes and papayas into bowls. "Or coconut milk. We won't go thirsty, or hungry either."

Lynn settled down cross-legged on the floor in front of the fire, waiting for the aroma of coffee to waft to her nostrils, and made a face. "I'm afraid that once we make it back to the States, I won't ever want to eat another piece of fruit," she pouted. Her eyes took on a faraway look. "Wouldn't bacon and eggs taste absolutely *terrific* this morning?"

"I think I'd rather have steak," Eliot said, his expression dreamy, too. He brushed his fingers through his hair, then tested the growth of his beard.

"Or maybe fried chicken," Lynn continued. "My mother makes the best fried chicken and milk gravy . . ."

Eliot drew her up from the floor and held her at arm's length, gazing into her eyes. "Whoa now," he chuckled. "Let's cut this out right now! We mustn't start thinking about what could be if we were back in San Francisco. That'll lead us to start worrying all over again about why we've not yet been found."

Lynn's gaze wavered. "Well, why *haven't* we?" she asked. "Surely they must have search parties out looking for us. If we could find this place, why can't the natives find us? They know this country far better than we do."

"I don't know the answers, Lynn," Eliot admitted. He pulled her gently into his arms and hugged her tightly to his chest. "That's why we can't belabor the subject. We *don't* have the answers. And because we don't, we have to make the best of the situation."

"It's not that I don't love being alone with you," Lynn sighed. "You ought to know that by now, Eliot . . ."

"Yes," he said huskily. "I know that."

The strong aroma of coffee drew Lynn's attention. She smiled sweetly up at Eliot. "The coffee," she murmured. "If I don't pour it right now, it's going to boil away and we won't be able to enjoy the last precious cup."

"We mustn't have that," Eliot laughed, releasing her, giving her a playful shove toward the fireplace.

Another low, threatening rumble of thunder suddenly seemed to rock the ground beneath Lynn's feet. She turned with a start and questioned Eliot with wide, frightened eyes. "Maybe I was wrong," she said softly. "Maybe it is going to storm. And if it does, I agree with you—this hut won't give us any protection at all."

Her anxious gaze traveled to the holes in the ceiling and the gaps in the walls. "In fact, it may blow down onto our heads," she added.

"Not if I have anything to say about it," Eliot said, picking up his trusty machete and walking purposefully toward the door.

"Eliot, where are you going?" Lynn asked, rushing to his side.

"I'm going to repair the roof," he said. Then he laughed awkwardly. "Well, let me rephrase that— I'm going to *try* to repair the roof."

"What about your coffee?" Lynn asked, nodding toward the fireplace.

"Pour me a cup then come on outside and keep me company while I work," he suggested.

"Can't I help?"

"All right," he said. "We can work together. We can get twice as much done in a shorter length of time."

Lynn turned on a heel and rushed toward the fireplace. "I'll be right with you, Eliot," she said. "Two cups of coffee, coming up."

Eliot grabbed a piece of pineapple and shoved it into his mouth on his way outside, stopping to stare up into the sky. It was an ashen color, but not yet dangerously threatening. The storm seemed still to be far away in the mountains.

"Maybe we'll have a full day to work . . ." he muttered to himself, then accepted the steaming hot cup of coffee which Lynn had brought out to him. He leaned against the hut, leisurely sipping his coffee.

"How on earth do you propose to fix that hole in the roof?" Lynn asked, stepping back and looking up at the tattered palm fronds and exposed beams. "You don't even have a hammer and nails."

Eliot laughed, almost choking on his coffee. He wiped at his mouth with the back of his hand. "Hammer and nails?" he said, looking at her with lifted eyebrows. "There wasn't a nail used in *that* roof. It was made by twisting and tying coconut and palm fronds together."

Lynn gave him a skeptical glance. "And you think you can do that, huh?" she said. "I bet you've never had to do a lick of manual labor in your entire life."

Eliot placed his coffee cup on the ground, went to a low-growing palm tree and began hacking leaves away from the trunk. "I was a boy scout, remember. I'm good at anything I put my mind to," he bragged.

"Yes, I've noticed that," said Lynn with a kittenish smile. "What can I do to help?"

"Just carry the leaves over next to the hut and then I'll climb on top and start laying them in place."

"I can do that," Lynn said eagerly. She rushed

inside the hut, brought out the rickety chair and placed it next to the outside wall.

"Be careful," Eliot growled. "That chair's not very sturdy."

Lynn picked up several branches, holding them in the crook of her arm, then stepped gingerly onto the seat of the chair. Scrambling frantically, she was finally able to climb on top of the roof. She stopped to steady herself as she felt the weakness of the limbs beneath her and gave Eliot a nervous grin. Then on hands and knees she began to inch her way toward one of the largest holes.

A sudden zigzag of lightning racing across the sky and the ensuing clap of thunder made Lynn leap clumsily to her feet with fright. Then, just as quickly, the roof gave way beneath her and she felt herself partially plunging through the dried palm fronds until one leg was dangling through the roof while the other supported her clumsily on one knee.

Tossing away all the palm leaves she'd so laboriously carried up, she struggled to free herself, but saw the danger of the roof completely giving way beneath her and paused to take a deep, trembling breath.

Still trying to support her weight on one knee and the palms of her hands, Lynn looked desperately around for Eliot. Why hadn't he seen her dilemma? But the steady chopping sound of the machete gave her a quick answer. The bolt of lightning had apparently encouraged Eliot to work harder and faster, and he'd moved away from the hut deeper into the jungle.

Lynn sighed heavily and her lips set in a straight line. If he saw her up there with one leg sticking through a hole in the roof, she'd never hear the end of it. What a klutz! And she'd wanted so much to be helpful. Maybe she could extricate herself without ruining the rest of the roof, or breaking her neck— or her leg, which seemed more likely.

But after a few tries, the ache in her dangling leg made her forget her pride. She had to have his help. There was no other way. She glowered at the gloomy, threatening sky and silently cursed it. If it wasn't for the approaching storm, there would have been no need for such haste in repairing the roof, and she wouldn't have been prompted to do such a crazy thing as to try to fix it herself.

"Lynn, how are you doing up there?"

Lynn tensed as her gaze moved hurriedly toward the far edge of the roof, expecting to see Eliot's head popping up at any moment. Oh! How she'd hate him to see her there, like a rat caught in a trap.

But when she once more heard the steady chop-chops of the machete, she realized that he had only called to her casually while taking a rest from his labors.

Doubling her fingers into tight fists, Lynn felt an irrational anger building up inside. "He doesn't care if I'm alive or dead!" she muttered. "Why did he ask me how I was doing if he wasn't even going to check on me to *see*?"

The dull ache rose upward into the inner thigh of the trapped leg, causing Lynn to flinch and bite her lower lip. She struggled once more to free herself, then closed her eyes and took a deep breath. She knew that she had no other choice. She yelled for Eliot.

*"Eliot!"*

Slowing her breathing, waiting for him to answer, Lynn grew angrier still, hearing him busy at work.

Wriggling, cursing, she tried again to pull her leg out. Suddenly the hardened tip of a palm stem cut through her pants leg and dug into the tender flesh of her outer thigh. The pain shot through her, as though someone had pierced her with the sharp point of an arrow.

Grabbing at her leg, she once more tried to get Eliot's attention. "Eliot, for God's sake!" she screamed. "Will you come here?"

She listened, then let out a deep sigh of relief when she heard only the sound of thunder in the distance. He had stopped chopping at last. He must have finally heard her.

She watched anxiously for his head to appear at the far end of the roof, but he was nowhere in sight. Apparently he hadn't heard after all.

"Eliot!" she screamed again. "Where the hell are you? I'm hurt! Come and help me out of this mess!"

"Lynn?" Eliot said, his voice suddenly coming from below her.

Looking through the small space on either side of her dangling leg, she could see Eliot inside the hut, looking up at her in astonishment. "Well, don't just *stand* there! Get me out of here," she cried.

In a flash, Eliot was outside the shack and climbing up on the roof beside her.

"Why on earth didn't you answer me, Eliot?" she snapped. "I've been yelling my head off!"

"I went to the lagoon for a fresh supply of water," he said. "How long have you been—uh—stuck?"

"Too long," she grumbled.

He leaned down and began inspecting the damage inflicted on her leg, and frowned. "It's going to hurt a little, Lynn," he said, "when I pull that damn thing away."

Lynn raised her eyes to the cloudy heavens. "Why do these things always happen to me?" she groaned. "You must think I'm the klutz of all time!"

"I don't think anything of the kind," he said soothingly, carefully tearing away the palm fronds to reach her imprisoned leg.

Lynn flinched when her leg gave way a bit beneath her and the sharp tip pierced deeper. Cold sweat beaded her brow and once more she found herself biting her lower lip from the pain. Then she forced a smile at Eliot. "You didn't even laugh at me this time," she said. "Lost your sense of humor?"

"Would you feel better if I'd laughed?" he asked. He placed his fingers firmly around her leg, trying to inch it out of the hole, then stopped, not yet having cleared away enough of the leaves.

"Well, maybe—then again, maybe not," she said. "If you *had* laughed, I wouldn't have thought it was so serious."

"Are you okay?" he murmured, stopping to give her an anxious, loving look.

"Sure," she said nervously. "I'm just fine."

"It doesn't look as bad as I was afraid it was," he said. "Only a flesh wound. I had thought it might be a nasty gash. But it wasn't as deeply embedded in the flesh as I had thought from my first look at it."

"That's the first encouraging thing I've heard today," Lynn laughed. She melted inside when Eliot dropped a soft kiss on her lips. "And that,

215

my love, is the next and the *best* thing," she added as he drew away from her.

"Well, let me get you out of here and then we'll see just what else we might be able to dream up that will encourage you today," he chuckled.

He gave her a wicked glance, his mouth forming a seductive smile. "If you know what I mean," he drawled huskily.

"You can think of sex at the strangest times," Lynn laughed. "For all I know when you get my leg free you'll try to make love to me right here on this flimsy roof."

"Ah, a touch of danger could make it even more interesting, don't you think?" he laughed, turning back to his efforts to free her.

"I don't think I need this kind of excitement," she said dryly. Then she touched his brow gently. "Anyway, you're all the excitement I need to warm my blood, even on solid ground. But you know that, darling."

"True, tell me again," he laughed. "Over and over again. I'll never get tired of hearing it."

Lynn grimaced when Eliot once more tried to pull her leg from its confines, then sighed with intense relief when she finally found it free and stretched out, throbbing before her. "You did it!" she said, moving the leg tentatively from one side to the other.

"How does it feel?" he asked.

"I think I'll live," Lynn laughed softly. "Just help me get down from this dreadful place!"

Eliot placed an arm about her waist and half carried her to the edge of the roof, then eased her down onto the seat of the chair.

"Ouch!" Lynn squawked, as she put her full weight on the injured leg. But then she smiled when she further tested its dexterity and realized that she wasn't in as bad shape as she had first feared.

Eliot was on his knees, looking down at her over the edge of the roof. "Well? How is it?" he asked, furrowing his brow.

"Okay," she said, gratefully. "But I think I'd better get inside and see about taking care of my wound."

"I'll help you," Eliot said, climbing down onto the chair next to her. He stepped to the ground and then lifted her from the chair into his arms. "Hang on. I'll take care of you. Ol' Doc Smith to the rescue!"

Lynn twined an arm about his neck, giggling. Resting her cheek against his chest, she relished his closeness and his concern for her welfare. "I didn't think you'd *ever* hear me," she sighed. "For a moment there, it was as though I was alone. It was such a horrible feeling, Eliot!"

"Did you honestly think I'd leave you?"

"Not really. But it *did* take a hell of a long time for you to answer."

Moving into the hut, Eliot eased her down onto the bed of leaves and fell to his knees before her. With deft fingers he pulled the torn material of her jeans away from the wound, already partially stuck to her skin with oozing, drying blood.

"I'll clean this right up," he said, "but first you'll have to remove your pants."

Lynn smiled, running her fingers teasingly through his thick, dark hair. "You know the dangers of my doing that," she whispered.

"I'm all business," he said, standing up, straight, a

wounded expression on his handsome face. "Honest Injun." A small smile of amusement lifted the corners of his mouth.

"Yeah. Sure," Lynn teased.

"Undress. Doc Smith's orders," he said, walking toward the fire. He lifted the coffeepot from the flames and poured the remains of the coffee into two cups, then washed the pot and refilled it with fresh water.

"What are you doing?" Lynn asked, slowly pulling her Levi's down and wincing as she moved her injured leg.

"I'm going to boil some water to cleanse the wound," he said. "The lagoon water looks pure enough but I'm not going to take any chances."

Tossing her pants aside, Lynn turned her leg and studied the cut. She ran her fingers around it, relieved. Eliot was right—it was just a surface wound. There was little chance of infection. Out here in the jungle miles away from civilization, she knew just how lucky she was. The thought of losing a leg from gangrene caused a sick feeling to grab at her insides.

"Thank goodness it's not bad at all," she said with a sigh. She felt Eliot's presence and smiled her thanks up at him as he offered her a cup of coffee.

A loud crash of thunder caused the hut's walls to vibrate and drew Eliot quickly to the door. He peered up into the sky, then turned and looked at Lynn. "I'm glad your leg isn't bad," he said. "But, darling, seems the weather isn't going to be cooperative. Looks like there's one hell of a storm headed our way."

Lynn put her feet on the floor and joined him by the door. When she looked up into the sky and saw the masses of dark clouds lowering above them, she shivered. "Do you think we might be in for a tropical hurricane?" she whispered, panic-stricken. "We might not survive, Eliot!"

"No, I think it's just a plain old-fashioned storm," he assured her.

Eliot went over to the fire and rescued the coffeepot, then poured some hot water into a bowl. He nodded toward it. "Lynn, you'll have to take care of your leg yourself," he said. "I've got to get back outside, on the roof. Somehow I've got to patch that roof, or we'll be washed away."

He walked to the door again and stuck his head out. "Damn! I thought it was going to stay in the mountains for a little while at least," he grumbled.

"Go on," Lynn said, edging her way to the table. Cringing with the pain, she settled down onto a chair. "Do what you can, but please be careful. That lightning is the worst I've ever seen, and I've seen some terrible electrical storms, believe me!"

"Don't worry," Eliot said. He kissed her softly on the lips then turned and disappeared from sight. Lynn could hear him climbing back up onto the dilapidated roof.

Lynn tried to focus her thoughts on other matters than the weather. She tore a strip of material from her shirt and soaked it in the steaming water. Then, wincing from the heat, she wrung it out and placed it gingerly on her injured leg. Another crash of thunder nearby caused her heart to lurch and her eyes to move to the roof. She laughed nervously as Eliot's face appeared above her, smiling down through the hole.

"That one didn't get me!" he chuckled.

# *Twelve*

SUDDENLY THERE was no breeze. The morning air had a sultry, muggy, oppressive weight to it that they hadn't felt earlier. Lynn slipped back into her jeans and went outside, watching Eliot who had finished patching the roof as he piled more palm and coconut fronds against the walls of the hut.

"Do you really think that's going to help?" she asked apprehensively, limping to his side. "One gust of wind and there goes the ball game."

"All I can do is try," Eliot said, stopping to mop his brow with the back of one hand. "I should have taken the time to do all this earlier."

Forked lightning zigzagged again across the purple clouds. The palm trees looked black against the sky. Lynn tensed, aware of the sudden silence. Only moments earlier the air had been filled with the jungle sounds she'd begun to take for granted. It was positively eerie.

"It's too quiet," Lynn whispered, licking her lips nervously. "I don't like it."

Eliot finished piling rocks against the stacked, cut fronds, then stepped back, wiping his hands on his pants. "I'd say I got this finished just in time," he said, glancing at the boiling clouds.

Another streak of lightning slashed across the sky and then the wind began to rise with a low, moaning sound, riffling the palm fronds overhead almost ominously.

"Let's get inside," Eliot suggested. He placed an arm about Lynn's waist and helped her limp into the hut and over to the fireplace. "You stay put. Keep a close eye on the fire. If the wind blows the walls in, this place could go up like tissue paper."

"All right," Lynn murmured apprehensively, settling down on the floor. She rubbed her aching leg as she watched Eliot begin dragging the table toward the door. "Why on earth are you doing that, Eliot?"

Turning the table on end and fitting it across the entranceway, he gave Lynn a quick glance. "You've just witnessed my magic act. This table has been turned into our door before your very eyes," he told her. "Not only will it help to keep the rain out, but it might prevent any creature the storm might scare out of the brush from joining us inside."

Lynn, eyes wide, watched him kick at one end of the table, making sure it was solidly in place. The only space left was at the top, where the dim light shone faintly over the edge of the table.

"And what if we need to get out of here in a hurry?" Lynn asked, shivering uncontrollably both from fear and from a sudden chill in the air that was whistling through many cracks in the walls and windows.

"It can be moved away just as quickly," Eliot said. He turned around and picked up the two cups he had placed on the floor. Noticing that the coffee hadn't been emptied out, he took them and placed them at the edge of the fire to reheat it. "We can drink the rest of this sludge while we await our fate," he added.

Lynn moved over a bit and patted the floor next to her. "Come and sit beside me, Eliot," she softly murmured. "Put your arms around me. I'm feeling kind of nervous, and I want to snuggle."

Eliot settled down beside her, chuckling beneath his breath. "Your wish is my command," he said, draping his arm around her waist and drawing her into his warm embrace. "Darling, snuggle for all you're worth. And you're worth a lot!"

He glanced down at her leg. "Has your leg stopped bothering you so much?"

Lynn made a face. "You know, with the scare of the approaching storm, I'd completely forgotten all about it!" she said.

Eliot snapped his fingers. "Darn! Me and my big mouth." Then he kissed her tenderly on the lips. "Sorry about that, babe. Forgiven?"

"At this moment, I'd forgive you anything," she whispered. "Just hold me, darling. Hold me tight."

"Everything'll be all right," Eliot soothed. He burrowed his nose into the soft curve of her neck and shoulder. "You'll see. The storm will pass quickly. Then we'll be just as happy-go-lucky as we were before."

"Sure," Lynn pouted. "Happy-go-lucky, lost in the jungle, with nothing to eat but fruit and no more coffee! Happy-go-*un*lucky would be a more accurate description."

"I thought you were enjoying our romantic isolation," he said.

"Eliot, the word 'home' sounds so good at this

223

moment," she sighed. "Please don't misunderstand, but I would give anything to be back home, walking beside the ocean, enjoying the sand between my toes and watching the seagulls soaring overhead . . ."

The sudden roar of heavy rain lashing against the roof and the walls of the hut drew Lynn's face quickly up and Eliot to a standing position. The fury of the high winds tearing and shrieking through the trees was like no other they'd ever heard before. The walls of the hut were quickly becoming soaked inside as the rain blew in the windows and through the cracks in the walls and roof that Eliot hadn't succeeded in mending well enough.

Eliot stretched out a hand to Lynn. "Here it comes," he said grimly. "Come on—stand next to me. I don't know what to expect will happen next."

Trembling, Lynn dashed into his arms and clung desperately to him. She could see the rain through the open window—it seemed to be driven in an almost horizontal direction, rather than straight down like normal, ordinary rain.

The walls squeaked and the roof groaned as the wind howled and moaned around the hut. Pools of water were forming all around Lynn and Eliot's feet, and falling rain drenched them both as part of the roof slowly disintegrated before their upturned eyes.

"Well, I guess I'm not such a great carpenter after all," Eliot said, trying to force a lightheartedness into his voice.

"Carpenters use *nails*," Lynn groaned, seeing another palm frond rip away overhead. "Oh, if only we'd had some nails! Maybe our house would have held together."

Eliot framed Lynn's face between his hands. "*Our* house," he said softly. "Do you realize what you just said? You called this *our* house."

"So I did," Lynn said, laughing nervously.

"Well, it is," Eliot said, drawing her once more next to him and hugging her tightly as she buried her face in his chest, refusing to watch the rest of the destruction as the rain fell all around them.

"This is our house. We've made it ours," he added. "Maybe—just maybe—one day we'll have a real house, darling, maybe on Nob Hill in San Francisco . . ."

A crackling sound overhead and the rush of water and more falling debris on Lynn and Eliot's heads forced them to scuttle quickly to one side of the room. Lynn coughed and sputtered and wiped her face.

"Are you all right?" Eliot asked, clutching onto her shoulders, looking anxiously down into her face.

"What happened?" Lynn asked, rubbing her eyes.

"We've just lost most of our roof," Eliot informed her. "I'm afraid we've got to get out of here."

Lynn began looking desperately around. "Eliot, my boots . . ."

"Grab them," he said, already working to pull the table away from the door.

"The garnets!" Lynn cried frantically, throwing palm leaves aside, searching for her boots and the stones beneath them.

"To hell with the garnets!" Eliot shouted. "Let's just get out of here, now!"

Lynn finally found her boots. She thrust one under each arm and reached for Eliot's hand as one wall came toppling over beside her. "But those stones are probably worth a lot," she argued feebly.

"So are our lives," Eliot growled, guiding her on outside. The wind began whipping at their bodies as though it was trying to rip them apart as it had their shack.

"Come on!" Eliot yelled, pulling at Lynn's hand. "Follow me. I know where to go where we'll be safe."

Lynn winced as a sharp pain tore through her leg. But she wouldn't cry out. She wouldn't let Eliot know that the pain grew worse with every step she took. But she couldn't help letting out a squawk when one bare foot made contact with a hairy thorn from a fallen branch of a tree.

Eliot swung around, eyes filled with concern. "What's the matter?"

"I've got to stop and put my boots on, Eliot," Lynn gasped, reaching to rub the sole of her foot.

"Here—lean against me," Eliot encouraged. "But hurry. We're in danger of a tree toppling over on us."

Lightning forked and crackled on all sides of them. The rain continued to fall in sheets, blotting out their surroundings with a steady curtain of water. Rain stung Lynn's eyes and filled her nose and mouth. She coughed and spit, feeling her drenched clothes clinging clammily to her shivering body.

Almost crying from the effort, she struggled with one boot and then the other until finally she had them both securely on. "I'm ready," she said, coughing again.

A loud crash from close behind her made her jump with a start. She clung to Eliot, peering through the rain, finally able to see from where the noise had come. A huge mahogany tree had fallen directly onto the hut, which now lay in a smoldering heap as the fire from the fireplace tried to fight against the rain, to take hold and finish the destruction begun by the storm.

A pang of sadness ate away at Lynn's heart. The ramshackle hut had gradually come to mean something very special to her. Though cursing it at times, she did know it would always be a special part of her dreams of Eliot. While they had lived in that hut, they had shared everything as man and wife . . . and even more than that. They had found out what the fight for survival really meant—the survival of the fittest. Well, so far, so good, she thought. We must be among the fittest!

"Well, that's that," Eliot sighed, combing his fingers distractedly through his hair. He turned Lynn firmly around and began moving her onward.

"Eliot, where are we going?"

"To the cave."

Lynn's eyes widened. "The cave?" she repeated. "But that's so far . . ."

"It only *seemed* far because we hadn't had it in mind when we had started out the other day," he said flatly. "Now we know it's there. We'll go directly to it. You'll see. It won't take nearly as long this time."

Lynn tugged at Eliot's arm. "Eliot, you forgot the machete," she cried. "You'll need it, won't you?"

Eliot spun around, doubling a fist at his side. "Damn!" he growled. "You're right—I do need that thing. It's the only tool we've got. Without it, we're in real trouble."

"I'll wait here till you get it," Lynn said, visibly trembling. She hugged herself with her arms, inwardly cursing the steadily falling rain.

"Don't you budge," Eliot ordered, cocking his head and, looking up at the sky overhead, relieved that in this spot at least, there wasn't so much danger of being crushed beneath a falling tree.

"All right," she said. "But please hurry!"

She watched him rush back in the direction from whence they come, then began rubbing her leg, realizing that it had become a bit swollen. It was then that she also realized that the rain was letting up, and, she began speaking a silent prayer of thanks as the winds began to subside and the rain became only a fine mist.

Eliot rushed toward her with the machete in one hand and the other hidden behind his back. "I've got something for you," he said with a twinkle in his eyes.

"For me?" Lynn said, wringing the water from the tail of her shirt.

"Yes. For you," Eliot chuckled, bringing the coffee can from behind his back with a flourish.

Lynn laughed a little awkwardly. "The *coffee can?*" she said. "Why on earth . . . ?"

"Look inside," Eliot said, offering it to her.

"More magic?" Lynn asked, taking the can and peering inside it. Then a .slow smile crinkled her nose. "Eliot," she sighed. "You found a garnet!"

"It was on the floor next to the machete," he laughed, "so I placed it in the coffee can. A precious—okay, semiprecious—jewel for my precious lady!"

Lynn threw her arm around his neck and pressed a

kiss to his lips. "Thank you!" she whispered. "You're the sweetest thing!"

"*Thing?*" Eliot chuckled, placing his hands around her waist. "I hope I'm more than a 'thing' to you, Lynn."

"You know you are," she said. Then she raised her eyes to the forest ceiling. "And look!" she cried. "I do believe I see a bit of blue sky breaking through."

"Just a little bit too late," Eliot said, leading Lynn on toward the lagoon.

"Too late?" she asked, placing the garnet safely inside her front right jeans pocket and dropping the empty can on the ground.

"Too late to save our shack."

"What are we going to do, Eliot?"

"We'll spend the rest of the day and the night in the cave, then we must move," he said.

"But where to?"

"Damned if I know!"

"But if you had thought we might find some signs of civilization by moving on, we would never have stayed here so long," she pointed out.

"Darling, the hut was the only reason I felt it was best to stay put," he said. "But now, we don't have a roof over our head. We must try to find something else."

Lynn trembled, afraid. "I don't like it, Eliot," she murmured. "I don't like it one bit!"

"I'm not exactly crazy about it myself," he admitted with a shrug. "But it seems we have no choice."

Tree limbs strewn in the path Eliot had previously cut through the brush were slowing their progress. Eliot helped Lynn over them, holding tightly to her elbow. The chattering of the birds and monkeys overhead had revived and steam rose upward from the forest floor, as dense as a London fog.

Lynn pulled at her shirt, hating the wet, sticky feel of it. "I'm sick of all of this," she said from between clenched teeth. "I hate these Levi's. I hate this shirt!"

Then she grabbed Eliot by the arm, stopping him in his tracks. "Eliot," she cried. "My hat! I forgot my hat!"

"So the snake has returned to his natural habitat for a proper burial," Eliot chuckled.

Lynn doubled a fist and hit the solid steel of his arm. "Eliot, that's terrible," she said, then giggled. "Do you realize that hat has helped us through all of this?"

"How so?"

"The snakeskin band has been the cause for some pretty terrible jokes on your part," she said. She stood on tiptoe and kissed him softly. "That's helped us through some tight squeezes, darling. If not for your warped sense of humor, I don't know how I could have gotten through the past few days."

Lifting her chin with a forefinger, Eliot returned her kiss, then said, "Has it really been so bad?"

"Right now is the worst. My leg's not doing so well."

"Well, baby, maybe I can do something about that."

"What do you mean?"

"If you'll carry the machete, I'll carry you."

Lynn laughed. "Are you serious, Eliot?"

"Try me."

Lynn gingerly took the machete from his hand

then stood before him with a gleam in her green eyes.

Eliot laughed huskily and swept her quickly up into his arms. "To the cave!" he said, taking wide, steady strides onward. *"Charge!"*

"All that's missing is a horse," Lynn giggled, clinging with one arm about his neck.

"A horse!" Eliot said, giving her a lifted eyebrow look.

"You sound like a Union officer leading his troops during the Civil War."

"Ah *hah*," he said. "So you're not a Southern belle after all, I see."

Lynn rested her head against his chest, laughing. "I'm feeling better already, Eliot," she sighed.

"Even without your hat?"

"I guess I can live without it," she said with a shrug.

"Good," he said. "When we get back to San Francisco, I'll buy you a *dozen* hats to make up for the loss of that one."

"Eliot, I'm beginning to doubt if we'll ever see San Francisco again," Lynn said sadly.

"Nonsense," he growled.

"They should've found us by now."

"They will," he mumbled. "In time. Keep the faith, baby."

Lynn raised her head quickly from its comfortable place on his chest as the roar of the waterfall reached her ears. Through a hazy mist rising from the crystal clear water of the lagoon, Lynn could see the magnificence of the steadily falling water. Miniature rainbows glistened through the mist, and tropical birds in their own rainbow colors were weaving almost magically in front of the waterfall in the first weak rays of sunlight.

"It's even more beautiful today," Lynn sighed.

"At least that's one thing the storm didn't play havoc with," Eliot said, stepping to the lagoon's edge. "In fact, the rain has enhanced the lagoon's paradise effect. The greens are greener and the colors of the flowers lining the lagoon seem even brighter, if possible. And look at the fish swimming to the surface—I've never seen fish like that. Maybe I could catch some for dinner."

Lynn grimaced. "I wouldn't try it. They might be piranhas!"

"Then I guess we better not risk a swim," Eliot said, nuzzling her neck teasingly. "On second thought, what better way to find out if they're piranhas or not?"

Eliot began swinging her playfully back and forth over the water.

Lynn tightened her hold about his neck. "Eliot," she squealed. "My leg! You wouldn't really throw me in, would you?"

Eliot dropped a kiss on the tip of her nose. "Of course not," he said gently. "And speaking of your leg, let's get you into the cave and take a look at it."

Eyeing the ledge behind the waterfall, Lynn's brow creased in a frown. "You'd better put me down. I don't think you could make it across that narrow ledge with me in your arms."

"Just watch me," Eliot chuckled, taking wide steps toward it. "You keep hold of the machete. We'll be needing it tomorrow when we head out again."

"The thought frightens me, Eliot."

"We'll just have to keep taking this one day at a time. We've made it so far, haven't we?"

"Except for my clumsiness," she said, looking wryly down at the torn leg of her jeans. At least the rain had washed most of the blood from it.

Then she clung tightly and barely breathed as Eliot began edging along the ledge behind the waterfall. Looking downward, Lynn grew somewhat dizzy when she saw the steady cascade of water tumbling below her. A whirlpool of sorts was created by the meeting of waters, causing Lynn's dizziness to heighten.

Closing her eyes, she pressed her cheek against Eliot's chest and then breathed easier when he took one last wide step and they were inside the cool, semidark confines of the cave.

The sound of steady dripping drew Lynn's eyes to the roof of the cave. "The rain even found its way in here," she grumbled. A damp chill seemed to penetrate her very bones. "This may not be such an ideal hideaway after all."

"We'll go farther back into the cave this time."

"But it'll be dark," Lynn argued, shivering.

"I'll gather up some dry twigs and build a fire."

"You won't be able to find anything dry after that storm we've just managed to live through."

"I'll search until I find something," he assured her.

"I wonder if those strange birds will fuss at us again," Lynn said, peering through the gloom toward the roof of the cave.

"They will just have to share their love nest with us this time," Eliot said as he moved his way between beautifully sculptured stalagmites and stalactites. After leaving the dripping behind, Eliot eased Lynn from his arms to the ground. He kissed her softly. "Give me the machete," he said. "I'll be back soon."

Lynn glanced quickly around her. Her heart thundered against her ribs but she refused to reveal her growing fears to Eliot. "All right," she murmured.

"Don't go away," Eliot teased.

Lynn watched his silhouette against the light that came through the cave's entrance, then sighed heavily as he disappeared from sight. She lowered herself to the ground and patiently waited, sifting sand nervously through her outstretched fingers. When she heard the crunch of rock close by, Lynn lunged quickly back to her feet, placing her fingers to her throat.

"Lynn, it's only me," Eliot reassured her. "I found some dry limbs. They'd been sheltered by overhanging rocks outside, next to the side of the cave."

Sighing with relief, Lynn once more settled onto the sandy floor. "Okay, let's see some more of your Boy Scout skills," she said. "No matches, right?" She couldn't see what he was doing but she soon saw sparks and then a small flame took hold in some of the dried twigs.

"Ah, success again!" Eliot laughed, adding more wood to the flickering flames.

Lynn relaxed a little as she saw the fire flickering on Eliot's face. Even with his incipient beard, she thought he'd never looked handsomer as his dark eyes glowed warmly back at her. Wet ringlets of dark hair framed his chiseled features, giving him an innocently boyish appearance. When he reached out a hand to her, she was drawn upward into the building magic of the moment.

"I love you," he whispered huskily, showering kisses over her face as his hands stroked her damp, tumbled hair. "Oh, how I love you!"

Lynn felt a giddiness inside her head as he lowered his lips to hers and kissed her sweetly. His fingers wove through her loosened hair, causing it to settle in waves around her shoulders. Then she leaned into his male hardness as he worked at her buttons, removing her wet shirt.

With a soft groan she welcomed his warm hands cupping her breasts. His thumbs pressed into the nipples, causing a sweet pain there, igniting sensuous flames inside her that leaped upward like wildfire, threatening to consume her with the heat of their mutual desire.

Letting her fingers travel over the corded muscles of his shoulders, then downward, Lynn found the buttons of his shirt, loosened them and pressed her fingers against his chest, loving the texture of the curls that grew there so profusely.

"I want you," Eliot whispered huskily into her ear. "I want you now."

Lynn arched her neck as his mouth pressed against the soft hollow of her throat. A soft moan of pleasure rose sensually from Lynn's lips as his mouth lowered to one nipple, drawing it slowly between his teeth.

"But where, Eliot?" she managed to whisper.

"By the fire. On the sand."

The flames of the fire cast haunting shadows on the ceiling and walls of the cave. Lynn was seduced by rapture as Eliot's hands continued their work of disrobing her, right down to her boots.

Then he straightened his back and eyed her, a gleam of passion in his dark, dreamy eyes. "And now, darling, it's your turn to undress me," he whispered, devouring her nudity with a gaze of intense approval.

With a tremor of all her senses, Lynn slowly pulled his shirt away from his shoulders, savoring the touch of her fingers against his flesh. A sweet ache of longing arose between her thighs. She swallowed hard and tossed his shirt aside, compelled to press her cheek against the expanse of his powerful chest.

Closing her eyes, she hugged him tightly to her then moved her head to let her tongue lap seductively at his nipples. When she heard a soft moan from between his lips and could feel the trembling of his body, she smiled and worked her tongue lower, flickering it in and out of his navel.

"Lynn . . . baby . . ." Eliot groaned. He dug his fingers into her shoulders as she unsnapped his jeans and slowly lowered the zipper. The sight and scent of him was slowly driving her wild. She slipped her fingers inside and felt the crisp hairs between them, then with pulses racing searched farther and discovered his throbbing, ready hardness.

With a skill that she had learned from their many sessions of uninhibited lovemaking, she rescued his shaft from its confines and kissed it with ardor. Another moan seemed to be wrenched from the depths of his being.

"Eliot, you'll have to finish undressing yourself," Lynn gasped. "I'm so weak now from the need of you, I'm not going to be able to do another thing until you're stretched out next to me."

The warbling of a bird above her drew Lynn's eyes quickly up. She saw the black bird perched on a rock ledge, watching, and she thrilled inside, welcoming Eliot's arms as they engulfed her and pressed her closer and closer to him. Tonight she would forget everything but Eliot and their audience of one—but tomorrow . . .

# Thirteen

THE AIR was shimmering under a harsh sun. A flock of colorful birds rose screaming into the sky. Lynn was limp from the intense heat, yet she forced herself to walk steadily alongside Eliot.

"How's the leg holding up?" he asked, stopping to get his breath. The jungle was thinning around them and the slope of a low-lying mountain range seemed to be the next major challenge.

"My leg is the least of my worries," Lynn sighed. She lifted the tail of her shirt and began fanning herself with it.

"Yeah, I know what you mean," said Eliot.

"Eliot, this is the time for truth," Lynn said, raking her eyes slowly around her and seeing nothing familiar about the terrain. "We're moving in the opposite direction to Leon, aren't we?"

"I can't say," Eliot confessed.

"I didn't think you could," Lynn sighed, slumping her shoulders in defeat.

"Come on," Eliot encouraged. He cupped her left elbow in the palm of his right hand. "We have to keep moving. I've got to get you to some sort of shelter before nightfall. Maybe we should have stayed at the cave . . ."

"And what happens if we don't find any shelter?"

"Let's keep hoping for the best. All right?"

Looking down at her soiled, ripped Levi's and her shirt with its rips and tears and sweat stains, Lynn groaned. "How can you stand to even walk next to me?" she asked. "I'm a terrible sight and I don't feel any better than I look. I'm hot. I'm tired. When is this going to end, Eliot?"

"Soon, I hope," he growled. He drew her into his arms and comforted her. "It's foolish to worry about your appearance. We're a matched pair, you and I. And remember," he said with an attempt at a grin, "beauty is only skin deep."

Lynn laughed softly, then tensed and looked quickly up into Eliot's eyes as she heard his sudden intake of breath. He held her even more tightly, as though his arms had turned to steel.

"Don't look now, but we've got company," he whispered into her ear.

Feeling a numbness seize her insides, she slowly turned her head. Her heart pounded wildly when she saw a dark-skinned soldier standing before them with a rifle pointed straight at Eliot's chest.

"A *Contra* . . ." she whispered harshly, glancing, wide-eyed, up at Eliot. She was relieved to see no fear in his eyes, and a solid strength in the hard set of his jaw.

"Just stay calm," Eliot whispered back, still staring in the soldier's direction. He slowly released his hold on Lynn and urged her around behind him as he faced the guerrilla soldier.

Lynn listened breathlessly as Eliot and the soldier

exchanged words in Spanish, all the while letting her gaze move over the stranger. He appeared to be well-fed, well-armed, and well-clothed in a dark green uniform. He was supplied with full field equipment consisting of a pistol and belt, canteen, knife and backpack. He wore combat boots and on his arm was the arm band that Adam had mentioned was the mark of all *Contra* soldiers, showing their loyalty to their particular band of guerrillas.

"*Como se llama usted?*" the soldier asked, glowering with his dark eyes back at Eliot. A thick mustache covered his upper lip and a green billed cap was pulled down low over his forehead.

"*Me llama* Eliot Smith," Eliot replied. "*Hable usted ingles?*"

The soldier shook his head back and forth then went into another flurry of Spanish, gesturing with the barrel of his rifle.

"What's he saying?" Lynn whispered.

"He wants to know what our business is here in the jungle," Eliot whispered back. "Ain't that a joke?"

Then he grew serious and tried to explain to the soldier that he and Lynn were lost and that they were no threat, that they were there purely by accident and that their motives were entirely peaceful.

The soldier nodded his head, pointed his rifle toward the machete and spoke in another rapid patter of Spanish.

Lynn saw the machete fall to the ground as Eliot released its handle.

"Why did you drop the machete?" Lynn whispered.

"He considers it a weapon."

Lynn felt her heart skip a beat and she glanced a bit sideways at Eliot. "And you said we weren't in danger of running into a *Contra!*" she whispered irritably.

"Everybody makes mistakes," said Eliot with a shrug. "This is no time to argue. What we must do now is look as friendly as possible. Smile!"

"How can I do that?" Lynn fretted. "My knees are as wobbly as jello. And I'm *not* used to having a rifle pointing in my face. I see absolutely nothing to smile about."

"Think happy thoughts," Eliot said. "And, darling, start moving."

"Moving? Where?" she asked.

"We've just been instructed to follow that jolly green giant on into the mountain pass."

"Oh, no," Lynn sighed. "Where do you think we're being taken?"

"To a *Contra* camp. Where else?"

Lynn blanched but fell in step close to Eliot as the soldier stood aside and let them pass on by him. A half turn of the head showed Lynn that their captor was only a few feet behind them, with the rifle still aimed at their backs, following at their heels.

"I knew I should've stayed in San Francisco," Lynn fumed. "Adam was right, you know."

"Sure. Adam knows everything," he growled. "Well, babe, Adam ain't here now so you'd better get your act together and remember that I'm the only one here besides that soldier who can speak Spanish and possibly get us out of this mess and back to Leon in one piece."

"And just how do you propose to do that?" Lynn

asked dryly. "You're the one who got us into this mess in the first place!"

Eliot didn't reply and Lynn closed her lips into a narrow line as she trudged along beside him. For what seemed like several long, dragging hours they walked through dark passages of moss-covered rocks jutting out above them in the continuing mountain pass and then out into an open sweep of green jungle spreading out as far as the eye could see.

"I wonder how much farther he's going to make us walk," Lynn whispered to Eliot, wiping her brow dry of perspiration with the back of her hand.

Eliot grabbed her around the waist and drew her quickly to his side. "Don't look now, but I think we've got *more* company," he said grimly, stopping to peer ahead through the thick foliage.

A long column of soldiers with semi-automatic rifles slung across their shoulders were emerging from the forest, coming silently up the same steep, winding path Lynn and Eliot had been forced along.

Dark stares from the soldiers made Lynn's insides grow cold. She so wished that she could understand the brief Spanish phrases being exchanged between the soldier at her back and those passing on by.

"We're very near their camp," Eliot said, leaning closer to her.

"How do you know?" Lynn asked.

"They were talking about a Commander Hernandez," Eliot said. "He's been waiting for our soldier who was sent out to scout the area."

Lynn laughed sarcastically, "Well, he sure found a

prize when he discovered us," she said. "We're such a serious threat!"

"*Mas aprisa!*" the soldier suddenly shouted at Lynn and Eliot.

Eliot looked over his shoulder and gave the soldier a scowl, then looked down at Lynn. "Come on," he said, urging her onward. "We've just been ordered to move faster."

"Eliot, I'm about to drop!"

"Just think of what lies ahead at the camp," Eliot tried to encourage her.

"Sure—imprisonment," Lynn scoffed.

"I keep telling you, think positive. Food. Water. And possibly a roof over our heads, Lynn."

"While we're prisoners, I'm sure," she insisted.

"They have no reason to hold us prisoner," Eliot argued. "Once their leader sees we're perfectly harmless gringos lost in the jungle, he'll treat us fairly. You'll see."

"I certainly hope you're right," Lynn sighed. "But I can't say I'm particularly optimistic."

Eliot ran his fingers nervously over the stubble of his developing beard. "Damn! If only Hank had gotten lost with us," he grumbled.

Lynn's eyes widened as she quickly glanced over at him. "What on earth makes you say that? What good could Hank possibly do us?"

"If Hank were with us, then at least we'd have a camera to shoot some of this," Eliot said, looking back at the soldier. "I bet a camera would soften him up a bit. These foreigners go nuts over cameras."

"Eliot, if we arrived in the *Contra* camp with a movie camera and announced that we were from a television station in the United States, we would probably be shot first and questioned later!"

Eliot laughed wearily. "Yeah, I guess you're right," he said. Then his expression became solemn as his eyes focused straight ahead.

"We seem to have arrived," he murmured, nodding his head.

Lynn followed Eliot's steady stare and took an involuntary step backward in fear. The camp carved out of the jungle was no larger than a football field. There were several small adobe houses and past the houses was a small open field. The whole area was ringed by towering mountains and dense green jungle. From time to time a military radio squawked noisily from one of the adobe buildings and soldiers were lined up in four rows of what appeared to be sixteen each, listening to a speech being given by an elderly man, who despite his apparent age was stout and square-shouldered.

Lynn felt the barrel of the soldier's rifle suddenly at the small of her back and was roughly directed on until she and Eliot stood directly in front of what appeared to be the *Contra* leader.

"Commander Hernandez, I believe," Eliot said, offering a hand of friendship to the man whose dark eyes reflected only deep mistrust.

"Who the hell are you?" Commander Hernandez growled in English, glaring from Lynn to Eliot. But before giving either of them a chance to respond, he began conversing in rapid Spanish with the soldier who had taken Lynn and Eliot captive.

Lynn intently observed the commander. He wore the same dark green uniform as the other soldiers but instead of a billed cap he wore a black beret on which was an insignia consisting of two crossed rifles.

On his left sleeve was a blue and white insignia bearing the initials FDN and he wore the same type of pistol belt and canteen as the others. His copper-colored face was lined with age and his dark hair was touched with gray. He bore these marks of age well and appeared to be a man who had dedicated his entire life to change—*his* designated changes. His full, bushy mustache curved downward at the corners of his mouth, giving him a slightly sinister appearance.

Commander Hernandez dismissed the soldier with a quick salute then clasped his hands tightly together behind him as he frowned from Lynn to Eliot. "So you say you're lost," he grumbled once again in English. "How does it happen that you're lost in the jungle?"

Eliot turned on all his considerable charm and smiled. "It's a long story, sir," he began.

"One I'm waiting to hear," Commander Hernandez said flatly, not returning the smile.

"Well, it's like this . . ." Eliot said, and then proceeded to tell exactly how he and Lynn had become separated from the rest of their party—leaving out the more intimate details, however.

When he was through with his explanation, he waited patiently as Commander Hernandez contemplated him in silence, while thoughtfully curling the tips of his mustache between his short, stubby fingers.

"Ancient ruins, eh?" Commander Hernandez finally murmured. He paused for a moment longer, then eyed Lynn speculatively.

"*Sí,*" he finally said. "That does *tener sentido.*"

Eliot took a brave step forward. "*Me llama* Eliot Smith," he said firmly, once more offering his hand in friendship. "It's a pleasure to make the acquaintance of such an astute commander as you." He then continued to speak in Spanish.

Lynn's eyes widened. She gave Eliot a quick glance as she realized his game plan. One look at Commander Hernandez told her that Eliot's attempt at diplomacy seemed to be succeeding, because his words had drawn a broad smile and a hearty handshake from Commander Hernandez.

"*Es favor que me hace,*" Commander Hernandez said, still flashing a wide, toothy smile. "*Me alegro de conocerle.* From the great city of San Francisco and a big television celebrity in my small camp? *Sí. Me alegro de conocerle.*"

Eliot laughed good-naturedly and gave Lynn a somewhat smug glance. He nodded toward her. "*Two* television celebrities in your small camp," he quickly corrected. "This is Lynn Stafford. She is my co-host on 'Morning Magazine,' a television show in San Francisco."

Commander Hernandez now offered his hand to Lynn. He squeezed her fingers tightly and began pumping her arm up and down. "*Sí, sí,*" he said, laughing. "Two television celebrities. And one a woman!"

The gleam in his dark eyes showed his approval of Lynn, though considering the way she looked she wondered how any man could find her the least attractive.

But then another thought occurred to her. As she had studied the camp she had noticed that there were no women in sight. Maybe she'd been safer in the wilds of the jungle than here among the possibly women-hungry guerrilla soldiers!

Slowly she turned her eyes to the men who were still standing at attention, waiting for further orders from their leader. A sense of relief flowed through her, since she saw no interest at all etched on their non-smiling faces. They appeared to be dedicated only to the *Contra* cause.

"Lynn Stafford, *me alegro de conocerle,*" Commander Hernandez said to Lynn, releasing her hand and making a stiff bow.

Lynn gave Eliot a questioning glance, not knowing what to say in return since she hadn't understood what he'd said.

Eliot leaned closer to her and spoke in her ear. "He says that he is very glad to meet you," he whispered.

"Oh," Lynn whispered back.

"You might say *muchas gracias,*" Eliot prodded.

"What does that mean?"

"Thank you very much."

"Oh," Lynn said again. She squared her shoulders and cleared her throat nervously, then said, "*Muchas gracias,* Commander Hernandez."

Commander Hernandez raised his eyes slowly to hers as he straightened his back. "*No hay de que, de nada,*" he said briskly, clasping his hands together behind him once more.

Lynn gave Eliot another puzzled look.

"He says you are welcome," Eliot whispered. "It's also a way of saying 'thank you'."

Lynn smiled back at Commander Hernandez, then jumped, startled, as he whirled suddenly around and began shouting out orders to his men. When one short, stout soldier stepped quickly to Eliot's side, cold fear flooded Lynn. The soldier looked threatening with his rifle poised in front of him, yet she forced herself to remember how friendly Commander Hernandez had just been, and hoped for the best.

"I have much to do today," Commander Hernandez said, looking from Lynn to Eliot, then back to Lynn. "But Rodriguez here will show you a place of shelter. We will talk later. Tonight while we sit around a fire, eating our evening meal together."

Eliot cleared his throat nervously and took a step forward. "*Gracias*," he said. "But, Commander Hernandez, I would like to know how Lynn and I can obtain safe passage to Leon. We're eager to return to the States. Could you help us?"

Commander Hernandez frowned and once more began toying with his mustache. "*Puede ser,*" he grumbled.

Eliot's face grew a bit pale. "What do you mean, *perhaps?*" he asked. "Surely you don't plan to hold us prisoner here at your camp. You know that we're no threat to you."

"The threat is that you now know where my camp is, *sí?*" Commander Hernandez said. "It is not good that you should know that."

Eliot cleared his throat again and forced an ingratiating smile. "There would be no reason whatsoever for us to reveal your location," he said. "You can trust us."

"You are ones who eagerly hunt for news for your *television estacion, sí?*" Commander Hernandez growled.

"Well, yes," Eliot mumbled.

"*Contras* is news, *sí?*"

"*Sí,*" Eliot agreed.

"You can still say you would not tell anyone of this *Contra* camp?"

"I can promise you that, sir," Eliot said. "But you will have to trust us."

Commander Hernandez kneaded his well-defined chin. "*Sí. Puede ser.* I will have to get to know you better to fully trust you," he said flatly. "Tonight. By the fire." He then flailed his arms into the air, giving more orders to the lone soldier at Eliot's side.

When Eliot was nudged in his ribs with the barrel of the soldier's rifle, he understood the silent message, took Lynn's hand and led her to an adobe house their guide pointed out.

"*Gracias,*" Eliot said politely as the soldier nodded toward the door. "*Muchas gracias.*"

Lynn stepped cautiously inside the house, relieved when from the corner of her eye she saw the soldier turn and leave her and Eliot alone.

"Well? What do you think of our newest home away from home?" Eliot asked as he looked around the one room, dimly lighted house.

"I have to admit it's a step up from the last one," Lynn said with a sigh, taking in her dismal, dingy surroundings.

And yet, compared to the crudeness of the hut and the cave that they had just left behind, this wasn't so bad after all, she decided.

"At least it's a roof over our heads," Eliot said, gesturing toward the roughly hewn, thatched ceiling. "Without holes, I might add."

"I know." Lynn walked around the room, gingerly

touching the handmade furniture. It was the same type of unpainted furniture that had been in the hut, yet in better condition and with one very welcome exception—a bed, with a layer of blankets thrown over a thin mattress, stood against the far wall, and above it hung a square, cracked mirror with a shelf beneath it upon which sat a half-burned candle in a holder made from a tin can.

"And matches," Lynn said, then laughed as she glanced toward Eliot. "No more boy scouting! This is real luxury—matches! Imagine!" She eyed the firewood piled next to the fireplace and then something else of even more interest caught her eye.

With a gasp of delight, she whispered, "It can't be! But it is, isn't it? Isn't that a *tub*?"

"A rough caricature of one, but yes, I believe that round wooden contraption over there might conceivably be referred to as a tub," Eliot said.

"Is it safe for me to take a bath?" Lynn asked eagerly. "Right now I'd sell my soul for hot water and soap!"

"Who knows what is or isn't safe here?" he grumbled. "But if you want a bath, my love, I'll see to it that you get one."

"How?"

"Just you watch," Eliot said cheerfully. He turned and left the house, and Lynn paced what seemed to her a full hour before he returned. Then, astonished, she stood aside and watched as soldiers began filing in one at a time with buckets of hot water which they poured into the tub. Once it was filled and she and Eliot were once more alone, Eliot went to the door, closed and locked it.

"How did you ever manage that?" Lynn whispered in awe.

"Charm, darling," Eliot chuckled. "Pure charm."

"You're a miracle worker, that's all," she sighed. "But won't you tell me what you said?"

Eliot came over to her and began unbuttoning her shirt, then slipped it gently from her shoulders. With a quick flick, his tongue touched one of her nipples. Then a lazy smile lifted his lips as he said, "I promised them each quite secretly, one at a time, that if they ever came to San Francisco I would see to it that they would be my guest on television. *That's* how."

"But, Eliot, surely none of them will *ever* come to San Francisco."

"Don't you know that most foreigners dream of being able to go to America one day?"

"Well, yes . . ."

"Well, these soldiers are no different," Eliot said. "They have their own private wants and needs, as we do."

Eliot cupped one of Lynn's breasts with one hand while the other began lowering the zipper of her jeans.

"Eliot, how can you think of doing this now when we don't even know our fate?" she protested.

"Isn't it a good way to put our worries behind us?" he asked huskily. "It'll work like a charm, believe me."

Feeling a slow flush rising, Lynn glanced quickly toward the door and then to the three windows of the house. She gently pushed Eliot away. "Eliot, *please*," she said uneasily. "I can't feel as loose as you do at the moment. And we're not exactly alone.

Anyone could walk by a window . . ."

A sudden knock on the door made Lynn wildly cover her breasts with crossed arms. "See what I mean?" she told him. "This isn't the time or the place. Now what do we do?"

Laughing softly, Eliot draped her shirt over her shoulders. "Just step back out of sight," he said. "I'll go and see what they want."

With a pounding heart, Lynn stepped into the dark shadows of the room as she watched Eliot open the door. She leaned closer, frowning when only a quick exchange in Spanish could be heard. But when she heard Eliot say a polite *"Muchas gracias,"* she relaxed a little, though she wondered why thank you's were in order.

When Eliot stepped back from the door and closed and locked it again, Lynn moved from the shadows and went to him. "What did he want?" she asked, then stopped and stared when she saw folded clothes piled neatly onto Eliot's outstretched arms.

"Clothes," Eliot said. "Commander Hernandez sent them. He had noticed that ours were slightly the worse for the wear, so he offered us these."

"How nice of him," Lynn said, eyeing the green khaki material. Then she tensed. "But these are *Contra* uniforms."

"True. Guess he didn't have time to go shopping."

"Surely he wouldn't be giving these to us to wear if he plans to let us leave here, to go back to Leon."

"Why not?"

"Don't you see, Eliot?"

"No, I'm afraid I don't."

"If we show up in Leon in *Contra* uniforms,

everyone will know we've been with the guerillas."

"So what?"

"Commander Hernandez stated quite boldly that his reason for hesitating to let us return to Leon was because he didn't want us to tell people we'd discovered his camp. How can we possibly explain these clothes? Say we picked them up at a rummage sale?"

Eliot placed the clothes on a table. He went to Lynn and cupped her chin in the palm of his right hand. "You've got it wrong, baby," he said thickly. "He said that he was worried about our possibly telling *where* his camp is. Nothing else. His main fear is that we might lead the authorities back here. We have to convince him that this is something we would *never* do."

"Will we be able to?"

"Only time will tell."

"And in the meantime, what do you propose we do, Eliot?"

His eyes gleamed and he chuckled throatily. "That's a dumb question," he said.

"Eliot, surely you don't mean what I *think* you mean," she whispered. "Not now. Not here. You have the most incredible one-track mind!"

"Afraid I do," he said, brushing his lips tantalizingly across hers. "While I'm with you, that is. I have been known to think about other things in different company."

Lynn glanced toward the windows. "Like I said before," she softly argued, "anyone could see."

Eliot playfully lifted one of her legs and removed a boot, then the other, and tossed them aside. "None of those soldiers are going to have time to peek," he assured her. "Commander Hernandez is too busy shouting out orders to them."

"You managed to get them to break away long enough to get the water," she argued.

"I just happened to catch them while they were changing guard," he said. "That's how."

"Excellent timing," Lynn scoffed.

"Isn't every good thing that happens in life almost always due to excellent timing?" he said, pulling her shirt away, then draping it across the back of a chair. His fingers went to the snap of her Levi's and then her zipper and when these were both out of the way, he slid his hand down, across her abdomen and lower, until his fingers were exploring where in spite of herself she ached and throbbed for him.

Bending her back, his teeth caught the nipple of one of her breasts. Feeling the passion rising like wildfire inside her, Lynn could not deny herself what her body craved. Unable to resist her response to him, she slowly shoved her jeans down over the sensuous curves of her hips and let them drop to the floor.

Eliot's fingers crept around and played across her hips, then gently eased her panties down until she stood totally naked before him.

As though consumed by a drugged rapture, Lynn helped him off with his clothes, then gasped softly as he scooped her up into his arms.

"And just where do you think you're taking me?" she purred, linking her arms about his neck. His scrubby beard, still short and rough, tickled her neck as he lowered a long, intimate kiss there.

Carrying her over to the tub, Eliot stepped in and

began lowering himself into the water, to Lynn's surprise.

"Eliot, what . . . ?" Lynn whispered, then giggled as he positioned her on his lap, settling into the bottom of the tub.

"We're going to give each other a bath and then, baby, we'll let nature take its course."

"I wouldn't exactly call this a hot tub," Lynn laughed, scooting from his lap. "There's not very much room for two!" She squeezed into the tub opposite him and reached for a bar of soap, sniffed it and wrinkled her nose in distaste. "And I wouldn't call this soap, either," she said, shuddering. "It smells disgusting."

"If it lathers, it's soap," Eliot said, taking it from her. "Here. Let's give it a try."

Feeling his eyes on her, Lynn closed hers and sighed as he began smoothing suds over her sensitive breasts, causing them to tingle. In slow circles his fingers caressed her breasts, occasionally teasing a nipple with a slight stroke of his thumbs. And as he eased the suds lower, pausing where her waist narrowed, then even lower, causing ripples of desire to float across her flesh, Lynn arched her neck and softly moaned.

Feeling the heat rising inside her, she reveled in his caresses, then melted into his arms as he placed a hand at the nape of her neck and drew her closer to him. Moving her body seductively against his, Lynn welcomed his lips bearing down upon hers with a frenzied urgency.

"To hell with this," Eliot murmured, nuzzling her neck. "You're right—there's not enough room for two!" He rose and stepped from the tub and hurriedly lifted her up into his arms, then carried her to the bed.

"But, Eliot, the soap suds . . ." Lynn whispered, running her fingers across her body, wiping suds onto the scratchy wool blanket stretched out beneath her. "I'm getting the bed all wet."

"In a matter of moments, you won't even notice," he chuckled, lowering himself down over her. Tenderly, he placed his hardness inside her and groaned as he felt the warmth of her enfold his sex, easing his entry with her sweet moisture.

Eliot molded her to him, feeling the surrender of her silken flesh beneath him. He stiffened his back and closed his eyes and the tension mounted inside him as he moved with her while she arched her body to meet his each and every thrust.

As Eliot's hands moved soothingly over her, Lynn let euphoria take hold. She slowly moved her head back and forth, moaning softly. She gripped his shoulders with her fingers and sank her nails into his flesh, urging his male strength deeper and deeper inside her until they were joined on a pinnacle of rapture, conscious of nothing but their mutual ecstasy. Then, spent, they lay aglow in one another's arms.

A loud knock on the door drew Lynn back to reality. She eyed the door warily, then looked at Eliot.

"Relax," he said, calmly. He rose from the bed and quickly started dressing in the green outfit that he had been given. He tossed Lynn the other pants and shirt. "Here—hurry. Get into these."

When the knocking persisted, Eliot went to the door and leaned his head close to it. "*Espere un momento,*" he called out.

Lynn's knees were weak from their lovemaking and her fingers trembled as she hastily buttoned the shirt which was much too big. "What did you tell him?" she whispered.

"To wait a moment," he said, slipping into his boots, then chuckled beneath his breath when he saw Lynn holding the waistband of her pants out away from her waist.

"I know," she grumbled. "The latest in jungle attire. How am I supposed to keep the darn things up?"

"They're only the slightest bit big for you, darling," Eliot teased. He removed the belt from his Levi's and tossed it her way. "Here. Put this on. We can make an extra hole in it later, to make it fit."

The knocking began again, this time louder. "Guess I'd better open it," Eliot grumbled.

Lynn hurried with the belt, yanked her boots on, then went and stood, outwardly poised but inwardly apprehensive, next to Eliot as he opened the door.

A tall, thin soldier with a scraggly beard looked at Lynn and handed her a small, black plastic bag. "*Dadiva*," the soldier said, smiling. "An *especial* gift for *senorita* from *Comandante* Hernandez."

Lynn accepted the bag, feeling mysteriously flat objects through its thin texture. "*Muchas gracias,*" she said, smiling her thanks at the soldier.

He bowed stiffly. "*No hay de que,*" he said. He straightened his back and smiled from Lynn to Eliot. "*Adios,*" he added, swung around on the heel of a boot and in military fashion walked stiffly away.

"Hmm," Eliot said, kneading his forehead in perplexity. "I wonder what that was all about?"

Lynn stepped back into the room, opened the plastic bag and reached inside it. Her eyes brightened and a happy, pink glow arose in her cheeks. "Eliot, it's a comb!" she cried delightedly.

She quickly took it out of the bag. "And a *mirror!*" she added, removing it as well.

Her fingers searched around inside the bag and found two small cylindrical objects. She shook the bag over a table and a tube of lipstick and a small bottle of perfume rolled out. She gave Eliot a wide-eyed, disbelieving stare. "Do you suppose these are standard guerilla equipment?" she asked.

Eliot laughed as he settled onto a chair next to the table. "Don't be too amazed," he said. "I bet these guys carry these CARE packages to draw women friends into their arms. You know they have to be away from their wives or girlfriends for months at a time."

"You've gotta be kidding!"

Eliot toyed with the comb. He shrugged. "I'm probably wrong," he chuckled.

"You and your one-track mind," Lynn scoffed. "I'm sure you are."

Holding up the mirror, she shuddered at the sight of the dark circles beneath her eyes and her sunburned nose, already flaking and raw-looking, not to mention her tangled hair. "Not that I care why our fearless leader has this in his possession—I'm just glad he gave these to me," she sighed, happily, then frowned. "Maybe he's trying to tell me that my appearance needs improvement."

Eliot rose from the chair and moved behind her and gently began pulling the comb through her hair. "I doubt it. It's just a friendly gesture. And, darling,

I feel this gift is a sign of good things to come," he said. "Now I'm sure they'll see that we get safely back to Leon. You seem to have been a big hit with Commander Hernandez."

Shadows fell across Lynn's face. "Is that really all that good?"

"Why wouldn't it be?"

"How can you for one minute even try to figure out how these soldiers' minds work?" Lynn said, lowering the mirror to the table. "I just hope that by this time tomorrow we'll be anywhere but *here* . . ."

# *Fourteen*

THE CAMPFIRE was glowing orange against the backdrop of the jungle which was black with night. A lone cry from a distant bird reverberated hauntingly through the air, causing goose pimples to rise on Lynn's flesh as she and Eliot made their way to the circle of men who were relaxing around the huge bonfire.

Commander Hernandez sat among his men, immediately recognizable by the beret on his grizzled head. He was sitting with his legs outstretched before him, crossed at his ankles, and was peeling an orange, pulling the peel off in a long, perfect spiral. With a brusque nod of his head toward Lynn and Eliot, he said, "Come. Join us. Soon we will eat and drink. But first let us talk. Get acquainted. *Ponerse el corriente* is *importante.*"

With an aching, growling stomach, Lynn caught the scent of food being prepared somewhere else in the camp. It had a rich, spicy smell and she knew that whatever their evening meal consisted of, it would taste like manna from heaven. At this point, smoked pork sausage with cornmeal fritters would taste every bit as delicious as Southern fried chicken, or the finest tenderloin. A diet of fruit was finally to be a thing of the past.

The strong aroma of coffee intoxicated her senses next, and she watched entranced as a huge, blackened coffeepot was lifted from the edge of the fire and slowly passed around to those with tin cups. How she wished she had a cup!

Commander Hernandez tossed his orange peel into the fire and began noisily biting into the orange sections as he plucked them away from the golden fruit. Some juice trickled from the corner of his mouth as he lifted an eyebrow toward Lynn and Eliot. *"Venir,"* he said genially. "Sit each of you on the side of me."

Lynn smiled nervously at him, then glanced at Eliot. He placed his arm gently around her waist and urged her to sit down beside Commander Hernandez, and she smiled tentatively at their captor and host. Then she watched as Eliot settled down on the other side of the commander. Suddenly she didn't like having been separated from him. Somehow she felt vulnerable.

*"Cafe, senorita?"*

Lynn turned with a start when she heard the voice behind her, and when she saw a kind-faced soldier offering her a steaming cup of coffee, she smiled up at him, nodded her head and murmured, *"Gracias."*

The cup was hot to her touch, reminding her forcibly of scorching her fingers on the lantern in the tent. How long ago that seemed, yet it was only a few days in the past . . . She leaned forward, looking past the commander to Eliot. Somehow that night in the tent seemed *weeks* ago. So much had happened since. The dangers she and Eliot had shared, the accidents that had left her with an aching leg and slight blisters on her fingers had been eclipsed by Eliot's skills in making love. She could still feel the lingering passion of Eliot's lips upon hers and the web of rapture he had spun around her heart.

When he leaned a bit forward and smiled at her, Lynn drew quickly back, blushing. It was as though he had read her mind. Maybe he had even been thinking about the very same things.

"But that's foolish," she told herself. "Right now, the only thing on his mind is our safety and getting us out of here, and I'm thinking of our sensual moments together. Guess I have a one-track mind, too."

"And now, my *Americano* friends," Commander Hernandez said, spitting orange seeds on the ground beside him, "we will talk of your return to Leon."

"I assume there is no major problem with that," Eliot said, looking across the brim of his tin cup as he sipped his coffee.

"No. No problem," Commander Hernandez said, eyeing first Eliot, then Lynn. He broke into a boisterous laugh as he once more focused his attention on Eliot. "You see, my *Americano* friend, I have realized I have nothing to fear from you. You would be incapable of leading anyone back to my camp. *Comprende?*"

A slow anger was rising inside Eliot; he felt as though he was being made fun of for some reason, as though Hernandez knew some joke which he was unaware of. He tightened his fingers about the cup. "No," he said as calmly as possible, "can't say that I do understand the meaning behind your words.

Might you want to enlighten me, Commander?"

"If you got lost once in the jungle, you would only get lost a second time," Commander Hernandez said, laughing again. "Now you *comprende?* How could you lead anyone anywhere?"

Eliot felt a slight color rising to his face. He placed the empty tin cup on the ground before him, then said, "Sure, Commander. I get your point." He laughed feebly.

"Then we can leave . . . go back to Leon?" Lynn said eagerly, her eyes lighting up with hope.

"*Sí,*" Commander Hernandez said, nodding his head vigorously. "*Manana por la manana. Pronto.*"

"He says 'Yes, tomorrow morning, pronto.' " Eliot explained to Lynn. When he saw the relief in her face he smiled and relaxed as well. He reached a hand to the commander. "*Muchas gracias,*" he said. "Lynn and I both appreciate your hospitality."

"*Sí,*" Commander Hernandez said, shaking Eliot's hand vigorously. "You can tell your *Americano* friends of the *Contras* with the warm and friendly hearts."

"Then I can make mention of you back in the States?" Eliot asked cautiously.

"*Sí,*" Commander Hernandez growled, removing his hand. "*Americanos* and Hondurans as well known we are here on Carmen Island but they do not know exactly *where.* I am proud of my cause. Publicity will not hurt me nor my men." He gestured with a wide sweep of his hand. "*De todos modos,* soon we will be gone from this place."

"Oh? How come?" Lynn asked interestedly, sensing a possible newsworthy story.

"The war of the guerrilla is one of mobility and

ambush," Commander Hernandez said. "One has to be able to move quickly at any time. When things get shaky here, we move someplace else."

Lynn noticed that the men sitting around the circle of the fire were watching intently as their commander was talking to his visitors, though she assumed few of them understood English. Some were now smoking cigarettes, and some were eating guava fruit they had picked from a tree. Most of the soldiers wore rosaries around their necks and one had two safety pins fixed on his cap in the shape of a cross, to show his commitment to the Roman Catholic faith.

"This group I command is called *Batalion Aguilar*, or Eagle Battalion," Commander Hernandez said, offering a cigarette to Eliot. When Eliot shook his head, Hernandez placed it between his own lips and lighted it with a burning twig he had pulled from the fire. Then he leaned back on one elbow. "*Batalion Aguilar* means to be strong," he boasted proudly.

Eliot stretched his legs out before him and also leaned back on an elbow. "I've read much about the *Contra* cause," he said. "But I'd like to ask you firsthand . . . What is it you hope to achieve?"

Commander Hernandez let smoke drift slowly from between his narrow lips, staring intently into the fire. "There is much repression," he growled. "Religion is totally suppressed and there is not enough food for the poor."

"And do you think you will be *victorioso?*" Eliot continued.

"We will bury the hearts of the enemy!" Commander Hernandez said hotly. "We are fighting a guerrilla war and in a guerrilla war, the name of the game, as you *Americanos* say, is staying power. Eventually, when people realize we will not be defeated, more of the *poblacion* will join us. *Sí*. We *will* in the end be *victorioso!*"

Eliot didn't know whether to wish him good luck or not since as an unofficial emissary of the United States, his position was somewhat ambiguous, to say the least. So he just smiled and let the commander keep on talking.

"Guerrilla warfare is an art," Commander Hernandez said enthusiastically. "You have to learn it and my men have learned it well."

A dinner bell cut through the calm of the evening.

"*Comida!*" Commander Hernandez said, rising quickly to his feet. "Shall we go eat, my *Americano* friends?" He half bowed and gestured with a sweep of his arm for Lynn and Eliot to pass on by him as Eliot helped Lynn up from the ground.

They were ushered into a large adobe house lighted dimly by two kerosene lamps on a long dinner table where a variety of food steamed in pottery bowls. At a fireplace at the far end of the room a big pot of beans was boiling over the fire and the cook was slicing up a tropical root called *malanga* into another pot which held what looked like vegatable soup.

"Help yourselves," Commander Hernandez said, sinking into a chair at the head of the table.

Lynn glanced behind her as Eliot pulled a chair from beneath the table for her. A row of rifles rested against the wall and cartons of ammunition were piled to one side.

As she settled onto the chair next to Eliot, Lynn

looked curiously from soldier to soldier. They had already begun eating from tin plates. She knew that only a portion of the soldiers were here, realizing that they ate in shifts all hours of the day and night. Some of them would probably be manning the guardposts, with shifts of four hours each throughout the night.

"How do you get supplies if no one is supposed to know your location?" Eliot asked as an assortment of spicy foods was piled on his plate and Lynn's by Commander Hernandez.

"Low-flying planes drop our supplies," Commander Hernandez said. "We have connections. We are well supplied with uniforms and all necessary armaments."

"Which government . . ." Eliot began, then stopped in mid-sentence when he saw Commander Hernandez's hand drop to the pistol at his waist as he glowered back at Eliot.

"*Lo siento*," Eliot quickly said, clearing his throat nervously. "I was out of line to ask such a question of the commander. Please excuse me."

A slow smile lifted Commander Hernandez's lips and the kerosene lantern lit up the deep lines of his face, making him look older and somehow less sinister. He reached for a bottle from the center of the table and patted it fondly.

"Let us *beber a la salud de brindar por* our success in life, my friend." He laughed raucously.

"Ah, yes. A toast. Right," Eliot said, lifting his tin cup for Commander Hernandez to fill it. He nodded toward Lynn. "Your cup, darling," he whispered.

"From the looks of things, I think a toast would be the last thing you'd want to share with that man," she whispered back. "For a moment there I thought we both were going to be shot!"

"Lynn, your *cup*," Eliot persisted, whispering at her out of the corner of his mouth.

"Oh, all right . . ." she murmured. She held her cup next to Eliot's, frowning as Commander Hernandez filled them both.

"*Aquardiente*," Commander Hernandez chuckled. "White rum." He placed the bottle on the table and then picked up a different one, holding it out for Lynn's inspection. "Or perhaps you would have preferred *vino de coyol*, sparkling wine not unlike French champagne. It is obtained from the sap of the coyol palm."

"This will be fine," Lynn said. She wished the meal were over so she and Eliot could return to the privacy of their little house. Then maybe the night would pass quickly and their trip to Leon would begin. She had noticed a battered jeep outside in the compound. Maybe, just maybe they would be treated to this means of transportation instead of heaving to walk or return by mule to Leon.

"Bottoms up, *senorita* Lynn and *senor* Eliot," Commander Hernandez said, swallowing his rum in one huge gulp.

Lynn lifted the cup gingerly to her lips, then flinched as the fiery liquid rolled down her throat and into her stomach. The burning in her throat brought quick tears to her eyes but she blinked them back and gasped quietly to herself as she placed the cup back on the table, only one-third emptied.

"Perhaps, *senorita* Lynn, now you are also ready for more nourishment that will stick to the *estomago,"* Commander Hernandez said, reaching his thick hands to the bowls of food in the center of the table.

"Yes, please," Lynn said, holding one hand against her throat, silently cursing the powerful alcoholic drink and only hoping the spices added to the food wouldn't add to the fire in her stomach.

Hernandez piled *tortillas* and *arepas* on her plate. The second helping was even bigger than the first, but when the fruit tray was passed to her, she readily spooned fried bananas, berries and nuts onto her plate, and then added hard-boiled eggs, dried pork sticks and beans in tomato sauce.

"I'm glad you're not on a diet," Eliot said, chuckling.

"I have been, remember?" she said. "A forced diet. I'm just making up for lost time." She began eagerly forking the food into her mouth, ignoring the soldiers' eyes on her, watching her. She didn't care if they thought she was a pig. She was hungry, and she intended to eat her fill now while she had the opportunity!

Eliot took another mouthful of beans. "Tomorrow, darling," he whispered. "We should be back in Leon by tomorrow."

"And San Francisco the next day," she sighed.

"I'm not sure that's the best place for us," he said quietly.

"Why on earth not?" Lynn asked, eyes wide. She bit into a fried banana and savored its sweetness on her tongue. "Aren't you as anxious to get back home as I am?"

Eliot slipped a hand under the table and squeezed one of her knees. "Yes and no. If you recall, when we were back in the States, we didn't exactly get along all that well."

"If *you'll* recall," Lynn said sharply, "that was because of what happened at the station. If you think I've forgotten that, or that my feelings about it have changed, you're mistaken."

"Are you referring to my replacing Adam or the fact that I was appointed Program Director?"

Lynn cast him a sour look. "Eliot, you know the answer to that," she whispered. "I've told you enough times."

"Both, huh?" he mumbled.

"You got it," she said dryly.

"What can I do to make you forget?" he asked. When he saw the blush rise to her cheeks, he chuckled. "I mean forget *forever*," he leaned his lips close to her ear, "not only when we're making love."

Frustrated, annoyed, and embarrassed, Lynn reached for her cup and took a quick swallow, forgetting how powerful its contents were. As the liquor scalded its way down her throat and insides, her eyes began to water. Knocking the cup over, she leaped up from her chair, clutching her throat and gasping.

"Lynn?" Eliot said, rising too, and grabbing her by a wrist. "I didn't mean to upset you so much!" Then he chuckled when he saw what the true cause for her seizure had been.

"Go ahead and laugh!" she rasped. "Very funny, I'm sure!"

Swinging around she rushed outside and took a deep, shuddering breath to cool her throat. She looked toward the sky, seeing an enormous full moon sailing overhead. In its silvery light, she saw Eliot hurrying after her.

269

"I'm sorry," he said, clasping her hands tightly. "I always seem to be rubbing you the wrong way and that's the last thing I want to do. Forgiven?"

"Eliot, please . . ." Lynn sighed. "Just go on back inside and finish your meal, okay?"

"Only if you'll go with me."

"I'm suddenly not so hungry any more," she said stubbornly.

Eliot released her hands and walked a few feet away from her, staring up into the sky at the moon and the sequined stars. "Funny," he murmured. "I'm not either." He turned and boldly faced her again. "Except for one thing."

Lynn set her jaw firmly and lifted her chin. "That's your answer to everything, isn't it?" she whispered.

"What do you mean?"

"Sex," she said flatly.

He strolled casually back to her and traced her facial features with one gentle finger. "Only when I'm with you," he said huskily. He kissed the tip of her nose. "Admit it, Lynn," he said. "It's the same for you. You know it is. You couldn't live without me now, could you?" His smile could only be described as smug.

"You are a conceited oaf!" she whispered harshly, jerking away from him, and stormed toward their adobe house where a soft, golden light glowed through the window from the one kerosene lantern they had lighted before leaving. Flinging the door open, Lynn hurried on inside. A distinct chill raced through her, as she became aware of the dampness of the night cloaking her in its sheer, colorless garment.

The house smelled pleasantly of woodsmoke,

reminding Lynn of the warmth she and Eliot had shared while building the fire in the fireplace. Now seeing only a few shimmering flames stroking the half-burned log, she went to the fireplace and placed several more logs on the embers. She settled onto the earthen floor in front of it and tucked one foot beneath her, watching the flames take hold and becoming almost hypnotized by the brilliant patterns they made as they danced and flickered.

At this moment she hated herself. Why had she gotten so angry at Eliot? Why did he bring out this unattractive aspect of her personality? There was no denying her love for him. He'd been right—without him, life would no longer have any meaning. Why couldn't she just give in to her feelings? But she *knew* why, didn't she? The fireplace and its magical allure was suddenly a reminder of just why she seemed to always be battling her emotional reactions to Eliot.

Remembering evenings before the fire in her Illinois home, sitting with Randy, sharing popcorn and sodas, Lynn felt a slow, agonizing tearing of her heart. Somehow if she let herself love Eliot so deeply, she felt she was being disloyal to her memories of Randy.

She closed her eyes tightly, trying to bring her dead husband's face into focus in her mind's eye. Cold sweat popped out on her brow as she thought harder and harder. But only Eliot's face would materialize. His roguish smile tantalized and teased her, angering her to the point of letting out an exasperated cry.

"Lynn, what on earth is the matter?" Eliot asked, suddenly dropping down on his knees beside her.

Feeling like a fool, Lynn turned her head and

271

avoided meeting his eyes. In the flesh, he was an even greater challenge to her sense. Oh, what was she to do? And tomorrow when *real* life began, all over again . . .

Eliot forced her head around with a forefinger beneath her chin. "Lynn, please don't start that again," he murmured.

Lynn's resolve wavered. His slightest touch made her tremble, draining her strength away, making her feel as though she were melting inside. Never since Randy had a man had such power over her—and it was at this moment that she at last felt resigned to the fact of Randy's death, ready to give her heart totally to another man. She felt she was finally able to put all antagonism behind her, this time for good, and from this moment on let her heart as well as her body accept Eliot and all the love he offered her.

"I'm sorry," she murmured. A tear sparkled at the corners of her eyes as she slowly lifted a hand to his cheek. "But, Eliot, sometimes you do drive me crazy!"

"Because I tease you so much?"

Lynn laughed softly. "Well, yes, that's part of it."

"And what's the rest of it?"

"I guess—I just didn't want to let myself love you so much," she whispered, slipping into his embrace. Suddenly she felt completely at peace and more content than any other time in her whole life, in spite of their precarious situation.

"But you do?" he said huskily. "It's not just the *aguardiente* making you so mellow and loving, is it?" he teased, burrowing his nose in the thickness of her hair.

A sigh escaped Lynn. "Eliot, there you go again,"

she said. "*Please* stop teasing me! I'm completely serious, and completely sober."

"Forgive me, Lynn," he said gently.

"I'm a woman," Lynn whispered. "And I want to be treated like a woman, not like a child who has to be humored and jollied along."

"I see no problem with that," Eliot murmured. "No problem at all."

"You don't?"

"No," he said. He looked deeply into her eyes. "Don't you think there's just a little too much light in here?"

"Too much light?"

"Yes," Eliot said. He rose to his feet, and went over to the kerosene lamp and turned it out. With a trace of a smile, he yanked a blanket from the bed and began spreading it on the earthen floor beside Lynn.

Lynn eyed him quizzically. "Now what are you up to, as if I couldn't guess?" she asked, watching as he smoothed the wrinkles from the blanket.

"One guess is all you get," Eliot said, softly.

"It's more than I need," said Lynn, laughing. "Experience has taught me to interpret that glint in your eye. You're like an open book, my darling— I can read you so well!"

Eliot settled down on the blanket and reached for her hand. "Which chapter are you on now?" he asked.

Lynn pretended to think deeply about his question, then said, "I'm about halfway through. A real page-turner. I can hardly wait to see what happens next!"

"Do you predict a happy ending, darling?"

"There may even be a *sequel*," Lynn giggled. As Eliot's hand lowered and cupped one breast through the heavy material of her uniform shirt, she caught her breath and shivered uncontrollably, and not from the cold.

"Come here, baby," Eliot said, his words thick with desire for her. His hands gently drew her down onto the blanket next to him.

"The windows . . ." Lynn softly protested.

"It's dark in here, Lynn. No one can see in."

"The fire lights the room as though it was daylight," Lynn whispered, slowly falling victim to the rapture she felt as Eliot framed her face between his hands and leaned closer to her, lavishing soft kisses across her face.

"The soldiers are busy eating and drinking. We have complete privacy. Don't worry, Lynn. Just let me love you."

"Yes," she whispered. "Love me!" She closed her eyes and arched her neck as Eliot's fingers unbuttoned her shirt and slipped it from her shoulders. With sexual excitement building inside her, Lynn welcome Eliot's eager lips on first one nipple, then the other as he caressed her breasts with sure, sweet strokes.

She felt the wild pounding of her heart as she lifted her hips to make it easier for him to finish undressing her until she lay, naked and trembling beneath his hot gaze. Then it was his turn to remove his clothes as she watched, impatient to feel the warm, hard length of his body next to hers. She had never needed or desired him so fiercely. As Eliot gathered her into his arms and lowered himself over her, she gasped, raising her body to meet his, easing his entry, moaning and writhing as she felt his hardness within her.

His hot lips tasted the flesh of her neck, his fingers caressed her swollen breasts. She writhed in rapturous response.

The flame of desire leaped between them, fusing their bodies together in heated passion. When Eliot's lips moved to hers and kissed her demandingly, she answered him with a quivering, intense surrender of her entire being.

Lynn twined her arms about his neck and clung to him. Her breasts felt on fire as his hand stroked and fondled them.

"I love you . . ." Lynn whispered, moaning as Eliot's lips moved from the hollow of her throat to her breasts and began sucking first on one nipple, then the other.

"Lynn, I need you so much . . ." he groaned against her flesh. He clasped her even closer to him, making her his willing prisoner, as his thrusts slowed inside her and became instead long, smooth strokes, as though he were trying to savor every movement, every sensation, making the moment last as long as possible.

"Eliot . . ." Lynn whimpered harshly, knowing that the instant of blissful, ecstatic release had come, "now, darling. Now . . . !"

Her eyes closed spasmodically and her breath caught in her throat as the magic of the moment carried her on the crest of a wave of passion like nothing she had ever experienced before, then burst into a million droplets of pleasure coursing through every vein.

When Eliot's pleasure was also spent, Lynn sighed

and snuggled next to him, as content as a child, innocent and without a care in the world. As Eliot's fingers gently stroked one breast, a joyous tremor rushed across her flesh.

"Cold?" Eliot murmured, drawing her even closer to him, against the hard contours of his body.

"How could I be after that?" she said, laughing softly.

"You just shivered."

"Because your hands do such crazy things to me."

"Will they always?" he asked huskily, letting his fingers graze the tautness of one nipple.

"Always," she whispered, raising up to kiss him softly on the lips. Then she giggled again as her hand ran across the coarseness of his whiskers. If they didn't get back to civilization soon, he'd look like one of the bearded guerillas.

Eliot reached up and rubbed his whiskers. "You like?" he asked.

"I like you with or without," Lynn murmured, nibbling at his shoulder, loving the manly taste of him.

Eliot lowered his head and began rubbing his whiskers teasingly from one of her breasts to the other. "How does that feel?"

Lynn laughed silkily. "If you don't stop, I'm going to turn into a sex fiend for the second time tonight!" she murmured shakily, feeling passion once more welling up inside her.

"I can stand it if you can," Eliot said huskily. "This will be our last night in paradise, so we'd better make the most of it."

"Anywhere you are would be paradise," she said.

"Even San Francisco?"

"Even San Francisco," she told him firmly.

"Then I don't mind going home," he said, leaning up on an elbow and looking down at her.

"Why should you mind?"

Eliot's face became suddenly shadowed remembering Lynn's involvement with Adam Lowenstein. Adam was waiting, threatening to destroy the happiness they had found.

"Eliot, you didn't answer me," Lynn persisted. "Why do you look so glum?"

Eliot scooped her into his arms and held her tightly. "It's nothing, darling," he said. "Absolutely nothing at all."

# *Fifteen*

HANGING ON to her seat for dear life, Lynn swallowed hard as the jeep careened in and out of deep ruts. First she was on the seat and then she was just as quickly bouncing off it again. Her teeth seemed to be rattling in her head. This road was a challenge that she hadn't planned on.

"I think I liked the mule better," she shouted to Eliot between spine-jarring jolts.

Eliot laughed as Lynn looked over her shoulder at him, a harried expression on her face. He had given her first choice of seats in the jeep, but she apparently wasn't getting an easier ride in the front seat, next to the driver, than he was in the rear.

"Very funny," she said, groaning as she fell sideways and her elbow hit the door with a loud crack.

"*Perdone,*" the driver said, giving Lynn a quick glance. "*Lo siento, Senorita* Lynn. The roads are *de mala calidad!*"

Lynn gave Eliot a questioning look over her shoulder and he quickly translated.

"*Poor,*" he shouted. "He says the roads are poor!"

"Oh," Lynn said, laughing nervously. She settled back into her seat, turning toward the soldier. "*Sí.*

They sure are!" She got even more nervous watching the careless way in which he was handling the steering wheel. It seemed to be going every which way.

"How much farther?" she asked, checking inside her front left pants pocket to see if the one souvenir of her adventure was still there. A warm glow inside her at the touch of the gemstone told her that it was. She had come close to discarding her ruined Levi's without rescuing the garnet from the pocket. But when it had bounced out onto the floor, she had been readily reminded that she had almost left behind a precious memento that could prove to everyone just how exotic their experience had been when she explained how she had managed to obtain it.

She repeated her question to the soldier. "How much farther?"

The soldier gave her a blank look, shrugged, then focused his eyes straight ahead.

Eliot moved to the edge of his seat and tapped the soldier's shoulder. "*Millaje, numero de millas?*" he shouted. He gestured with a hand. "*Numero de kilometros.* How many more miles?"

"*Mucho,*" the soldier shouted back at him.

"Nice," Lynn sighed. "Real nice."

"You understood that, Lynn?"

"*Mucho* has to mean a lot," she grumbled.

"But at least we're on our way back," Eliot said, reaching to lift her hair from the nape of her neck.

"Yes. Thank God!" Lynn said, closing her eyes, and relishing the touch of his hand on her flesh. As he kneaded her tense muscles, she felt her shoulders relax a little. But only a delicious, cool shower would relieve her of that heat and the oppressive effect of the jungle humidity. It was as though a heavy weight was pressing in on her, threatening to stifle her completely.

Eliot once more tapped the soldier on the shoulder. In Spanish he explained that it would be a good idea to stop and rest a while. With an eager nod, the soldier pulled the jeep to a clanking halt.

"Well, *finally*," Lynn murmured.

Eliot jumped from the jeep and helped Lynn over the side. Together they struggled through the deep ruts of this crude road that had been carved out of the side of a low, spreading mountain.

"The rainy season took its toll on *this* road," Eliot growled. "We're damn lucky it's not raining now, or we just might be stuck here for days."

"It feels so good to stretch my legs," Lynn sighed. She placed a hand on the small of her back and tried to rub the ache out of it.

Eliot pointed. "Look, Lynn," he said. "Way off in the distance you can catch the shine from the buildings of Leon. We really don't have that much farther to go!"

A low drone overhead caused Lynn to look up. Against the backdrop of the brilliant blue sky she could see the most welcome sight in many days—an airplane with the bold red insignia of Southern Airlines on its side. One of those planes would take Eliot and Lynn back to the States.

"Oh, if we were only at the airport now," she sighed beneath her breath.

"What's that?" Eliot asked, putting an arm around her waist. "What did you say?"

"Do you see that plane?" she said, shielding her eyes with one hand as she watched it growing smaller and smaller as it receded into the distance. "Tomorrow we'll be flying out of here!"

"Can't help but see that big bird in the sky," Eliot chuckled. "It may not be as colorful as the birds here in the jungle, but it's a damn sight prettier to these anxious eyes."

Lynn linked her arms about his waist and rested her cheek against his chest. "This *is* a lovely place though," she sighed.

"Having second thoughts?"

"About what?"

"About going back to civilization?"

Lynn gave him a half smile as she looked up at him. "Eliot, you've *got* to be kidding," she said. "It's not that pretty!"

"You have to admit that it hasn't been all bad," he chided, kissing her forehead. "Now was it?"

"I learned a lot about myself and you while we were lost in the jungle," Lynn said quietly. She was letting her eyes absorb the lush green of the rolling, verdant jungle below them, the glitter from some distant waterfall, possibly even the one they had found, and the purple shadows of the highest mountain peaks farther in the distance. It was a panorama of breathtaking loveliness and somehow, ironic as it seemed, she was feeling a pang of sadness at the thought of leaving it all behind.

"Like what?" Eliot said, drawing her around to face him.

Seeing the bearded guerilla who was leisurely smoking a cigarette and leaning against the jeep, looking at them with interest, Lynn lowered her eyes. "Not here, Eliot," she whispered. "Not with an audience."

Eliot glanced back at the man, smiled absently toward him and nodded a silent 'hello'. Then he once more turned his full attention to Lynn. "I see what you mean," he murmured.

"I have so much to say to you, Eliot," Lynn said, smiling up into his eyes. "But later, when we're alone."

"And I have a lot to tell you, too," he said, wanting so badly to kiss her. But the eyes boring into his back made him realize that this too would have to wait until he and Lynn had some privacy.

Lynn turned once more to let her eyes take in the setting, memorizing every feature of the landscape. "I wonder exactly where we were out there," she said, gesturing with a sweep of her hand. "It all looks alike now, as though nothing could penetrate that thick blanket of green."

"I wonder how we happen to be on this mountainside," Eliot mused. "Seems the best guides are the guerilla soldiers. They sure could give the guides hired to lead the expedition in and out of the jungle a lesson or two."

"It doesn't matter," Lynn sighed. "We will soon be home! And I for one can hardly wait!"

The soldier interrupted their peaceful talk, saying in Spanish that it was time to move on. There were dangers in staying in one place too long. Remaining on the mountainside, in plain view, was a danger it itself.

Lynn climbed back into the jeep, preparing herself for the rough ride ahead. She glanced down at her attire, imagining the reaction of the guests at the hotel when she entered the lobby dressed like a guerilla soldier. If Hank were still there, he'd probably whip out his camera to film their arrival back to civilization. Instead of just filming newsworthy events, they had become the news themselves.

"We're off," Eliot said from behind Lynn, as he held onto the back of her seat. "From now on it'll be downhill all the way now. Hang on to your hat."

"I would," Lynn laughed. "If only I still *had* my hat!"

Eliot had a moment of consternation when he saw a long row of *Contras* suddenly come into view at the side of the road, seemingly out of nowhere, as the jeep made a quick turn. Like the others he and Lynn had seen, they carried the semiautomatic rifles slung across their shoulders. Then the jeep moved on past them and around more curves and up and down more hills, swerving and bouncing recklessly from side to side, and Eliot and Lynn both heaved a sigh of relief.

"The ruts are getting worse," Lynn shouted, clutching tightly to the seat. "It hardly seems possible!"

Eliot moved over to the left side of the jeep and began shouting in Spanish to the driver, trying to direct him which way to turn the steering wheel in order to miss the ruts, afraid the jeep might topple over the side of the mountain at any time.

"Bad ruts on the right," he said in Spanish, then, "Washout on the left!"

Washouts began to be even more prevalent and troublesome. Sometimes they were on both sides of the road at once. Steep dropoffs loomed as the jeep wound down the mountain road. Eliot knew that the penalty for a wrong turn of the wheel could be very high—fatal, in fact.

"Eliot," Lynn cried, glancing anxiously back at him. "Ahead. Look ahead!"

Eliot's eyes widened, seeing one of the worst double washouts yet. *"Parar las ruedas,"* he shouted to the driver. All three were jolted forward as the jeep came to a sudden halt.

"Come on, Lynn," Eliot said, reaching a hand to her. "We'll have to get out and guide him down the middle of what's left of the road."

"Good Lord!" Lynn groaned, stepping out onto the ground. She inched her way along the side of the jeep, looking down into the deep gorge below. One misguided footstep, one slip of the jeep's wheel, and they would be lost—this time forever.

"You direct him on one side while I take the other," Eliot ordered.

"I'll try," Lynn said, stepping cautiously over and then down the side of the washout to get to the other side of the road. Trees clinging to the side of the hill behind her made her feel somewhat safer. She grabbed a limb and leaned in front of the jeep waving her hand as Eliot did the same. The jeep inched ahead, careened sideways, then proceeded at a snail's pace until all four wheels were on solid ground. Lynn sighed with relief, climbed back into the jeep and grinned nervously at Eliot.

"I'm beginning to wonder if we'll reach Leon in one piece," she murmured.

"We'll get there," he assured her, patting her shoulder. "Just seems to be taking longer than I thought it would."

"You think a jeep would make better time than

those pokey mules," she said irritably.

"Consider it an object lesson in why mules were used in the expedition," he said, clinging to the side of the jeep as it once more began to bounce its way along the road.

"As I said before, a mule would even be welcome!" she laughed. Then her laugh turned into a groan when the jeep again stopped abruptly. She heard the driver grumble what had to be obscenities as he looked over the side of the jeep. It seemed to be stuck.

"Not again!" Eliot groaned. He too looked downward, then cast Lynn a harried look. "It's a concrete culvert of all things," he added gloomily.

"Now what do we do?"

"We'll see," Eliot said, jumping out as the driver began pressing his foot on the accelerator. Smoke filled the air as the wheels spun furiously, but the wheel only sank even more deeply into the rut just in front of the culvert. It appeared to be stuck for good.

Lynn climbed from the jeep and inspected the damage. "Eliot, I don't like the looks of that," she said, nodding toward the tire that was partially exposed above the deep rut. "In Illnois, where I grew up, we had rules for driving in winter—always take a shovel and a bag of sand. It gives you traction on the ice. But since there's no ice in the tropics, I guess there's no sand or shovel, right?"

Eliot combed his fingers wearily through his hair. "Right," he echoed. He gave the soldier a half smile as he climbed from behind the wheel to join in inspecting the damage.

Eliot and he exchanged many words in Spanish

and Lynn's heart sank when she saw the driver shrug and shake his head from side to side. She went to Eliot's side and touched him gingerly on the arm. "What is it, Eliot?" she asked apprehensively.

"Well, this guy says that the road is 'very good now' in comparison," he said, laughing. "I guess it really gets bad when it rains."

"Why was he shrugging his shoulders and shaking his head like that?" she persisted. "You're not telling me the whole story, are you? He was telling you that it's hopeless, wasn't he?"

"Lynn, I'm not keeping anything from you," Eliot said. "All he said was that the road wasn't all that bad. Honest."

"So if it's not all that bad, why aren't we on our way to Leon instead of standing here staring at a damn jeep in a rut?" Lynn fumed, crossing her arms across her chest and tapping her foot.

"We'll get out," he mumbled. "Somehow."

"Any suggestions?"

"We'll have to start pitching everything in sight beneath the wheels," Eliot said, already picking up stones and throwing them into the rut. "Stones, leaves, sticks—anything to give us traction."

Lynn began helping, cursing as her fingers were scratched by the rough-textured leaves and the sharp edges of the rocks. Eliot was digging into the sand at the side of the road with his fingers, dumping handfuls of it beneath the wheel, and Lynn started working beside him.

The only solution seemed to be to build a kind of bridge across part of the gulley. More sand was scooped up and then packed around the rocks. Eliot stamped it down over and over again, then fell once more to his knees, shaping and forming the sand beneath the wheel.

After a while, Eliot, sweating and exhausted, rose to his feet and wiped his hands on his pants. "There," he wearily announced. "That should do it." He went over to the driver and told him that it appeared their labors were over and that the jeep should be drivable now.

Lynn stood back and watched intently as the jeep's motor began whining and the tires spun and spun on the debris beneath them. "Let's give it a push, Eliot," she suggested, willing to do anything to get underway once more for Leon. If they failed, she knew there was no way to call AAA for a tow.

"Sure?" Eliot said, lifting an eyebrow at her.

"I've pushed cars out of ruts before," she said stoutly. "At home in Illinois. Remember? I was my father's 'son'."

Eliot chuckled and said, "Okay. What are we waiting for? Start shoving, sonny-boy!"

Leaning her full weight against the jeep, Lynn shoved and pushed, helping Eliot rock the vehicle back and forth. The jeep lurched, bounced and rocked over the washout. For one horrible second, the right rear wheel had been spinning on thin air. And then it was back in the rut again.

Lynn's back ached and sweat poured from every inch of her body. It seemed like hours before the jeep finally rolled free, and when it did, the sudden movement caught Lynn unawares. She stumbled and fell clumsily in the dirt.

Cursing under her breath, she glared at Eliot who was standing over her, smiling amusedly. "What's so funny?" she hissed.

"You look real cute sprawled there," Eliot said, offering her a hand up.

"That's one compliment I can do without!" she snapped as she got to her feet with his help. "Don't you have even *one* clumsy bone in your body? It seems I'm always the klutzy one."

"Poor baby," Eliot crooned, pulling her into his arms.

Lynn pushed against his chest. "Eliot, I'm all sweaty!" she said. She wiped the perspiration off her face with the sleeve of her shirt. "I must not only smell terrible but I probably look terrible as well."

Eliot ran his hand caressingly over her hair. "You still look good to me—smell good, too," he said.

"Well, I'd argue that," Lynn said. She eyed the soldier who was looking impatiently back at her and Eliot as he sat waiting, the jeep motor running. "Eliot, let's go," she urged, swinging around and walking toward the jeep. "It surely can't be much longer now."

Once they were settled in the jeep, it moved clumsily on down the mountainside and then onto flat land. They splashed across two streams that happened to flow right across the road. An occasional hut could now be seen in the clearings where leather-faced farmers worked the land.

"*Campesinos*," Eliot called them, meaning farm workers.

Just as quickly as the flat land had been reached, the jeep was climbing another steep grade once more, overlooking a dense, rolling vista of green. But something else caught Lynn's eye. It was the sight of distant buildings—the city of Leon!

288

"We're almost there," Lynn cried, looking delightedly back at Eliot.

"I see . . ." Eliot said, then bit down unexpectedly into his lower lip when he was thrust against the front seat as the jeep made a dangerous lurch and came to a sudden halt in another double washout.

When a groan of pain and frustration, Eliot pulled himself up from the floor of the jeep. He ran his tongue over the wound in his lip and tasted the saltiness of blood. He caught Lynn's eye as she sat staring back at him with an expression of deep concern on her face.

"You ought to be laughing, you know," Eliot grumbled.

"Eliot, I have a heart," she said softly. "Are you hurt badly?"

"No, I suppose I'll live," he muttered. Then he said, "Are you saying I *don't* have a heart just because I laughed at you under the same sort of circumstances?"

"I don't feel like laughing at anything right at this moment," Lynn sighed. "Haven't you noticed? This darn jeep is stuck again. And it appears to be worse than the last time. It looks as though we'll never get to Leon!"

Eliot licked the blood from his lip and climbed from the jeep. Upon closer inspection, he discovered that the right side of the road had been sheered off. There was no way the jeep could proceed.

The driver started gesturing with his hands and rattling off in Spanish so quickly that Lynn's head was spinning. She questioned Eliot with her eyes.

"He says we can't go any farther," Eliot said, scowling down the side of the embankment. "He wants to back up the way he came and leave us to find our way alone into town."

Lynn's insides froze at the thought. She looked longingly toward the glimmer of buildings in the distance. Knowing that they would probably have to proceed on foot made them look much farther away now.

"You can't be serious," she murmured.

"He also said that this was about as far as he was planning to bring us anyway," Eliot continued, "even if we hadn't run into more road problems."

"What?" Lynn gasped.

"He can't take a chance on getting any closer to Leon for fear of someone possibly seeing him and following him back to the camp," Eliot said. "It makes sense, Lynn, from his point of view. Seems we have no choice. I guess we ought to feel lucky we've made it this far. A bit farther on foot won't be all that bad."

"I suppose you're right," she sighed. "It seems we have no choice." She gave the *Contra* soldier a wavering smile, then said a polite *"Muchas gracias,"* as she climbed out of the jeep once again.

*"Sí, no hay de que,"* he said, bobbing his head up and down.

Lynn stepped cautiously over the hills and valleys of ruts to Eliot's side and clung to his arm as she watched the jeep rock back and forth until it suddenly shot backward. As it wound up the hill and out of sight, Lynn looked up into Eliot's eyes and said, "Well, I believe that's the last we'll see of the *Contras*."

"They weren't really such a bad lot, you know," Eliot said, scratching absently at his chin whiskers.

"Well? Shall we get going?" Lynn asked, gesturing with a weary hand toward the battered road.

"Yes. Let's," Eliot said, swinging into stride next to her.

They struggled through the ruts and gulleys until suddenly there was no road at all, just a drop-off that led down to the flatter land of the dense jungle.

"Now what?" Lynn groaned.

"Not much choice," Eliot shrugged. "Seems we have to go down there if we're going to get back to Leon."

"If you say so," Lynn said, laughing nervously.

"We have our bearings this time," Eliot reassured. "We know which way to go. There's no chance of our getting lost."

"If you say so," Lynn said dubiously, then accepted his hand as he began helping her down, away from the road.

Lynn wanted to inch down the hillside but it was so steep that she soon was scrambling, ducking loose rocks that tumbled after her, some hitting her shoulders or the top of the head. Her foot slipped and she let out a shriek as she fell the rest of the way down, gashing her thumb on a rock. When she landed at the bottom, smack on an anthill, she found that her sudden arrival had not been received particularly well. The indignant ants began swarming around her, stinging every exposed inch of flesh.

"Ouch!" she cried, fighting them off. "Eliot! God, help me, will you?"

Eliot came to the rescue, dusting off the ants as best he could. Then he sat down on the ground beside her, laughing until tears rolled down his face into his beard.

"You did it again!" she hissed.

"What?" he said, almost choking with mirth.

"Laughed at me!" she cried. "Eliot Smith, how could I *not* have laughed at you? I should have. You always find my misfortunes so damned funny!"

"Sorry," Eliot said, wiping tears from his eyes with the back of a hand. "But I've never seen so many ants!"

"I didn't have to see them—I felt them," she grumbled. She stretched out a hand before her and inspected the growing welts. "As if I don't already have enough injuries as a result of this trip! Now I have *ant* bites!"

"Well, I imagine you'll live," Eliot said, rising and helping her up from the ground.

"Sure. I'll live," she said, pulling angrily away from him. "No thanks to you!"

"I scared away all those nasty critters, didn't I?" he teased.

"Now that was quite an accomplishment, wasn't it," Lynn said sarcastically. "You should receive a medal for valor!"

"Enough, already," Eliot laughed. "Come on, darling. Let's make tracks and see how fast our legs can carry us back to civilization."

"You have no machete this time," Lynn reminded him.

"To hell with a machete," he grumbled. "I'll tear these vines and creepers away with my bare hands if it means getting us back to Leon!"

"You're really anxious to get back to your position as program director, aren't you, Eliot?" Lynn said icily.

"Oh, Lynn, for God's sake!"

Lynn swallowed hard and hung her head. "I know," she said. "I shouldn't have said that. It just kind of popped out."

"That means you still . . ."

Lynn turned to him and sealed his lips with a sweet kiss, then withdrew hastily as he winced, remembering the wound inflicted on his lip as the result of the jeep's sudden stop.

"You really *did* get hurt, didn't you?" Lynn whispered, touching his swollen mouth.

"No," he assured her. "Nothing but a scratch." Then he took her by the hand. "Let's see what we can do to get us out of this place before nightfall."

Lynn tensed. "Surely it won't take that long," she said, scrambling over a fallen log as they moved onward.

Eliot laughed. "I was only kidding," he said.

"One day . . ." Lynn said, glaring at him, eyes flashing warning signals.

"I know," he chuckled. "I know. I'll get mine. Right?"

"You got it," Lynn said, then raised her head, letting her golden hair trail down her back. She couldn't help appreciating the darting, colorful birds overhead and the antics of the spider monkeys swinging from branch to branch. Things had a way of being lost from one's memory so quickly when one was absorbed in the busy schedule of "real life" . . .

A sparkle of blue ahead caught her eye. "A lagoon," she said.

"Want to take a swim?" Eliot asked. "This may be our last chance to enjoy the beauties of nature."

"I'm ready for some water, all right, but the kind

that comes out of a shower in an honest-to-goodness bathroom," she said. "Just keep walking. Don't you let any erotic ideas start floating around inside that raunchy head of yours."

"My brain is always swarming with erotic ideas," he said, drawing her next to him. "But I'll tell you about them tonight in the comforts of a bed in an air-conditioned suite."

The humidity didn't seem as bad today to Lynn, but perhaps it was only because she knew they were drawing closer to Leon. Now she saw fenced-in houses surrounded by small plots of farmland; there were squared-off plots of land where ripening bananas hung from stalks. Workers were busy in the fields, harvesting them, and mule-drawn carts were moving away from the fields out onto the same dirt road that Lynn and Eliot had just discovered and were now traveling on.

Lynn sighed with relief. "I just can't believe it!" she said. "We've just about made it. Two days ago I would have said it was impossible. I thought we were gone—lost forever."

"I'll try to flag down a ride," Eliot said, then ran over to one of the mule-drawn carts and conversed in rapid Spanish with the driver. When he waved for Lynn to come ahead, she hurried her pace and gladly climbed aboard the cart next to him. Dangling her feet from the end, clasping onto one side of the cart, she took one of Eliot's hands and squeezed it affectionately with her other free hand.

"It won't be long now," she said. "What a relief to be off our feet and on solid ground away from that blasted jeep!"

Houses multiplied at the side of the road and the

road turned into a cobblestone street as the cart moved slowly on toward the downtown district of Leon.

When the taller buildings began to draw near, Lynn wanted to jump from the cart and run head-long to the Saint Francis Hotel, but Eliot stopped her and smiled, shaking his head. "Darling, we'll get there soon enough," he said. "Be patient."

"Do you think everyone on the expedition has flown back to the States?" she asked, looking anxiously over her shoulder.

"Most likely," Eliot said.

The traffic had thickened now. Speeding taxis with their shouting drivers and an occasional pri-vately owned vehicle wound their way along through the widening streets. And when Leon's business district came into view, Lynn realized that, yes, they *had* made it back! It wasn't just a mirage. The sight of the Saint Francis Hotel confirmed this.

Eliot spoke a quick *Muchas gracias* to the driver of the mule cart then took Lynn's hand and jumped with her onto the street. Dodging swerving vehicles, they rushed on toward the hotel entrance.

Lynn took in the majestic facade of the building and its glittering cleanliness. Then she looked down at the way she was dressed and the dirt and filth of her ill-fitting clothes. When the eyes of passersby began turning her and Eliot's way, she felt a blush rising to her cheeks and hurried her pace into the hotel lobby, ducking her head.

Fortunately the lobby was almost void of people. Eliot went up to the front desk and asked whether his and Lynn's rooms were still being held in their names. At that point the hotel management realized just who these two dirty, disreputable-looking people were.

In a matter of minutes, reporters were swarming all over the lobby, their flashbulbs blinding Lynn. She covered her eyes with her hands, wishing she'd had a chance to get more presentable before being confronted with the barrage of questions.

But then a familiar voice reached Lynn's ears through the excited babble, and her heart leaped as she slowly lifted her hands from her eyes and spoke his name in a surprised, soft whisper.

"Adam!" she said. "Adam Lowenstein! Is it really you?"

Eliot set his jaw grimly as he saw Adam moving quickly toward Lynn, his arms outstretched in delighted welcome.

# *Sixteen*

IGNORING THE crowd around her pushing and throwing questions, Lynn rushed to meet Adam. Her heart beat excitedly as she took in his dear, familiar face, clear blue eyes and his short, gray hair. His beige sport coat and open shirt were wrinkled as though he might have slept in them, and she knew that he must have acquired such a disheveled look while worrying about her safe return.

"Oh, Adam!" she cried as she rushed into his embrace. "It really is you!" She hugged him tightly, resting her cheek against his chest. She closed her eyes and savored the warmth and security of his surrounding arms.

"Lynn, you're all right!" Adam said against her hair. "I've just about gone nuts with worry. And your parents—they're worried mindless!"

Lynn gave him one more quick hug, sighing happily. For so many years Adam had been her pillar of strength, the best friend anyone could ever hope to have. He had always been there, offering a shoulder to cry on if she needed one. And now he was there again, to comfort her.

Pulling gently away from him, Lynn gazed up into

his eyes. "Adam, why are you here? How . . . ?"

"KS90 sent me here on an assignment."

"Oh?"

He placed a finger to her chin. "You, my dear, are that assignment," he said. "I guess you must know that you two are the top news story all over the country."

Lynn laughed. "Yes, I kind of figured that."

Adam quickly bent over her, whispering in her ear. "Lynn, you're on camera. It's Hank. Turn around and give it all you have. Everybody will be seeing this, you know."

Being the professional she was, Lynn turned around and faced the camera, smiling radiantly at Hank. He had stayed on, hoping for their safe return and intending to capture it on film for KSFC-TV.

Forgetting her disheveled appearance, Lynn straightened her shoulders and began answering questions as Adam asked them. It seemed so right to be with Adam again in front of the camera. They were once more a team as they'd been for so many years.

Then suddenly Lynn caught a glimpse of Eliot, standing on the sidelines glaring at her. She and Adam were stealing his thunder, and not only that, but she remembered Eliot's jealousy of Adam. She knew that after her display of happiness at seeing Adam, Eliot's suspicions had been renewed.

Eliot gave her a wry smile along with a mock half salute and pushed his way through the crowd on his way to the elevator. Lynn felt frantic inside. She gave Adam a desperate look and started to move from his side to follow Eliot, but Adam's firm grip on her elbow caused her to remember the camera and the story the world was waiting to hear.

Forcing a smile, she glanced toward the elevator and when she no longer saw Eliot there, a slow ache began to form about her heart. At this point, there was no way to draw attention to him since he was no longer there. If anyone asked her, how could she possibly explain his absence?

Realizing Eliot's professionalism, Lynn was surprised to see that he had given up his part in this story so easily—and not only the story, but *her*. How could he?

"And that uniform you're wearing, Lynn . . ." a reporter shouted out at her. "Where did you get it? What happened to your own clothes?"

Knowing that she had to compose herself, Lynn blinked her eyes and cleared her throat before answering. Then, getting a grip on herself, she said, "A guerilla commander was kind enough to lend me this uniform because my own clothes had gotten ripped and were quite filthy."

Gasps and a murmur of startled comment at the mention of the guerillas made Lynn aware of what was to come. She was prepared to deal with it, yet she longed to rush to Eliot, apologize, and urge him to return to the lobby with her. Strangely enough, she felt that it wasn't Adam who belonged there at her side, but Eliot. She was feeling more and more disloyal by the moment . . .

"How did you happen to meet this guerilla commander and what was his name?" a newscaster shouted at her above the building excitement in the hotel lobby.

Lynn was wondering why no one had asked about Eliot's part in their adventure. Didn't anyone realize that they'd gone through it together? It was the same way she had felt when she had defended Adam during the contract dispute, only now it was Eliot who deserved her loyalty and dedication. He was her rightful co-host and, above all else, she *loved* him!

"Lynn, you didn't answer the question," Adam whispered into her ear.

She shook her head, trying to orient herself. "What question?" she whispered back, truly not remembering.

"About the guerilla commander—how you met him and what his name was."

Lynn focused her eyes straight ahead, trying to put Eliot out of her mind. He'd chosen to not be a part of the interview. It wasn't her place to force him to, was it?

But the battle inside her would not be won. She set her jaw firmly and said, "*Eliot Smith* and I were rescued from the wilds of the jungle by a *Contra* soldier. We were taken to a guerilla camp and that is how we became acquainted with their commander."

"His name," someone shouted. "What was his name?"

"I can't disclose that information," she said.

"Why not?" asked another reporter.

"Because I gave my word that I wouldn't."

"Were you mistreated by the guerillas?" "How long did they hold you at their camp?" "How did you escape?"

Lynn's head began to swim from the steady flood of questions. She looked longingly toward the elevator, now unable to see its doors because of the crowd. Her loyalty to Eliot caused her to move quickly away from Adam, to push her way through the grabbing, eager hands.

"Lynn," Adam shouted. "Where are you going? The cameras . . ."

"To hell with the cameras!" Lynn whispered to herself as she shoved and pushed and finally reached the elevator door. When she was alone inside the elevator, she tapped her fingers nervously against her leg until it finally stopped at the floor she and Eliot had originally occupied. With tears sparkling at the corners of her eyes she rushed to Eliot's door, which she noticed was partially open. Without hesitation she hurriedly moved on into the living room of his suite, but she was disappointed to find no signs of Eliot anywhere.

The silence unnerved Lynn. She eyed the door that led into the bedroom. Maybe he was in there. Maybe he was getting ready to take a shower . . .

Almost breathless, Lynn hurried into the bedroom. Her heart plummeted when she saw the bureau drawers hanging open, empty. With a wild beating of her heart, Lynn went to the closet and slid the doors open, to discover all the clothes gone from the hangers.

Her gaze moved to the floor. "Even his luggage!" she whispered. A strange sort of sob tore from her throat. "God! He's gone!"

But then a small ray of hope lighted her misery when she glanced across the room to the door that led into her suite.

"Maybe he's in there," she whispered tremulously. Her footsteps were muffled by the thick carpet beneath her boots as she moved toward the door, encouraged to see that it was also standing partially ajar. Only Eliot had the key.

Stepping gingerly into her suite, she felt the icy grip of desperation. This room was just as empty as Eliot's suite had been.

Then another thought struck her. Maybe, just maybe, all their things had been moved to other rooms when word of their disappearance had reached the hotel. Maybe these suites had been needed by the hotel management. Maybe Eliot was waiting for her in another suite. She hadn't taken the time to ask the desk clerk.

"There's one way to find out," Lynn said, anxiously moving into her bedroom. But one look around gave her the answer she was seeking. Everything was exactly as she had left it. Her cologne, hair dryer and brush, along with the rest of her toiletry items were on the dressing table.

"He's gone," she whispered. She bit her lower lip in frustration. "He's packed and gone."

Circling her fists at her side, she cried aloud, "How could he? What's he trying to prove? Does he have so little faith in my love for him?"
But she was remembering all the times she had argued with him, throwing accusations at him, defending Adam, and revealing her anger at his having taken over her position as Program Director at the station.

"None of those things matter any longer, Eliot," she whispered, blinking tears from her lashes. "I told you that! What you have done tells me only one thing—your love for me wasn't strong enough. If you truly loved me, you would have fought to be by my side downstairs!"

Footsteps behind her made her hands fly to her throat. Her heart pounded wildly and she began to smile as she whispered his name, turning slowly around. "Eliot, you didn't leave . . ." she said. Then her face became a mask of confusion when instead of Eliot, she saw Adam standing in the door that led into Eliot's suite.

"Lynn, what's this all about?" Adam asked, coming into the room.

"How did you get in?" she asked.

"Into Eliot's room?"

"Yes."

"The door was open. Before coming to see you I thought I'd better check things out there, to see if anything was wrong," Adam told her. He reached for her hand and flinched when she pulled quickly away.

"And obviously there *is*," he added. "What is it, Lynn? Where's Eliot? And why is this connecting door open?"

Lynn turned away and clapped her hands over her ears. "Questions!" she cried. "Please, Adam, no more questions. Just leave me alone. Do you hear? *Leave me alone!*"

Adam went to her and gripped her shoulders, turning her around to face him. "Lynn, this isn't like you," he said gently. "You've never shut me out before. I'm always here to help you—or have you forgotten?"

Lynn wiped at her nose with the back of her hand, sniffling. With wavering eyes she met Adam's and forced a quivering smile to her lips. "Yes, you've always been there when I've needed you," she murmured. "Even now, Adam. I would never have expected to find you on Carmen Island.But here you are, with the same broad shoulder for me to cry on. You're·a special man, Adam, and I appreciate you so much . . ."

"Even if KS90 hadn't sent me here, I would've come anyway," he said thickly. He reached a hand to her brow and brushed a strand of hair back from her eyes.

"My parents," she suddenly said, paling. "I've got to call my parents!"

"Before I came up here I took the time to give them a quick call," he assured her. "They're eager to talk to you themselves, but they're ecstatic that you're all right."

"You even did that?" she whispered, smiling warmly at him. Then she tensed, hearing the sound of a plane overhead. With a racing pulse she rushed to the sliding glass door, quickly opened it and stepped out onto the terrace. Shielding her eyes from the harsh rays of the sun she looked up. When she saw the Southern Airlines airplane in the sky directly overhead, she was certain that Eliot was on board, returning to the States without her.

"Eliot . . ." she whispered, feeling as though a part of her heart was being torn away. She watched the plane until it was just a speck against the brilliant blue sky, then went back into her suite and closed the terrace door behind her.

"Lynn, you and Eliot Smith," Adam said softly. "Did you . . . ?"

Lynn fell into Adam's arms and cried softly against his chest.

"Oh, Adam, I love him," she whispered. "He's the first man since Randy that I've let myself feel anything about. And now he's gone."

"You and . . . and Eliot Smith?" he repeated, shock apparent in the strained texture of his voice.

"I know," she said, laughing awkwardly, drawing gently away from him. "How could I possibly love such a dreadful man, right?"

"You said it, not me," Adam grumbled.

"Well, Adam, he's not at all like you and I first suspected."

"You obviously changed your mind only because you were stranded all that time alone with him," Adam scoffed. "In the jungle, I imagine any man looks pretty good."

"No. It's more than that, Adam," she said softly. "He's warm, charming and so protective of me. He's truly everything I ever wanted in a man."

Adam shook his head, laughing softly. "God, I can't believe this!" he said. "You and Eliot Smith! No. I *can't* believe it."

"Well, it doesn't matter if you believe it or not, because apparently Eliot doesn't either, or he wouldn't have left."

"Why *did* he leave so suddenly, Lynn?"

"Who knows?" she murmured, avoiding his eyes.

She couldn't tell Adam that Eliot's sudden departure was for the most part because of Adam himself. Yet she had to tell someone or she felt as though she just might burst. She eased out of his arms and went to stand by the wide expanse of window, looking out past the tall buildings and on into the intense greens of the jungle. Lynn felt as though those days and nights with Eliot hadn't really happened at all, as though it had all been a figment of her overactive imagination.

Cassie Edwards

As though of their own volition, her fingers moved to her front pants pocket where the garnet lay, waiting to be rescued and admired all over again. She curled her fingers around the gemstone, positive proof that none of this had been a dream. If she closed her eyes she could recreate the scene in her mind—she and Eliot were swimming nude, searching the lagoon bed for more stones. Remembering his caresses beneath the water and his sweet kisses made her heart ache even more. Suddenly she felt more angry than hurt. How dare he treat her so poorly!

"Lynn," Adam said, once more clasping her shoulders, "you'd better get a hold of yourself. The press is still waiting. Come on—I'll go down with you."

"I don't want to talk to them quite yet," she said, tensing. "You know that their questions will eventually swing back to Eliot, and what am I supposed to tell them when they ask why he flew back to the States without me?"

"Maybe it's because he wants to be the first to arrive at the station with the story," Adam suggested, dropping his hands to his side. Then he absently kneaded his chin. "Damn him! That has to be the reason."

"No. That's not it," Lynn murmured, settling down onto a chair. She struggled with one boot, yanking and pulling at it. Her boots seemed to have shrunk a full size—or maybe her feet had grown! Swollen most likely.

"Why would you doubt that, Lynn?" Adam grumbled. "It sounds like something that conceited ass would do."

"Without Hank and the film?" Lynn said. "No, I'm

306

the one who has the true advantage here. Adam, you must know that."

Adam sank down onto a chair and drummed his fingers nervously against its arm. "Then why?" he said. "What is it you're not telling me?"

Lynn flung the boot across the room and began pulling at the other one. Then she paused to meet Adam's questioning stare. "For one thing, Adam, we stole Eliot's thunder downstairs," she said dryly. "We were once again a team, as though we were deliberately leaving Eliot out of the picture."

Adam's brow furrowed and his fingers became idle. "Yes, I see what you mean," he said quietly. "I hadn't thought about that."

Lynn continued to struggle with the boot, lowering her eyes from Adam's. "Secondly, Adam, it's because of *you*," she murmured. "Eliot is jealous of you. And the way I ran into your arms downstairs in the lobby—well, that must have seemed to confirm all his previous suspicions about the two of us."

"Good Lord!" Adam said, rising to pace back and forth.

"Adam, you know that so many people through the years have thought we had something going between us."

"Yes, I know."

"Well? Why is it so hard to believe that Eliot does too?"

"Yeah. I guess you're right," Adam said. "But, Lynn, I had to come, Eliot or no Eliot. You understand, don't you?"

Lynn tossed her other boot aside and leaned back in her chair. She sighed heavily as she curled her toes into the plush carpet at her feet. "Don't blame yourself for any of this," she said. "Eliot is to blame. Fully. He just didn't have enough faith in my love for him to carry our relationship to its logical conclusion. And if that's the way he wants it, well, that's that."

"Is there anything I can do to help?" Adam said, leaning forward, eyeing her with a lifted eyebrow.

"No. I can handle it," Lynn said.

Her gaze traveled over her guerilla uniform and she laughed softly. "I must be a sight," she murmured. "I'd better get in the shower. But first I must call my parents."

She smiled warmly at Adam. "And thank you again, my very special friend, for calling them for me," she said. "You knew that I was in quite a state, didn't you?"

"Well, yes, I did. I do know you quite well, Lynn, after all."

"You probably know me better than anyone," she sighed. She rose slowly from the chair. "Even better than most husbands." She strolled to the window and gazed from it.

"Lynn, about that shower," Adam said. "The interview might be more effective if you would stay the way you are. You know, just the way you came out of the jungle?"

Lynn swung around and faced him. "Adam, do you realize just how long it's been since I've worn a dress?" she sighed.

"But you do want to come across on the screen in the best way possible, Lynn, you know—for effect," Adam continued. "Remember the ratings."

Lynn's lips curved into a stubborn pout. "Adam,

do you want to know something?" she said. "Suddenly I don't give a damn about ratings or much of anything else. I just want to go home to my beach house. I need time to think. Do you understand?"

"Yeah. Guess I do." Adam shrugged. "So you're not going to agree to any further interviews?"

"My heart just isn't in it, Adam."

Adam drew her into his arms and hugged her affectionately. "Whatever you decide, I'll go along with," he said. "You know I always want what's best for you."

"Even if I'm cause for *your* ratings to drop?"

"Lynn, I'm only on the radio, remember?"

"But, Adam, downstairs, in the lobby, I felt as though we were partners again," she whispered. "You have to know that any of that footage could help your career. I feel as though my refusing to do more interviews is the same as stabbing you in the back, career-wise."

"That's nonsense," Adam scoffed. He held her gently away from him. "When do you want to fly back home?"

"The next plane, please, Adam?"

"As good as done," he said. "I'll make the arrangements. We'll both be on the first flight available."

"Thanks, Adam," Lynn said, reaching a hand to his cheek. "You're so good to me."

"You deserve the best of everything, Lynn."

"Tell Eliot Smith that," she sighed. "Seems he doesn't agree with you."

"I just may," Adam said under his breath.

"Did you say something, Adam?" Lynn questioned.

"No. Nothing," Adam said, swinging around. He

headed toward the door. "I'm just down the hall. Room 804. Give me a buzz on the phone when you're ready to go get a bite to eat. I'm afraid we've a few hours to wait before the next flight back to the States."

The ache was renewed around Lynn's heart. "Yes," she murmured. "I know." She walked Adam to the door and gave him a kiss on the cheek. "I'll call you. Soon. And, Adam, thanks again. For everything. Especially for understanding."

He winked. "Anytime," he said, then left the room, leaving Lynn alone with her tortured thoughts of Eliot.

# *Seventeen*

THOUGH IT was Lynn's first afternoon back in San Francisco, she had decided not to put off telling Taylor of her decision. It hadn't taken long for her to decide that she could not, would not appear on "Morning Magazine" with Eliot after his departure from Carmen Island without an explanation. She had yet to hear from him and, being of a stubborn nature, had chosen not to approach him until he first contacted her.

Wearing a pale taupe dress of nubby silk by Maria Rodrigues with a classic dark brown fedora that hid her hair beneath it, handsome sterling silver earrings and matching cuff bracelet, Lynn walked determinedly toward Taylor's closed office door. The sound of her brown suede pumps were muffled by the thick carpet beneath her feet as she swept past Taylor's secretary's desk and into his office unannounced. She no longer had to worry about his reaction. In a matter of minutes she would no longer be under his thumb. She would be a former employee.

Lynn lifted her chin haughtily as she met Taylor's surprised stare from where he sat behind his desk.

"Well, what have we here?" he said, removing his cigar from between his lips. "It's about time I've heard from you in some capacity. No phone calls. Nothing! Hank said that you even refused to be interviewed. What the hell's wrong with you, Lynn? Have you forgotten why you were sent to Carmen Island?"

"How could I forget?" she said dryly. And she most certainly hadn't forgotten him or his superior attitude. Millionaire or not, it didn't make him any more pleasant to be around. He continued to glare at her through thickly lensed horn-rimmed glasses perched on his bulbous nose. The dark toupee covering his bald head seemed to accentuate the heaviness of his face.

"So? Why did you refuse to cooperate with the press?" Taylor growled, once more chomping on his cigar. He lifted a thick, shaggy eyebrow, waiting for her answer.

Lynn placed the palms of her hands on Taylor's desk and leaned closer to him. "Because it was something I just decided to not do," she said. "And, Taylor, I don't regret that decision. Not one damn bit!"

"You didn't help your position here at the station, let me assure you of that," Taylor growled.

Lynn let a cynical, soft laugh rise from her throat but let him rant on as he was wont to do whenever he was thwarted.

"I had big plans for that story, Lynn," he continued, "from the very first when word reached me that you and Eliot were missing."

"I'm sure your major concern was the ratings, not our safe return," she scoffed.

"When I heard that you and Eliot might possibly have strayed into guerrilla territory and that the islanders refused to search for you, I was damned worried," Taylor said, jerking his cigar from his mouth.

"Why, Taylor? Because you saw the chances of losing a great story or because you feared for our lives?"

Taylor rose quickly from his chair and nervously straightened his tie. "Enough of this," he said. He walked around the desk and offered her a hand. "Damn glad to have you back, Lynn!"

Lynn ignored his hand and went to stand by a window. Seeing the outline of the Golden Gate Bridge through the low-hanging fog made her appreciate the fact that, yes, she was home, all right. But the word "home" didn't have the same happy sound as it had while she had been in the thick of the jungle. She had thought that once she and Eliot arrived in San Francisco their future as man and wife would be assured. Without him, Lynn couldn't find the heart to be happy about anything. She was bitter and disillusioned. She only hoped that she could get this thing with Taylor over and done with without running into Eliot face to face.

Feeling a desperate need to escape back to her beach house, Lynn turned and boldly faced Taylor. "Taylor, as of this moment I am resigning from the staff of KSFC-TV," she stated. She watched his ruddy face turn pale with shock. "In fact, I'm taking some time off from any sort of a job. I need a rest."

"*What?*" he gasped, teetering as he reached to steady himself against his desk. "You can't *do* that!"

"Oh, yes I can," Lynn said. "Even without two weeks' notice. I resign. Now." She laughed softly. "That wasn't so hard," she said. She moved briskly toward the door but was stopped by the firm grip of Taylor's hand on her shoulder. She turned and frowned at him.

"I take it you didn't watch 'Morning Magazine' this morning," he said slyly.

"No, I didn't," she replied. "My plane landed shortly after the show aired. But even if I had been in town I wouldn't have watched it. Why do you ask?"

Taylor's shoulders slouched as he stubbed out his cigar and settled back into the chair behind his desk. He placed his fingertips together before him and stared at Lynn glumly. "So you didn't hear the announcement that Eliot has left us too," he grumbled. "He's gone back to Seattle."

Lynn took a step backward, feeling as though someone had slapped her in the face. Her pulse raced, her throat became suddenly dry. "What did you just say?" she said.

"So you see why *you* can't leave us, Lynn?" Taylor went on.

Lynn moved slowly across the room to Taylor's desk. Trembling a bit, she leaned against it. "Taylor, I ask you again," she whispered. "What did you say about Eliot?"

"He wasn't even professional enough to tell me in person!" Taylor growled. "He sent a memo. A damn *memo!* He's got some nerve. He said contracts are made to be broken, or some such rot!"

Lynn sank down into a chair, feeling weak-kneed

and light-headed. "Eliot? Back in Seattle?" she murmured, shaking her head to try to clear her thoughts. Then she looked questioningly toward Taylor. "Why, Taylor? What reason did he give?"

"He didn't say," he snapped. "Just said he was headed back to his old job in Seattle."

"But he was good on 'Morning Magazine,'" Lynn murmured, confused.

"Well, it's all yours now," Taylor said flatly. "I wasn't serious when I said that you had hurt your position here at the station. I won't bring anybody else in. The show is yours. All of it. And the position of Program Director is all yours, too."

Taylor drew a folded contract from a drawer. With deliberate movements he unfolded it and spread it open before Lynn's eyes. "And here's that contract you've always wanted," he said. "Top dollar, Lynn. I mean to hold onto you, no matter what it costs."

Lynn began a slow boil. "You and your damn contracts!" she fumed. "*Now* you give me what I've always wanted but only because you can't have Eliot Smith!"

Anger flashed in her green eyes as she rose from her chair. "Taylor, you can shove that contract!" she hissed and rushed from the office, almost in a state of shock. Blindly she ran down the long hallway and only when she was finally in the confines of her private office did she let the tears begin to flow freely.

"Eliot, why . . . ?" she whispered, doubling her fists at her sides. "Didn't you ever really love me? Was going after this job and me just a passing fancy, a test to see how much you could achieve? What the hell are you trying to prove?"

She focused on a cardboard box on her desk. "I've got to get out of here," she whispered. "And fast!"

With trembling fingers she began opening and closing drawers, emptying their contents into the box. Once everything was packed and nothing personal remained in the office, she gathered the box and her purse into her arms and rushed toward the elevator.

"I need a new hat," she whispered under her breath. "If ever in my life I needed to buy a new hat, this is the time."

Ignoring questioning glances and greetings, she stepped into the elevator. As soon as it reached the ground floor she rushed out to her car and headed toward Jan's Millinery only a few blocks away.

"It all sounded so exciting on the news!" Cathy exclaimed as she sat sipping a glass of wine in Lynn's living room. "Lost in the jungle with a hunk like Eliot Smith. Lynn, tell me all about it!"

Lynn hadn't counted on having a visitor so soon. She had just hidden her box of office memorabilia away in her bedroom when Cathy had come knocking on the sliding door off Lynn's terrace. While jogging, Cathy had spied the light from Lynn's windows and knew that her best friend was finally home from her adventures.

Lifting her fedora from her head, Lynn placed it on a table, then reached inside the hat box for her new one.

"And a new hat?" Cathy was puzzled. "What prompted its purchase, Lynn? And why are you so glum? God, Lynn, *say something!*"

Lynn felt that she wanted to scream. She was so

keyed up from all that had happened that she felt she might explode. But instead she swallowed hard and turned to face Cathy. "Cathy, I'm fine," she said. "But, please—no more questions, okay. I'm sick to *death* of questions!"

Cathy set her glass of wine on a table and shoved the sleeves of her sweatshirt up above her elbows. "Oh, you mean all the reporters," she said. "I'm sure you've really been bugged, Lynn." Then she frowned. "But, Lynn," she quickly added, "you refused all those interviews. It's all in the news—how you've refused to answer any questions about your time in the jungle with Eliot Smith." A slow, teasing smile touched her lips. "Come on, Lynn. You can tell me. What's behind all this secrecy, huh?"

Lynn set her jaw firmly and flashed Cathy a harried look. "Cathy, I don't want to talk about this to anyone," she murmured. "Please just drop it. Okay?"

Cathy rose from the chair and went to Lynn and took one of her hands. "Lynn, something happened between you and Eliot, didn't it?" she asked.

With a heaviness pressing on her heart, Lynn turned away from Cathy and placed her new hat on her head. She purposely ignored Cathy's questions. Lynn didn't want to even speak Eliot's name aloud. It hurt badly enough just thinking about him, much less speaking about him.

Lynn strolled to the mirror behind her bar and looked at her reflection. "Do you like this one, Cathy?" she asked, admiring the striking yellow, big-brimmed creation. When she didn't hear any response, she turned to see what was absorbing Cathy's attention. Then she grew cold inside as she saw Cathy examining the translucent garnet that Lynn had carelessly left on the bar.

"Lynn, this is beautiful," Cathy sighed. "Where did you get it? What kind of stone is it?"

Lynn jerked her hat from her head and dropped it back in its box, then began pulling the pins from her hair, once more ignoring Cathy's questions. "I'm going to change and join you jogging," she said, shaking her hair free and hurrying toward her bedroom.

"But, Lynn . . ."

Facing Cathy with a set, cold stare, she said, "Cathy, like I said. *No more questions.*"

Shrugging, Cathy put the garnet back down on the bar. "Sure, Lynn," she murmured. "Whatever you say."

"I'll change. I'll be back in a minute." But when Lynn saw the hurt in Cathy's eyes, she went to her friend and took her hands, squeezing them affectionately.

"I'm sorry, Cathy," she murmured. "But I've had a pretty rough time lately. I quit my job today."

"You *what?*" Cathy gasped.

"I'll tell you everything later, okay? But for the moment I just want to put it out of my mind."

"But your *job*, Lynn . . ."

"I know," Lynn murmured. She pulled her hands from Cathy's and went into her bedroom.

"But, Lynn, *why?*" Cathy asked, following at Lynn's heels.

"It's really such a long story, Cathy. I *will* tell you later. Honest," Lynn said as she changed from her dress into shorts and halter. Then a few brief strokes of a brush through her hair and she was ready to go and try to run some of her frustrations off.

Once out on the beach, barefoot, enjoying the warmth of the sand sifting between her toes, Lynn finally began to relax. She loved the sound of the surf, the cry of the soaring seagulls, the early evening sun on her bare shoulders and face. It evoked a different sort of peace than she had found in the jungle. The effervescence of the foamy wavelets lapping at her feet as the tide began to rise and the salty wind blowing in from across the bay had filtered through her dreams even while she had been sleeping next to Eliot on their bed of palm and coconut fronds.

Shaking her head to clear her thoughts and not wanting to remember the rapture she had known with Eliot, Lynn forced a soft laugh. "And you said you're doing fine on your own, Cathy?" she said, glancing at her friend running next to her. Jogging hadn't helped Cathy's weight problem but her separation from her husband had given her a relaxed, special glow.

"Yes," Cathy said, puffing as she labored to keep pace with Lynn. "Pete's moving out is the best thing that's ever happened to me. I've been having a wild time dating!" She gave Lynn a wide smile. "Lynn, there's a lot of hunks out there and *available*," she added. "I could introduce you to a few."

The same, familiar ache tore through Lynn's heart. "I'm not interested," she murmured. "Men! You can have 'em."

Cathy wiped beads of perspiration from her brow. "I'll take 'em, I'll take 'em," she laughed. "With Pete giving me the house and a monthly allowance, I've got it made, Lynn. I'm having a ball!"

The sun was now an orange disc on the horizon,

looking as though it were being swallowed up by the ocean. Streaks of purple and crimson mingled with the darkness of night settling in over the ocean. Lynn couldn't help remembering the sunsets on Carmen Island. How had Eliot described them? "As though you could reach out and touch them . . ."

A tormented loneliness filled Lynn's heart. Why was it that everything reminded her of Eliot? All she had to do was close her eyes and he would be there, kissing her, loving her. She would never forget the sunlight on his hair nor the passion in his eyes.

Lynn swallowed a lump in her throat, tossing her hair back from her eyes. The salty taste of her lips was a mixture of both the seawater breeze and tears. She came to an abrupt halt and turned her back to Cathy, not wanting to reveal her streaming eyes to her friend. Though Cathy had just recently gained her freedom and was enjoying it, Lynn couldn't enjoy her own recently acquired freedom. It seemed that her short time away had changed the lives of both Cathy and Lynn.

"Lynn, what's the matter?" Cathy asked. She stopped and placed a hand on Lynn's arm. "You're crying! What is it? Can I help in any way?"

Lynn brushed the tears from her face and squared her shoulders. "I'm going to have to work this out alone," she murmured. "I just *have* to. I can't go on like this."

"You're in love, aren't you, Lynn?" Cathy asked. "Only a man could cause such pain in your eyes."

"Yes," Lynn finally confessed. "A man. But I'm going to forget him. I must."

"But why? What *happened*, Lynn?"

Lynn shook her head. "I really don't know," she

said. "I'm so confused. Maybe I should call him. Maybe I've been too stiff-necked. I'm pretty sure I know why he ran off the way he did."

She turned her gaze to Cathy. "But my damn pride just won't let me call him. I will *not* go begging a man to love me!"

She almost choked on the words, silently cursing Eliot for putting her in this position. Until Eliot, she had been content to live alone. But now every moment without him seemed an eternity.

"It is Eliot Smith, isn't it?" Cathy murmured. "You're in love with *him*. Well, what do you know!"

Words were not needed. The pain deepened in Lynn's eyes at the mention of Eliot's name. Then a movement in the distance, another runner on the beach, distracted Lynn's attention. In only jogging shorts and sneakers, there was something familiar about the way the man held himself, so tall, so sure, and—oh, God, now that she realized who it was, she couldn't help but remember the times she had let her fingers explore the corded muscles of those broad shoulders . . .

Her heart began to pump wildly as he drew nearer to her. Now she could see his tanned, chiseled features, cleanly shaven now, the thick chest hair curling around the nipples Lynn had so often run her tongue over.

As the muscles of his legs flexed with each stride, bringing him ever closer, Lynn felt a slow melting beginning inside her. She knew that he was on the beach, this particular stretch of beach, for only one reason. To see *her*. He knew her habit of jogging. And what more casual, comfortable way to meet than on the beach?

It was now apparent to Lynn that it was Eliot's stubbornness as well as her own that stood in the way of their getting together again. By happening to run into her on the beach, he could make it appear that he had not sought her out, that their meeting was merely an accident.

"Lynn, what is it?" Cathy asked, then turned around and suddenly found herself face-to-face with Eliot Smith as he stopped at Lynn's side, panting for breath.

"Well. What a coincidence," Eliot said, combing his fingers through his hair. His eyes devoured Lynn, mesmerized by her beauty. His loins ached with need as his gaze drifted to her breasts, remembering their sweet taste, their yielding softness. Then he looked into her eyes and saw an answering passion in their green depths.

Lynn's body was engulfed by a river of sensation as she let his dark eyes make love to her. No touch was needed, no contact at all. The secrets revealed by their shared, rapturous gazes were those that nothing or no one could ever destroy. Lynn now knew just how foolish she had been to let even one day pass without trying to iron out the differences between them.

"Why, Eliot?" she finally managed to say. "I don't understand."

Eliot glanced toward Cathy. Cathy laughed nervously. "I really must go, you two," she said, clumsily backing away. She lifted a hand and waved. "See you around, okay?"

"Okay," Lynn murmured and then turned back to Eliot.

"Can we talk?" he asked, nodding toward her house.

"Where'd you park your car?"

"Down on the beach road."

"That wasn't necessary. Why didn't you just come to my house? Don't you know I've been dying to see you?"

"I do now," he said hoarsely. "I guess I had to gauge your reaction at seeing me first."

"And that was?"

"That you've missed me as much as I've missed you," Eliot said. He hesitated, then grabbed her and drew her roughly into his arms, crushing her mouth beneath his.

Breathless, Lynn twined her arms about his neck and pressed her body against him, returning his kiss with all the passion she had locked inside her since their last moments together that night at the guerilla camp.

A low moan rose from deep inside Eliot as he pulled his lips slightly from hers. "Baby, I've missed you so!" he said, his voice trembling with emotion. His hands caressed her back almost frantically. He cupped the firmness of her buttocks, then moved back up again, to twine her hair around his fingers.

"Eliot . . ." Lynn whispered, almost sobbing, "don't ever, *ever* leave me again!"

Once more his lips bore down upon hers. Her mouth opened and welcomed the warmth of his tongue, meeting his with her own in a sensuous intertwining. She sighed pleasurably when he withdrew from her long enough to scoop her up into his arms. Then she leaned her head against his chest and welcomed one of his hands inside her halter, cupping a breast, driving her almost mindless with ecstasy.

Eliot took the terrace steps two at a time and went inside her house as though it were his own. He moved on into her bedroom and placed her gently on the bed.

"Eliot?" Lynn whispered, feeling almost drunk with passion.

Eliot sealed her lips with a forefinger. "No questions now," he murmured. "I'll give you the answers, all of them, after we've made love."

"But, Eliot . . ." Lynn persisted, leaning up on an elbow.

"You do want me, don't you?" Eliot asked, placing his thumbs inside his jogging shorts, ready to pull them down.

"God, yes!" Lynn said, not believing the huskiness of her own voice.

As he stepped from his shorts and shoes, she quickly shed her own, then stretched out on the bed and held her arms out to him. "Darling, please . . ." she whispered.

Eliot lowered himself slowly over her, tenderly cupping one breast while his lips found the nipple of the other, taut and ready to receive him. Lynn writhed in pure ecstasy, craving the consummation of their love and knowing that she had never needed him more than at this very moment.

His hardness pressed against her abdomen and as he seductively slid himself up and down the satin flesh of her thigh, she could feel his pulsating heat. She opened herself fully to him as he entered her gently, yet fiercely.

Twining her arms about his neck, she clung to him and lifted her hips to take him fully inside her. If she closed her eyes she could almost hear the cries of the macaws and quetzal birds in the jungle and the splash of the waterfall in the distance. The aroma of exotic, lush flowers was an intoxication in itself, so real that it was as though they were lying on a bed of orchids and she was a flower herself. The memory of their jungle paradise was so fresh in her mind that she was transported back in time, living it all over again.

"Eliot, love me, darling," Lynn cried, almost delirious with happiness that he had come back to her. She no longer cared why he had left. He was here now and she would never let him go again.

She devoured his face with her eyes. He was lost in ecstasy, his eyes closed, his jaw set. Tiny beads of perspiration lined his brow and his lips were tightly drawn. Lynn traced a finger around one of his nipples and she felt and saw his delight by the slight tremor of his flesh.

And when his eyes slowly opened and looked into hers, dark with passion, Lynn drew his mouth down to hers and kissed him deeply. She could feel his heart hammering against her breasts. Their flame of love burned ever higher, making her heart-beats keep pace with his, and she welcomed his thrusts within her. As the whirlwind of rapture spun them both in its vortex, they shuddered in unison, then lay spent and panting in one another's arms.

"I still can't believe you're here," Lynn whispered, running her fingers through his hair.

"You can thank Adam Lowenstein for that," he

said hoarsely. He leaned on an elbow and watched her reaction.

"What do you mean?" Lynn murmured. "What has Adam got to do with it?"

"He flew to Seattle and talked to me about—well, uh, *things*," Eliot said, cupping one of her breasts.

Lynn gasped softly. His touch was pure magic. "What things?" she whispered.

"That you and he were never lovers but just loyal, dedicated friends and coworkers."

"But Eliot, I had told you the same thing over and over again," Lynn sighed.

"Adam wasn't alone on his flight to Seattle," Eliot said. "His wife was with him and one of their grandsons, three-year-old David."

Lynn's heart began to race, realizing what lengths Adam had gone to to prove to Eliot that she was free. Adam was indeed the best and truest of friends! "Did he really do that?" she murmured.

"He's a fine man, Lynn," Eliot said softly, lowering a brief kiss to her lips. "I understand now, baby. Will you forgive me for my stupidity and jealousy?"

"It hurt me so deeply when you left me in Leon. I didn't know where to turn or what to think."

"I had to," he said. "When I saw you and Adam together on camera, how right you two looked together, I felt that I had been wrong all along to have come between you."

Lynn placed a hand on his cheek. "But you were wrong on both counts, weren't you, Eliot?" she softly laughed.

"What do you mean?" he said. "You and Adam can co-host 'Morning Magazine' again now that I'm out of the picture."

"That would be a bit impossible now," Lynn said.

"Why? What's to prevent it?" he asked, raising his eyebrows.

"Eliot, I'm no longer with KSFC-TV either," she said, watching as his face registered shock.

"You're *what?*" he gasped.

"I told Taylor to shove it," she giggled, still amazed at her temerity

Eliot sat bolt upright, still facing her. His chin quivered and then he began laughing. When he'd sobered somewhat, he drew her into his arms and hugged her to him. "What made you do such a crazy thing?"

"If you weren't going to be on 'Morning Magazine' I didn't want to be either," she whispered, resting her cheek on his chest. "And besides, I needed time away from everything, to think. I've missed you, oh, so much, Eliot! How could I have gone to work each day while I was tortured inside with the need of you?"

"Come back to Seattle with me, Lynn," he said huskily. "Let's get married."

Lynn looked up at him, wide-eyed.

"The weather is terrible there, but together we'd make our own paradise, darling," he continued.

"I want to, Eliot . . ."

He drew away from her and pleaded with his eyes. "Then, for Christ's sake, Lynn, do it!"

"Are you sure about your feelings for me, Eliot?" she quavered.

"You've become the most important thing in my life, baby," he said. "Without you these past few days, I've felt like a lost soul."

Lynn's heart began to race wildly. "If you're sure, Eliot . . ." she whispered.

"Then what are we waiting for?" he shouted, jumping from the bed. "Pack your bags, and let's go! We've wasted enough time as it is!"

In a state of semishock, Lynn rose slowly from the bed. "But, Eliot, I can't just take off like this," she murmured. "There are things I have to do . . ."

"We'll come back and do them later," he said. "Just lock your car in your garage—we'll get it when we come back."

"Do you have a rental car?"

"Yes. And two plane tickets back to Seattle," he chuckled, stepping into his shorts.

Lynn eyed him, astonished. "You were that sure of me then?"

"Yes. I knew you'd come back with me," he said, then chuckled once more. "But I didn't think you'd be able to stay, I thought it would just be for the length of time required for us to get married. I had no idea you'd quit your job."

"I'll have to find work in Seattle, Eliot," she said distractedly. "I'm not much for sitting idly by, doing nothing—at least not for long, that is."

"Being my wife is nothing?" he teased, framing her face between his hands.

"I don't know about you, but I'm dying to tell the world about our experiences on Carmen Island," she said. "I know that Taylor has Hank's films, but he doesn't have our personal story about being picked up by the guerillas, or the rest of our experiences." Then she frowned. "Unless you've already broken the story at your TV station. Have you?"

Eliot laughed. "Baby, it's *our* story, remember?"

he said. "Yours and mine. We'll tell it together."

"How?"

"I was saving this for a surprise, but I'd better tell you now. I've already spoken to KMRK's management in Seattle and they agreed on a husband/wife team 'Morning Magazine' type show, if I could persuade you to stay. How about it, Lynn? Think we can share the spotlight again?"

"Oh, Eliot!" Lynn cried, then threw herself into his arms. "Yes. *Yes!*" she shouted.

"Then maybe on to New York and the big time if we're a hit in Seattle. How does that grab you?"

Lynn drew away from him and smiled delightedly up at him. "Now, darling, don't get greedy," she teased.

Eliot moved his lips to hers and gently kissed her, then murmured, "I guess you're right. Who needs New York anyway? All I need is you!"

Wrapped in each other's arms, they sank back onto the bed.

"Eliot," Lynn murmured against his lips, "we'll miss that plane . . ."

# HISTORICAL ROMANCE
## *BITTERSWEET PROMISES*
### By Trana Mae Simmons

Cody Garret likes everything in its place: his horse in its stable, his six-gun in its holster, his money in the bank. But the rugged cowpoke's life is turned head over heels when a robbery throws Shanna Van Alystyne into his arms. With a spirit as fiery as the blazing sun, and a temper to match, Shanna is the most downright thrilling woman ever to set foot in Liberty, Missouri. No matter what it takes, Cody will besiege Shanna's hesitant heart and claim her heavenly love.

_51934-8                                              $4.99 US/$5.99 CAN

# CONTEMPORARY ROMANCE
## *SNOWBOUND WEEKEND/GAMBLER'S LOVE*
### By Amii Lorin

In *Snowbound Weekend,* romance is the last thing on Jennifer Lengle's mind when she sets off for a ski trip. But trapped by a blizzard in a roadside inn, Jen finds herself drawn to sophisticated Adam Banner, with his seductive words and his outrageous promises…promises that can be broken as easily as her innocent heart.

And in *Gambler's Love,* Vichy Sweigart's heart soars when she meets handsome Ben Larkin in Atlantic City. But Ben is a gambler, and Vichy knows from experience that such a man can hurt her badly. She is willing to risk everything she has for love, but the odds are high—and her heart is at stake.

_51935-6     **(two unforgettable romances in one volume)** Only $4.99

# HISTORICAL ROMANCE
## *HUNTERS OF THE ICE AGE:*
## *YESTERDAY'S DAWN*
### By Theresa Scott

Named for the massive beast sacred to his people, Mamut has proven his strength and courage time and again. But when it comes to subduing one helpless captive female, he finds himself at a distinct disadvantage. Never has he realized the power of beguiling brown eyes, soft curves and berry-red lips to weaken a man's resolve. He has claimed he will make the stolen woman his slave, but he soon learns he will never enjoy her alluring body unless he can first win her elusive heart.

_51920-8                                   $4.99 US/$5.99 CAN

# A CONTEMPORARY ROMANCE
## *HIGH VOLTAGE*
### By Lori Copeland

Laurel Henderson hadn't expected the burden of inheriting her father's farm to fall squarely on her shoulders. And if Sheriff Clay Kerwin can't catch the culprits who are sabotaging her best efforts, her hopes of selling it are dim. Struggling with this new responsibility, Laurel has no time to pursue anything, especially not love. The best she can hope for is an affair with no strings attached. And the virile law officer is the perfect man for the job— until Laurel's scheme backfires. Blind to Clay's feelings and her own, she never dreams their amorous arrangement will lead to the passion she wants to last for a lifetime.

_51923-2                                   $4.99 US/$5.99 CAN

**LOVE SPELL**
**ATTN: Order Department**
**Dorchester Publishing Co., Inc.**
**276 5th Avenue, New York, NY 10001**

Please add $1.50 for shipping and handling for the first book and $.35 for each book thereafter. PA., N.Y.S. and N.Y.C. residents, please add appropriate sales tax. No cash, stamps, or C.O.D.s. All orders shipped within 6 weeks via postal service book rate. Canadian orders require $2.00 extra postage and must be paid in U.S. dollars through a U.S. banking facility.

Name_____

Address_____

City _____ State_____Zip_____

I have enclosed $_____in payment for the checked book(s).
Payment <u>must</u> accompany all orders.☐ Please send a free catalog.

# TIMESWEPT ROMANCE

## *TIME OF THE ROSE*
### By Bonita Clifton

When the silver-haired cowboy brings Madison Calloway to his run-down ranch, she thinks for sure he is senile. Certain he'll bring harm to himself, Madison follows the man into a thunderstorm and back to the wild days of his youth in the Old West.

The dread of all his enemies and the desire of all the ladies, Colton Chase does not stand a chance against the spunky beauty who has tracked him through time. And after one passion-drenched night, Colt is ready to surrender his heart to the most tempting spitfire anywhere in time.

_51922-4 $4.99 US/$5.99 CAN

# A FUTURISTIC ROMANCE

## *AWAKENINGS*
### By Saranne Dawson

Fearless and bold, Justan rules his domain with an iron hand, but nothing short of the Dammai's magic will bring his warring people peace. He claims he needs Rozlynd—a bewitching beauty and the last of the Dammai—for her sorcery alone, yet inside him stirs an unexpected yearning to savor the temptress's charms, to sample her sweet innocence. And as her silken spell ensnares him, Justan battles to vanquish a power whose like he has never encountered—the power of Rozlynd's love.

_51921-6 $4.99 US/$5.99 CAN

# FROM LOVE SPELL
## FUTURISTIC ROMANCE
### *NO OTHER LOVE*
**Flora Speer**
**Bestselling Author of *A Time To Love Again***

Only Herne sees the woman. To the other explorers of the ruined city she remains unseen, unknown. But after an illicit joining she is gone, and Herne finds he cannot forget his beautiful seductress, or ignore her uncanny resemblance to another member of the exploration party. Determined to unravel the puzzle, Herne begins a seduction of his own—one that will unleash a whirlwind of danger and desire.

\_51916-X                                         $4.99 US/$5.99 CAN

## TIMESWEPT ROMANCE
### *LOVE'S TIMELESS DANCE*
**Vivian Knight-Jenkins**

Although the pressure from her company's upcoming show is driving Leeanne Sullivan crazy, she refuses to believe she can be dancing in her studio one minute—and with a seventeenth-century Highlander the next. A liberated woman like Leeanne will have no problem teaching virile Iain MacBride a new step or two, and soon she'll have him begging for lessons in love.

\_51917-8                                         $4.99 US/$5.99 CAN

**LOVE SPELL**
**ATTN: Order Department**
**Dorchester Publishing Company, Inc.**
**276 5th Avenue, New York, NY 10001**

Please add $1.50 for shipping and handling for the first book and $.35 for each book thereafter. PA., N.Y.S. and N.Y.C. residents, please add appropriate sales tax. No cash, stamps, or C.O.D.s. All orders shipped within 6 weeks via postal service book rate. Canadian orders require $2.00 extra postage and must be paid in U.S. dollars through a U.S. banking facility.

Name _____

Address _____

City _____ State _____ Zip _____

I have enclosed $_____ in payment for the checked book(s).

Payment <u>must</u> accompany all orders.☐ Please send a free catalog.